THE BLOOD RED INDIAN SUMMER

THE BLOOD RED

INDIAN SUMMER

DAVID
HANDLER

MINOTAUR BOOKS

A THOMAS DUNNE BOOK

NEW YORK

This is a work of fiction. All of the characters, organizations, and events portrayed in this novel are either products of the author's imagination or are used fictitiously.

A THOMAS DUNNE BOOK FOR MINOTAUR BOOKS
An imprint of St. Martin's Publishing Group.

www.thomasdunnebooks.com
www.minotaurbooks.com

Library of Congress Cataloging-in-Publication Data

Handler, David, 1952–
   Blood red Indian Summer : a Berger and Mitry mystery / David Handler. — 1st ed.
      p. cm.
   ISBN 978-0-312-64835-0 (hardback)
   1. African American football players—Fiction.   2. Berger, Mitch (Fictitious character)—Fiction.   3. Mitry, Desiree (Fictitious character)—Fiction.
4. African American police—Fiction.   5. Connecticut—Fiction.   I. Title.
   PS3558.A4637B58 2011
   813'.54—dc22

                                                            2011018786

First Edition: October 2011

10   9   8   7   6   5   4   3   2   1

For my dear friend David Thompson, who has taken up permanent residence in Slip F-18, Bahia Mar, Lauderdale

THE BLOOD RED INDIAN SUMMER

PROLOGUE

SHE WOKE UP WITH a gasp, her heart pounding. Sweat poured from her as she lay there in bed under a single sheet. It was that awful nightmare—again. The one where he came for her in the night, hungry for her. The one where he did those horrible things to her. And she couldn't stop him no matter how hard she fought him or—

Scritch . . . Scritch . . .

Except this was no nightmare. It was real. He was out there in the hallway turning the knob on her locked door, first one way, then the other.

Scritch . . . Scritch . . .

She scrambled up to a seated position, knees hugged to her chest, her breath quick and shallow, eyes wide with terror. It was 3:13 A.M. according to her bedside clock. Moonlight streamed in the open window.

Scritch . . . Scritch . . .

Such a tiny noise. But her senses were so alive that it had yanked her awake. Because she was expecting it, fearing it. That was why she'd locked her bedroom door.

Scritch . . . Scritch . . .

He was being real quiet so he wouldn't awaken anyone else. The bastard. She stared at the door in the moonlight, defenseless and alone. She couldn't cry out for help. If she did, then it would no longer be a secret. And it had to stay a secret. Just had to. That was the only thing that was saving her right now. That no one knew. Although they would soon enough, because there was no way she could hide the awful truth that was growing inside her right at this very—

Plink . . . Plink . . .

A different sound. Now he was, what, inserting a key in the lock? *He had a key to her door.* How? No point in wondering how. He always figured out how to get in when he wanted her. Had there ever been such a vile man on the face of this earth? No, never. She had to get out of here. Just had to.

Plink . . . Plink . . .

Desperately, her eyes searched for a way out. There was the door. There was the window—a second-floor window with its priceless waterfront view of Long Island Sound smack dab at the mouth of the Connecticut River. It was, what, a fifteen-foot drop out the window to the stone terrace below? She'd break both legs for sure. She *could* try to climb out the window and up onto the roof. Except she wasn't Catwoman. She was a flesh and blood girl. A flesh and blood girl who was about to be brutalized yet again.

Kerchunk . . .

He'd done it now. Unlocked the door.

Hurriedly, she lay back down, stiff as a board in her sleeveless T-shirt and panties. Pretended she was asleep as, oh-so slowly, he swung the door open. Every cell in her body screamed at her to run. Yet she forced herself to remain motionless, breathing slowly and evenly. She couldn't overpower him. He was too strong for her. Unbelievably strong. She had to outfox him. He was incredibly wily. But she had to try.

He tiptoed toward her bed, silent like the predatory night creature that he was. She could smell his sweaty animal scent. He *was* an animal, not a person who had any genuine feelings or sense of decency. He tiptoed closer and closer, her heart hammering inside of her chest as she lay there motionless. He came around to one side of the bed. Now he was right there next to her nightstand, reaching for her. . . .

She bolted out of the other side of the bed and made a dash for the open door. She caught him by surprise. He dove for her but missed her. She ran out the door and down the hallway to the stairs, silent on her bare feet. She had no idea where she was going. Just away. Down the stairs she ran, hearing him coming after her. Toward the kitchen, then out the kitchen door onto the fieldstone terrace, where she tripped over a garden hose and went down hard, scraping both knees. But she sprang right back up and kept on running as he barreled out the door after her. She ran across the lawn toward the water, hearing her own frightened gasps. She was not a fast runner. And he was so shockingly quick that within seconds he'd caught her from behind, ripping her T-shirt as he tackled her to the damp grass.

"Why do you make me chase you?" he whispered, pinning her body to the grass with his knees. His hands gripped her tightly by both wrists. "You know you want me."

"Why can't you leave me *alone?*" she moaned, squirming in his grasp.

"Because you're mine." One of his hands went to her throat, squeezing it so hard she couldn't breathe. "You'll always be mine." He let go of her throat and fell on her like an oak tree, nuzzling her neck, his breath reeking of alcohol.

She writhed beneath him, shuddering with revulsion as he rubbed himself against her, making her feel how aroused he was. He ran a hand up and down her bare leg, his fingers finding her panties. When she started to scream he clamped his other hand over her mouth.

"So beautiful," he whispered, rising up onto one knee to unzip his pants.

That was when she took her best and only shot—kneed him in the groin as hard as she could. He let out a groan of pure pain, releasing his grip on her. She scrambled out from under him and started running again. There was only one means of escape. She took it. Dashed across the narrow ribbon of sand and dove head-first into the water, shocked by how cold it was. She started to swim, the salt water stinging her scraped knees. Her stroke had never been smooth. It wasn't much more than a frantic dog paddle, her arms and legs working hard, nose up out of the water. But it got her where she was going, *away*, as she watched him over her shoulder.

He stood at the water's edge, fully clothed. "Come back, girl," he called to her softly. Didn't raise his voice. That would wake people up. He always remembered to keep quiet. He was pure evil that way. "Come on, stop this foolishness." He watched her for another moment before he took off his shirt and yanked off his shoes. But by now she was at least a hundred feet out and he wasn't much of a swimmer. He changed his mind and didn't come in after her. Just stood there and waited, knowing she'd eventually get tired and cold and would have to come back.

Except she wasn't coming back. He wasn't going to have her. Never again. She swam farther and farther out, *away*, until she could no longer see him standing there. All she saw were a few porch lights twinkling here and there at neighboring houses. All she heard was her own breathing, hard but steady, as the river's current sent her farther out into the Sound. Free of him. *Free.*

She turned over onto her back and floated, gazing up at the half-moon and stars that were poking through the hazy sky. The water didn't seem as cold to her now. She just felt numb. Also terribly aware. It was all so clear to her now. How she could never be truly free of that evil bastard. Never escape the awful reality of what he'd done to her. It would never, ever be good between her and the man she loved once he found out the truth. And he would soon enough. Everyone would. She wouldn't be able to hide it much longer. And then she'd lose him and that smile of his that made her melt. He would never smile at her again. Never love her. No man would.

Leave town. That's what she should do. Move to a place far, far away where nobody knew her and the evil bastard couldn't find her. She could take a new name and start all over again, truly free. Who was she fooling? She'd never be free again. Never be able to forget what he'd done to her. She'd had so many beautiful dreams for her future. Now they seemed like nothing more than stupid schoolgirl fantasies. *This* was all there was. *This* life. *This* evil bastard who would not leave her alone. There was no getting away and she knew it as she floated there, letting the current take her farther out to sea—so far out that she could barely see the twinkle of lights on shore.

Except, wait, she did have control. The absolute truth of this smacked her with a sudden sureness that was unlike anything she'd ever felt before. She had a choice. Sure she did. She could choose to let the sea take her away. Then he'd never be able to touch her again. And she'd never have to confess her terrible secret. No one would ever have to know. She *could* get away. Yes, she could. All she had to do was keep swimming. It seemed so perfectly clear to her. She wasn't wigging out or anything. She was being completely rational and mature.

I am taking control of my own life.

And so she started swimming again, farther and farther out into Long Island Sound. She swam and she swam, the current helping her along. Swam until her arms and legs felt heavy. Swam until every breath came hard. But she wasn't scared. She was calm and at peace. Safe. There was no fear. Just this water and that sky up there. It felt good. It felt right.

I am taking control of my own life.

She was many miles out now. Her arms and legs were lead weights. She could barely move them. Kept sinking below the surface, salt water streaming into her open mouth. Briefly, she fought to stay afloat, sputtering and gasping, flailing her exhausted limbs. But not for long. Because she was ready—and she wasn't afraid.

I never have to be afraid again.

And so she let the water have her. Sank below the surface for the very last time thinking, just for a fleeting instant, that her foot had scraped against the jagged edge of a rock. But by then she'd already surrendered.

She was gone.

24 Hours Earlier

CHAPTER 1

WHEN SHE HEARD THE floorboard creak outside her bedroom door, Des dove for the loaded SIG under her pillow, instantly awake. A prowler. A prowler had broken into the house. It was 4:02 A.M. according to her digital bedside clock.

"Coffee's ready, Desiree," a voice called to her through the door.

It wasn't any prowler. It was the ghost of Buck Mitry.

Des stashed her weapon back under the pillow, breathing in and out. She'd slept with it there for years. Felt safe with it there. Happiness was a warm gun. But she'd have to lock it away from now on because she did not, repeat not, wish to blow his fool head off. It merely felt that way sometimes.

"Desiree, are you up?"

"I am now, Daddy." She flicked on her bedside light and fumbled for her heavy horn-rimmed glasses. Reached for the covers that she'd thrown off in the night and pulled them over her. Her room was warm even with the windows wide open. It was freakishly balmy for late October. An official Indian summer, the weathermen were calling it. "Come on in."

Buck Mitry came on in. He wore a fleece-lined jacket over a V-neck wool sweater, plaid shirt and wool slacks. He was always cold these days, no matter the temperature. He'd lost weight since the surgery. The lines in his face were deeper and made him look ten years older to her.

"Daddy, it's four o'clock in the morning."

"You said you wanted to get up early. But if you'd rather sleep . . ."

"No, this is great. We'll have a chance to sit and chat for three hours until the sun comes up."

His lower lip began to quiver. "I-I'm sorry."

"No, *I'm* sorry. It's fine, really. I'll be up in a sec, Daddy."

Not that this meek stranger was her daddy. Her daddy was deputy superintendent of the Connecticut State Police—the highest-ranking black man in the history of the state. A fierce, six-foot-four-inch hard-ass known as the Deacon. The Deacon was feared by everyone. Including his only child, who was the resident trooper of bucolic Dorset, the historic jewel of Connecticut's Gold Coast. He was staying with her while he recuperated from quadruple by-pass surgery. Doing real well physically. Getting his appetite and stamina back. His cardiologist felt he'd be ready to resume a light office schedule in another ten days. There was only one problem: He'd undergone such a radical personality transplant that Des hardly knew him. The Deacon she knew was strong-willed and demanding, a tower of strength. This Deacon was hesitant, emotionally fragile and listless. He didn't do a thing all day long. Didn't sleep at night. Mostly, he just stared at the television. He'd lost his edge. And if he went back to work in this condition his enemies inside of the Waterbury Mafia would kick his butt around the block.

Des wanted the old Deacon back. True, the old Deacon could make her crazy. But at least he was the Deacon who she'd always known and loved. This one was a stranger.

She padded naked into her bathroom and splashed some cold water on her face, gazing at herself in the mirror. She was an inch over six feet tall, long-legged, high-rumped and, these days, all ribs and hip bones. She'd lost six pounds in the past two weeks. That was her thing. When she was stressed she stopped eating. She returned to her room and put on a cropped T-shirt and gym shorts, her stomach in knots. There was that ghost out there prowling her halls. There was the "urgent" work thing that First Selectman Bob Paffin, an all-around dick, had insisted she attend this morning at eight o'clock. And then there was the situation with the man in her life. A biggie that practically had her jumping out of her skin.

Her cottage overlooking Uncas Lake was airy and open. She'd torn down several walls so that the living room, dining room and kitchen were all one big room. Ordinarily, she shared the place with Bella Tillis, the seventy-eight-year-old Jewish grandmother and fellow cat rescuer who'd been her neighbor back in Woodbridge when Des's husband, Brandon, had left her. Bella was out on the West Coast for the month, attending the weddings of two of her nine grandchildren.

The coffee smelled good. The Deacon liked it strong and black. Her three live-in cats, Christie Love, Missy Elliot and Kid Rock, were noses down in their kibble bowls, thrilled that someone, anyone, was up this early. He poured her a cup, the mug practically disappearing in his hand. The Deacon had the hugest hands she'd ever seen on any man. He'd played first base in the Cleveland Indians organization before he'd joined the state police.

She went out onto the deck and sipped the coffee, gazing out at the blackness of the lake below. The air felt soft and muggy. It was supposed to hit ninety today. The Deacon sat down in one of the Adirondack chairs out there. Kid Rock immediately jumped into his lap and began kneading the Deacon's stomach with his paws. The Deacon stroked him, sipping his coffee in stony silence.

"Are you going to repair that section of railing for me today?"

"If I have time," he answered in a distant voice.

"You carpenters sure are hard to pin down. What *are* you going to do?"

"Same thing I did yesterday—sit here with my buddy and wonder what the point is."

"The point of what, Daddy?"

"My life."

Des felt her stomach clenching. "Have you thought about talking to that therapist your cardiologist recommended?"

He made a face. "I don't deal with shrinks."

"Maybe you should try. He said it's real common for people to feel a sense of letdown after this surgery. Nothing to be ashamed of."

"I'm not ashamed, Desiree. And I don't need any help."

"We all need help sometimes."

"I'm done talking about this. I'm fine."

"Sure you are," she snapped. "We're all fine. The whole fucking world's fine."

"Watch your mouth, young lady," he warned her, flaring slightly.

She let out a gasp. "Well, how about that? I finally got a rise out of you. Maybe I ought to start dropping F-bombs more often."

Instead, she went back inside the house before she totally lost it. Since she was up so nice and early she thought about spending some quality time with her sketchpad and a hunk of graphite stick. She'd been neglecting her portraits of murder victims lately. But she just couldn't seem to focus on shapes and shadows while the ghost of Buck Mitry was skulking around the place. Instead, she went down to the gym in her garage and did three punishing circuits of twenty-four reps each with twenty-pound dumbbells until her muscles were popping and the sweat was pouring from her. Then she showered and got herself ready for work, which took her almost no time. Des kept her hair short and nubby and never wore war paint on the job. Rarely wore it, period. Didn't need it. She had almond-shaped light green eyes, a smooth, glowing complexion and a wraparound smile that, in Mitch's words, made Julia Roberts look like ZaSu Pitts. Whoever the hell ZaSu Pitts was. Des dressed in a summer-weight poly/wool blend uniform. Her necktie was the same shade of royal blue as the epaulets on her slate gray shirt. Her high gloss square-toed oxfords were black. So was the Sam Browne duty belt on which she holstered her SIG. Her big gray hat with its band of royal blue and gold waited for her on a table by the front door.

The Deacon was sitting right where she'd left him, his eyes on the water, Kid Rock dozing contentedly in his lap.

"I'm heading out now, Daddy. Have yourself a good one, okay?"

He said nothing in response. Didn't so much as nod.

Des wasn't even sure that he'd heard her.

Turkey Neck Road was one of Dorset's choicest spots—a bucolic country lane of rolling green meadows and gnarly old trees set behind fieldstone walls that were centuries old. Long, winding driveways led to multimillion-dollar estates that looked out onto the mouth of the Connecticut River and Long Island Sound. Many of the estates had private docks. Turkey Neck was a slice of Yankee heaven. Incredibly peaceful.

Or it used to be. Des ran smack dab into the freak show as soon as she steered her silver Crown Vic off of Old Shore Road. Satellite trucks and news vans lined both sides of Turkey Neck. Camera crews from Connecticut's local news stations, from ESPN and from a dozen assorted cable news networks and tabloid TV shows were crowded around the security gate outside one of those long driveways, along with a wolf pack of paparazzi, print reporters and celebrity gawkers. The gate was new. So was the eight-foot chain link fence topped with razor wire that surrounded the entire twelve-acre estate. A trooper from Troop F barracks in Westbrook was trying to keep the traffic moving along. Another was guarding the gate. The troopers were there at the request of First Selectman Paffin.

Des idled there in the standstill traffic with her windows rolled down, a tropical breeze wafting gently off the water. It was so warm out that it was hard to believe the pro football season was already half over. And what an unusual season this was for Tyrone "Da Beast" Grantham, the famously volatile superstar linebacker who'd been wreaking havoc on the gridiron ever since he was a fifteen-year-old gangbanger back in the mean streets of Compton, California. Da Beast, a six-feet-four, 240-pound meat-seeking missile, was the most dominant, fearsome middle linebacker in the National Football League. A perennial Pro Bowler who last year, at age twenty-nine, had signed a seven-year, $135-million contract extension that made him the NFL's highest paid defensive player.

Truly, the man had it all—including a boatload of personal baggage. Tyrone Grantham had a history of violent personal conduct dating back to his freshman year at USC. He'd gotten into highly publicized physical brawls over the years with not only his teammates and coaches but with any number of adoring fans—in bars, airports, parking lots, wherever they found him. He'd been placed on probation so many times that he'd entered the language of the street: Getting probation was known as getting "Beasted." During his rookie year in the NFL, a New Orleans cocktail waitress had charged him with sexually assaulting her in his hotel room. The charge was later dropped after an undisclosed sum changed hands, but another woman soon lodged a similar complaint against him at the Pro Bowl in Honolulu. Da Beast was ordered to undergo anger management counseling. He did. It didn't help. The man didn't just have anger issues. He had alcohol issues, as in a pair of DWI arrests. He had illegal drug issues—marijuana was found in his car both times he was nailed for drunk driving. He had problems keeping his mouth shut. His frequent on-air interviews and tweets were inflammatory and profane. He had problems with the low-life male company he kept. During a routine traffic stop an unlicensed handgun was found in a friend's car that Da Beast was riding in. The friend was a convicted felon. As for female company, he'd fathered six young children with five different baby mamas, none of whom he was married to.

And then came this past off-season, when Tyrone Grantham had gotten into it with a 150-pound computer programmer named Stewart Plotka at a Dave & Buster's restaurant in Westbury, Long Island. Supposedly, Plotka, a resident of Forest Hills, Queens, was now permanently blind in one eye and had lost the use of his right hand. Da Beast had escaped criminal assault charges—no witnesses had come forth to back Plotka's version of what happened. But he still faced a mammoth civil suit from Plotka, who was claiming that Grantham had "defiled" his fiancée, a nursing student named Katie O'Brien, at a celebrity pro-am golf tournament in 2008. Plotka had hired himself New York City's heaviest hitting limelight lawyer, Andrea Halperin. Not a day went by when she wasn't turning up the heat to pressure Tyrone Grantham into a seven-figure settlement. Thus far, he had stubbornly refused.

Seemingly, Da Beast didn't care about anyone or anything. But an image-conscious NFL did. Already reeling from the unsavory behavior of the likes of Michael Vick, Plaxico Burress and Ben Roethlisberger, the league decided it could no longer afford to look the other way—especially because Grantham played for one of the New York area's two very high-profile teams. And so the commissioner had suspended him from league play for the entire season due to "conduct detrimental to the integrity of and public confidence in the league." It was a season in exile that, in the view of Da Beast's critics, was long overdue. According to his lawyer, the "chastened" football star intended to use this time off to demonstrate to his fans that he really, truly understood the responsibilities of being a modern-day sports celebrity. Da Beast was going to get his act together.

Except he'd chosen to get it together in an ultramodern, eight-bedroom estate right here on Turkey Neck Road in Dorset, much to the dismay of his straight-laced, early to bed and early to white neighbors. Neighbors who cherished privacy and quiet and were immensely displeased by the media horde that had invaded their happy, privileged home. Grantham had said all of the right things when he'd moved in two weeks ago with his new bride, Jamella, who was currently seven months pregnant with his baby. He said he'd turned over a new leaf. He said he wanted to be left in peace.

But his new neighbors were not happy. Especially the conservative blowhard in the house just past his on Turkey Neck—Justy Bond, proud owner of Bond's Auto Mall across the river in Old Saybrook, which was Connecticut's highest-volume GM dealership, not to mention Toyota, BMW and Volvo. It was Justy Bond whom Bob Paffin had asked Des to speak with this morning. She couldn't miss the man as she inched past the media crush and pulled into the driveway of his rambling, circa-1820 natural-shingled cape. The auto dealer was standing out on his front lawn hollering his head off at the snowy haired, weak-chinned Paffin, who'd been first selectman for twenty-four years and wouldn't know how to get or hold a real job if his life depended on it. Des and Bob were not exactly close. Bob was a malevolent noodge who'd done nothing but disrespect her and undermine her from her first day on the job. Right now, he was trying to placate Justy, who was a big-time local celebrity thanks to those grating commercials of his that ran 24/7 on the local TV stations. Justy starred in them personally, always accompanied by a young, scantily clad "Bond Girl" who'd vamp for the camera and repeat his famous slogan: *Just ask Justy.*

Justy Bond was accustomed to getting his way. And if he was pissed off, then Bob Paffin was supposed to do something about it. *Just ask Justy.*

Des parked her cruiser and got out. Justy immediately started across the lawn toward her with a big, bright smile on his face—a car dealer through and through. He was a tall, handsome one in his mid-fifties who was trying way hard to come off as boyish in his yellow Ralph Lauren Polo shirt, khaki slacks and Top-Siders. The man's thinning black hair was artfully poofed. His shoulders were thrust back, tummy pulled in. It was, Des supposed, what came from having a hot new trophy wife like Bonita, a former Bond Girl who was twenty years younger than Justy. And had broken up his first marriage, according to local lore. Once she became Mrs. Justy Bond, Bonita relinquished her on-camera role to a former Syracuse cheerleader named Darlene Franklin. Darlene had lasted only a few months before she'd been replaced by Callie Kreutzer, an art student at the Dorset Academy, who happened to be the girlfriend of Justy Junior—or June as he was known. June, age twenty-four, worked for his dad as a salesman.

"Glad you could make it, Master Sergeant Mitry!" Justy's dazzling white smile went all of the way up to his eyes, where it died a sudden death. "I appreciate you making time for me."

"Yes, very good of you, Des," Bob Paffin concurred, baring his own mouthful of dull, yellow teeth. The Dorset old guard didn't whiten. She had no idea why. Just knew it was so.

Justy led them around to the backyard on a bluestone path. There was a swimming pool back there, a patio with a lot of teak furniture and an acre or so of lawn leading down to the water, where a thirty-two-foot Coronado, the *Calliope,* was tied up at Justy's dock. A tanned, shaggy-haired young man in swim trunks was scrubbing the sailboat's deck. Des waved to June Bond. He waved back. She and Mitch had socialized with June and Callie. Mitch knew Callie's mom and had helped Callie find a place to live when she'd enrolled at the academy.

"What's that damned kid still doing here?" Justy fumed. "I swear, he cares more about that fool yacht than he does the family business. He even sleeps out on the damned thing, even though we have a half-dozen perfectly nice bedrooms in the house."

"A young fellow likes to have his own patch of turf," Bob said.

"A bit of ambition wouldn't hurt either." Justy shot a glance at his Rolex. "When I was his age I'd have made my first three sales of the day by now."

The view from there was pretty spectacular. Des could see downriver all of the way to the lighthouse on Big Sister Island. Upriver, she could make out the picturesque railroad bridge that had been spanning the Connecticut River on its sturdy granite pilings since 1907. She could also see the newly lengthened dock right next door where Tyrone Grantham's flaming orange cigarette boat, *Da Beast,* was tied up. It was a rather menacing-looking thing—more than forty-five feet long, low to the water and emblazoned from stem to stern with images of snarling lions and tigers. Also faintly silly. Like something out of a comic book.

Justy's gaze followed hers. "I hate that I can see that stupid thing from here. And you should *hear* it. First time he took her out I thought a jumbo jet was about to crash into our house."

He turned his back on the view and sat down at a teak table by the pool. Des and Bob joined him there.

"What can I do for you gentlemen?" Des asked, setting her big hat on the table before her.

Bob cleared his throat and said, "Have you met this fellow yet?"

"Tyrone Grantham? No, I haven't."

"We were thinking you might want to drop by and introduce yourself."

"And why would I want to do that?"

"To welcome him to Dorset, of course."

"I'm the resident Connecticut State Trooper here, Bob. If you want the Welcome Wagon give Eve Todd a call. She does a very nice job."

Justy heaved an exasperated sigh. "Oh, for crissakes, can we just talk plain?"

"Fine by me," Des said.

"I have had nothing but trouble with this *individual* since he bought the place. The man does whatever he wants and nobody dares say no. He lengthened that dock of his without town approval. That penitentiary-style fence he's put in between us is two feet taller than the building code allows. *And* it's topped with razor wire, which isn't allowed either. A twenty-foot stretch of the darned thing is at least eighteen inches over my property line. Plus the cheese heads who installed it mutilated a half-dozen of my trees. Why, I must be spending half of my time every day over at Town Hall filing one official complaint after another. Meanwhile, I've got the paparazzi and who knows what other human filth camped outside of my house twenty-four hours a day."

"You have my sympathy, Mr. Bond."

"I don't want your sympathy. I want you to *do* something."

"I don't see a role for me here," Des told him. "You do have a traffic situation, but I just saw two troopers out there trying to help out. I don't know what else can be done. We can't strong-arm the media. All we can do is keep the road clear and try to move the gawkers along. My advice is to be patient. They'll move on to another story in a few days and your life will return to normal."

"My *life* will never be normal as long as that man is living next door," Justy said tightly. "I should *not* have to put up with this. I have rights, too."

"Of course you do," Bob assured him. "That's why we thought you might have a talk with the gentleman, Des."

"A talk about what, Bob?"

Justy glared across the table at her. "Are you purposely playing dumb?"

"I'm not 'playing' at anything. I'm the resident trooper. If Mr. Grantham phones 911 and requests my presence I'll oblige him. If he breaks the law I'll—"

"He's broken several laws. I can give you a list as long as my arm."

"You're talking about possible building code violations, Mr. Bond. Those aren't criminal matters."

The two men exchanged an uneasy look before Bob said, "Des, I want to assure you that what I'm about to say is in no way racially motivated . . ."

"No, of course not," Des managed to say, her face revealing nothing.

"But we have . . . concerns about the criminal element Mr. Grantham has been known to associate with. We want to make sure he behaves himself."

"And he has," Des said. "Tyrone Grantham is not wanted in connection with any crime. He's a high-profile sports celebrity, period."

"What about his posse or crew or whatever it's called?"

"I believe it's called his wife and family," she replied crisply. "What about them, Bob?"

"Well, one worries about gang-related activity."

"Like one of those drive-by shootings," Justy said, nodding his head. "Bonita hasn't been able to sleep a wink since they moved in next door. She just wanders around the house all night, scared out of her wits."

"I'm unaware of any such gang-related activity," Des said, hearing the crunch of gravel out front as a car pulled in and parked. A car door slammed shut and footsteps started toward them on the bluestone path.

The footsteps belonged to Bonita, who was just back from an early morning tennis game at the country club. Or so her sleeveless white polo shirt and trim little white tennis shorts suggested. Bonita was thirty-six trying real hard to look twenty-six. Her day-glo tangerine lip gloss and nail polish were a bit too young for her. So was the matching tangerine scrunchie that held her shiny blond ponytail in place. Bonita was tall and slim with nice tanned legs and a perky little ass. Good, high cheekbones, a kitteny little nose, playful blue eyes—a vanilla princess through and through. Just the sort of pampered blond bitch whom Des had resented her entire life. But Dorset's many vanilla princesses were not all the same flavor, she'd discovered. Some were actually very nice people. Others were even nastier than she'd ever imagined.

"Hi, darling." Bonita gave Justy a big, smoochy kiss, mussing his carefully coiffed hair. "Greetings, Bob. Hey, Trooper Des," she added coolly.

Des said hey back—with equal coolness. She'd had to pull Bonita over on Route 156 last year for exceeding the posted speed limit by more than twenty mph—and driving on the wrong side of the road. She'd flunked her Breathalyzer test and had not been particularly gracious. In fact, she'd called Des a "hostile twat."

"How was tennis?" Justy asked her, smoothing his hair back down.

"*Really* hard." Bonita's mouth got all pouty. "And my little pink toes are *so* hot." She sat on the edge of the pool, took off her sneakers and anklets and dipped those little pink toes in the water, sighing contentedly as she paddled her smooth bare legs back and forth.

Bob Paffin couldn't take his eyes off her legs. The old goat was practically drooling. Justy, Des noticed, paid her no attention whatsoever.

Des also noticed that Bonita had a nasty scalp wound on the back of her head. "What did you do to your head?"

"Cracked it on the kitchen counter," Bonita answered lightly. "I was looking for a muffin pan in the cupboard down below. That'll teach me to cook. What are you three up to?"

"Talking about our new neighbor," Justy replied.

Bonita rolled her eyes. "Are you still obsessing about him? Let it go."

"Your husband was just telling me you're so upset that you can't sleep."

"I'm fine," Bonita assured her. "We're fine."

"We're not fine." Justy narrowed his gaze at Des. "What's more, I resent your cavalier attitude toward this crisis."

"There *is* no crisis, Mr. Bond. But you've asked me to weigh in so I'm going to. If you're so worried about Tyrone Grantham being a good neighbor then why don't you act like one yourself? Stroll on over there to welcome him to the community. Bring his new bride some flowers. Maybe a lucky horseshoe to hang over the front door. I understand that's a quaint tradition here in Dorset. Seriously, have you done *anything* other than holler bloody murder about him over at Town Hall? How about you, Bob? Have you rung his bell and introduced yourself?" On their stony silence Des shook her head and said, "We had a word for men like you when I was growing up—wusses."

"God, am I loving this or what?" Bonita whooped.

"Shut your mouth!" Justy snarled at his young wife.

Des parked her big hat on her head and said, "If you folks will excuse me, I'll be going."

June Bond came shambling across the lawn toward them now in his swim trunks, all sun-browned and sweaty. June was lean and broad-shouldered. His jaw was strong, his smile genuine. "Good to see you, Des," he said warmly.

"Back at you, June," Des responded.

Bonita eyed him rather humidly from the edge of the pool, her blue eyes roaming over his tanned, muscular frame. June's own eyes carefully avoided hers. Des would have sworn they had something going on if she hadn't seen for herself how much June and Callie adored each other.

If Justy was aware of anything he wasn't letting on. He was too busy showing who was in charge. "June, what in the hell are you still doing here? You should have been on the showroom floor a half hour ago."

"Just have to jump in the shower, boss. I'll be there in a flash."

"See that you are. Or go find yourself another job. In this family we *work* for a living, hear me?"

June's mouth tightened. "Yes, sir." He started toward the house at a brisker pace.

"Why are you so rough on him?" Bonita asked.

"I treat him like any other employee. I expect him to move merchandise."

Des tipped her hat and said, "Have a good day, folks."

"Des, what if you were to pay Mr. Grantham a simple courtesy call?" Bob thumbed his receding chin thoughtfully. "You know, just to see if there's any way you can be of service to him regarding the gawkers and so forth."

"The man's not stupid, Bob. He'll see right through that."

"What if he does? I should think he'd be flattered. I know I'd be. Would you do that for us, Des? Ask him if there's any way you can help out? And while you're at it, just, well, see if you can persuade him to accommodate his new neighbors a bit more?"

"The answer is still no, Bob."

"It would be in your best interest, you know."

"*My* best interest? How so?"

"Because if there's an incident of some kind, God forbid, it will reflect very poorly on your management skills. Your troop commander will take note of that when it comes time for your performance review. Especially because I'm quite certain he'll be made aware of it." Bob Paffin showed Des those yellow teeth of his again. At that moment he reminded her very much of a cornered Norway rat she'd had to shoot one night in the Frog Hollow projects. "Do we understand each other?"

CHAPTER 2

THE TRAFFIC WAS BACKED up all the way to Old Shore Road. A state trooper was trying to move people along. Whatever. Mitch waited there patiently in his bulbous kidney-colored 1956 Studebaker pickup. He was delivering cartons of nonperishables from the Food Pantry to the Joshua sisters, who lived in the waterfront estate just this side of the Grantham place, and he was in no hurry. Quite honestly, Mitch saw very little point in ever being in a hurry. It was the single most important life lesson that Mitch Berger, a child of the streets of Manhattan, had learned since he'd taken up residence in his antique caretaker's cottage out on Big Sister Island.

He reached for an Entennman's powdered donut, munching on it contentedly. Until a few months ago, Mitch had been the lead film critic of the most prestigious newspaper in New York City—as well as the buffed, primped on-air reviewer for its parent empire's cable news channel. But he'd said good-bye to all of that. These days, he was perfectly happy to write two essays a week for the e-zine that Lacy Nickerson, his former editor at the newspaper, had launched. Right now he was putting together his annual Halloween Scare-a-palooza, which was something that he, his readers and Netflix had all come to look forward to. Mitch always tried to avoid the obvious candidates like *Psycho* or *The Shining*. He'd choose fright films that were a bit more obscure, offbeat or just plain bizarre. And he'd come up with some good ones so far, like *The Maze* with Richard Carlson and Hillary Brooke, a 1953 William Cameron

Menzies 3D non-classic that had a real jolter of an ending (spoiler alert: You won't feel like eating frog legs for a really long time). And 1980's *Can't Stop The Music*, starring The Village People, Valerie Perrine and Olympic gold-medalist Bruce Jenner, which had to be the most outright terrifying Hollywood movie ever made.

Mitch helped himself to another donut, pleased by how relaxed he felt even though The Big Event was a mere day away. True, his forehead was breaking out for the first time in fourteen years. True, he'd just inhaled his fifth donut since he left the house. But, hey, it wasn't every day that his parents flew up from their retirement village in Vero Beach to meet the new woman in his life. *And* her father.

I love Des. I love my parents. Why am I freaking out?

Chet and Ruth Berger were terrific people who had devoted thirty-four years of their lives to giving inner-city schoolkids a chance. His dad taught Algebra at Boys and Girls High in Brooklyn. His mom served as school librarian at the Eleanor Roosevelt Middle School in Washington Heights. They raised Mitch in a two-bedroom rent-stabilized apartment in Stuyvesant Town. Scrimped and saved so he could attend Columbia. Took their pensions when they were sixty-two, and were now enjoying the Florida retirement they so richly deserved. In fact, this would be the first time they'd been back to New York in over a year. They were staying in Mitch's apartment on West 102 Street for a couple of days and coming out to Dorset tomorrow. He'd booked them a nice room at the Frederick House Inn.

I love my Des. I love my parents. Why am I freaking out?

It wasn't as if they didn't know she was a Connecticut state trooper who knew at least eighteen different ways to kill a man with her bare hands. Or that she wasn't Jewish. Mitch's beloved wife, Maisie, who'd died of ovarian cancer, hadn't been Jewish either. But, well, she *had* been white. And there was no way tomorrow night's real-life version of *Guess Who's Coming to Dinner?* wasn't going to be tense.

Not that Chet and Ruth had flown north solely to meet Des. They also had a couple of "appointments" to take care of in the city. "Appointments" that they'd been stubbornly tight-lipped about when Mitch tried to press for details over the phone. As in, perhaps one of them was in town to see a specialist regarding a grapefruit-sized tumor. Then again, perhaps Mitch was just a bit spooked. After losing Maisie he had every reason to be. Not to mention what Des had just gone through with the Deacon. One day, he was fine. The next day he was on the operating table having quadruple-bypass surgery. That was how these things happened when they happened. *Bam.* You never saw them coming.

Slowly, the traffic crept its way near Stalag Grantham, with its eight-foot chain-link fence topped with razor wire and festooned with KEEP OUT signs. All it needed was guard towers manned by helmeted storm troopers. Outside of Da Beast's front gate the news crews and paparazzi were jabbering and jostling like a slavering mob at a freak show. Which, in fact, was what they were.

Finally, Mitch was able to inch close enough so that he could pull into the long gravel driveway that belonged to Da Beast's neighbors, Luanne and Lila Joshua, a pair of wifty spinsters in their sixties. The Joshuas were one of Dorset's most distinguished founding families. Old, old money. Not that you'd know it by the condition of their place. The tall weeds in the rutted driveway brushed the undercarriage of Mitch's truck as he bumped his way toward their three-story center-chimney mansion, which dated back to the early 1700s and, you'd swear, hadn't been cared for since. It was a moldering wreck with broken windowpanes, missing roof shingles, peeling paint, rotting door frames, rotting sills, rotting everything. It was sad to see what had happened to such a fine old colonial showplace.

But the Joshua sisters happened to be penniless due to a toxic combination of poor investments, soaring property taxes and almost no income beyond the monthly Social Security check that their beloved seventy-two-year-old brother-in-law, Winston, received. The three of them would be starving if it weren't for the Food Pantry deliveries Mitch made three times a week. And the rent money they were receiving from their boarder, Callie Kreutzer, an art student at the renowned Dorset Academy. Mitch had a hand in that, too. Callie's mom, an art critic, was tight with Lacy, his editor.

Callie's bicycle was parked by the sagging front porch. So was the sisters' ancient blue Peugeot station wagon. Winston's vintage MGTD ragtop was parked there, too, though it no longer ran.

Which was just as well. Winston, who'd been married to Luanne and Lila's late sister Lorelei, was in no condition to drive it or any other vehicle. He'd been a celebrated *New Yorker* cartoonist back in his heyday, a dashing and colorful personality with a signature handlebar moustache. Near as Mitch could tell, both Luanne and Lila had harbored schoolgirl crushes on him when Lorelei was alive. These days they functioned as his full-time caregivers. He needed full-time caregivers. At first, folks around Dorset had attributed Winston's increasingly peculiar behavior to his tippling. He did like his liquor. And Dorset was no stranger to elderly drinkers who liked to kick up their heels after eight or ten martinis. But Winston's case took an extreme turn. One day, he ran stark naked down Turkey Neck in broad daylight shouting about how badly he wanted to stick his pecker in "some*one* or some*thing*." Actually made it all the way to the mini-mart on Old Shore Road before Des was able to corral him. Then he took to behaving badly in the dining room at the Dorset Country Club. Groping the breasts and bottoms of the waitresses. Groping himself. And then—the final straw—diving under a table and burying his face between the enormous wattled thighs of Amanda Heyer, age eighty-two.

Quite simply, the poor man seemed to have lost all sexual inhibitions. It wasn't Alzheimer's disease, as some around town had speculated. It was frontotemporal dementia. There was no cure and no effective way to slow its progression. All that the doctors could do was try to manage Winston's behavioral symptoms with medication. All that the sisters could do was try to keep him calm, clean and fed—and watch him get steadily worse. They'd have to put him in a nursing home when they could no longer handle him.

Mitch climbed out of his Studey, gathered up the two cartons of food he'd brought and let himself in the front door. Like a lot of the old houses in Dorset, the Joshua place had wide-planked oak floors and low ceilings. Unlike a lot of the old houses it reeked of mildewed rugs and cat urine. Nearly a dozen cats dozed here, there, everywhere. The sisters needed them. They had mice here, there, everywhere. Also spiderwebs and dust bunnies like he'd never seen before. If they owned a vacuum they hadn't used it since the dawn of the twenty-first century. There was an eerie, lost-in-time aura about the Joshua place. Maybe it was all of those antique, hand-wound wall clocks that were tick-tick-ticking away in every room, each one keeping its own sweet time. Or maybe it was all of those empty spaces on the walls. Luanne and Lila had been forced to sell off many of the old family paintings. A lot of their antique furniture was gone, too. He could still see the depressions in the rug where their dining table once stood.

He called out to them.

"Good morning, Mitch!" Luanne responded cheerily.

"We're in the kitchen, dear!" Lila chimed in.

They were sipping their morning coffee at the kitchen table, each of them immaculately turned out in a crisp summer dress, freshly made-up, coiffed and perfumed. Luanne and Lila were always very particular about their appearance. They were also unfailingly gracious and upbeat. Both sisters were blue eyed and silver haired, but the resemblance ended there. Lila, the younger of the two, was slender, shy and had a fluttery, clueless manner. Luanne, her big sister, was stockier, calmer and gave the impression of being on top of things. She wasn't. They were equally helpless. As far as Mitch knew, neither sister had ever held a job. Or lived anywhere else. All they had was each other and this old house, which they refused to sell but couldn't afford to keep up. To save on heat during the cold months they occupied a mere half-dozen of its twenty-eight rooms. There were entire wings of the place that Mitch felt certain they hadn't entered in years. He couldn't imagine what manner of wildlife lived up in the attic.

There was a glassed-in sun porch off the kitchen that the sisters were letting Callie use as a studio. She liked to work on her free-form paintings in there. Fling paint, in other words. It was all over the windows, walls and floors. Think Jackson Pollack. Think projectile vomiting.

"It's a beautiful day, is it not, Mitch?" Luanne exclaimed, petting the black cat that was sprawled on the kitchen table.

"Yes, it certainly is," agreed Mitch, who was starting to feel lightheaded. It wasn't just their heavy, fruity perfume. It smelled *awful* in there, as if something had died in one of the cupboards. He deposited the cartons of provisions on the counter. The canned goods, cereal and bread were courtesy of the Food Pantry. He'd bought the milk, eggs and orange juice at the A&P with his own money. Not that they knew. There was no reason for them to know.

"This is so *kind* of you, Mitch," Lila said in that trembly voice of hers that always reminded him of Katherine Hepburn in *Stage*

Door. He kept expecting her to come out with: *"The calla lilies are in bloom again."*

"My pleasure," he said, edging over toward an open window for some fresh air. From there he could see their stone patio and the two acres or so of lawn that he'd mowed for them last week. Beyond the lawn there was a sliver of beach at the water's edge. And an incredible panoramic view. On a clear day you could see Long Island. A dense thicket of trees stood between the Joshuas and their new neighbor. "How is Winston doing this morning?"

"Fine and dandy," Luanne replied. "I just shaved him with that nice Norelco you picked up for us. You're so clever." A decline in personal hygiene was another symptom of Winston's dementia. The sisters had been unable to shave him with a blade because he refused to sit still. "Right now he's having a good soak in a hot tub. Or I should say a warm tub. Our furnace is on its last legs. Assuming, that is, furnaces have legs."

"Ours does. It most certainly sits on legs." Lila glanced at him hesitantly. "Mitch, I hate to bother you but have you noticed a slight odor?"

"Why, no, I haven't."

"That silly sink of ours is backed up again. Could you? . . ."

Mitch had a look. And a whiff. The sink had two inches of fetid brown water in it. "Where do you keep your plunger?"

"In the cupboard under the sink," Luanne said.

He could hear all sorts of scurrying around in there as he searched for the plunger, shuddering inwardly. There was no telling what lived under there. Or how sharp its teeth were. He took the plunger to the clogged drain and brought up a fist-sized clump of either stringy vegetable matter, hair or, possibly, the earthly remains of a drowned mouse. He didn't know. Didn't want to know. But that black cat *was* watching him from the kitchen table with keen interest. Mitch bagged it—the clump, not the cat—and took it out to the trash. Then he ran the faucet for a minute to make sure the drain was clear.

He was just about to take off when he heard a loud thud upstairs.

"Ah, that'll be Winston," Luanne said. "Mitch, would you mind lending us your strong back? He's a bit heavy for us to hoist out of the tub."

There were at least eight bedrooms on the second floor. The bath that adjoined Winston's room was right at the top of the stairs.

He was sitting in an old claw-footed tub calmly soaking away. Winston was a big man, well over six feet tall. He'd rowed at Princeton and still had the broad shoulders to prove it. But the rest of him resembled a sagging old water buffalo. His skin hung from him in loose, billowing folds. Winston's hair, what little there was of it, was white. So was his handlebar moustache, which Mitch noticed looked kind of ratty and uneven.

Luanne noticed it, too. "Winnie, have you been chewing on our moustache again?"

"I'd rather chew on yours," he replied, his blue eyes twinkling at her.

"Now don't you be naughty, dear."

"What's that man doing in my bathroom, Lorelei?"

"I'm Luanne. Lorelei is gone, remember?"

"Then what are *you* doing in here?"

"Helping you take your bath."

"In that case, get out of that dress and hop in." Winston reached for her with his wet, soapy hands. "We'll go for a little spin."

"Behave, Winnie. You'll get me all wet." She bent down to wipe him with a washcloth. He immediately reached for her left breast and gave it a good squeeze. "And *please* remember you're a gentleman."

"You're mistaken. No gentlemen here. Who is that curly haired fellow?"

"Why, that's Mitch," Lila answered.

"*Who?*"

"Brubaker," Mitch said. For some reason, the old fellow had taken to calling him that.

"Oh, sure." Winston grinned at him. "How are you, Brubaker?"

"Just fine, sir. And you?"

"Horny beyond belief. And I really have to take a piss."

Luanne shook her finger at him. "Not in the water again, hear me?"

"Okay," he grumbled. "But only because you've got great tits."

Luanne sighed wistfully. "And to think there was a time when I would have sold my soul for just one night in the feathers with this man."

"Don't *you* get all earthy, too," Lila said to her primly.

"You're one to talk," Luanne shot back. "Considering that wild fling you and he had."

Lila reddened. "Winston and I did not have any fling, wild or otherwise. That was entirely Lorelei's imagination."

"Did you or did you not go to Scranton together for the weekend back in seventy-eight?"

"Strictly to look at a wardrobe cupboard that he wished to buy for her. Antiques have always been a passion of mine, as you know perfectly well. Winston wanted my advice. We stayed in separate rooms at the inn. Why, we never so much as . . . as . . . ." Lila's fine-boned face got all scrunched up. Then she ran from the bathroom, sobbing.

"I guess I have to stop teasing her," Luanne murmured. "She's getting so sensitive."

"She's always been sensitive," Winston said. "And she had the loveliest titties I've ever seen. Milk white, with a birthmark right here under her left nipple."

Luanne looked at him in alarm. Possibly, it was that specific mention of Lila's birthmark. "He's just spouting nonsense now, Mitch. He was always faithful to our Lorelei. Weren't you, Winnie?"

"We spent that weekend in Scranton screwing our brains out," he answered happily. "Hey, Brubaker, have you checked out those hot new babes next door? They stretch out by the swimming pool wearing next to nothing. And they're *colored* girls."

"You mean women of color," Mitch said.

"You can see them through the trees if you get over next to that fence."

"Winnie, I want you to leave those people alone. They have enough trouble with those awful reporters. Besides, we haven't been introduced."

"Sometimes they even get up and dance," he prattled on. "Shake those butts of theirs. You don't see butts like those on white girls. By God, I'd like to take a great, big bite out of—"

"Okay, we're done here," Luanne announced firmly. "Mitch? . . ."

Mitch grabbed Winston by one wet, slippery armpit while she reached across him for the other. They'd just managed to hoist the old fellow up onto his feet when Callie Kreutzer came bouncing past the open door on her way to the stairs.

Callie didn't seem the least bit fazed by the sight of the naked old man standing there in the tub. "I'm off to the academy, Luanne!"

"Have a lovely day, dear," Luanne responded sweetly.

"Don't go running off again!" Winston called out as Callie started down the stairs. "I've got something *huge* here for you!"

"Winston, *behave!*" Luanne barked as she began to towel him off. "I can take it from here, Mitch. Thank you so much."

By the time he'd made it outside Callie was getting ready to ride off on her bike, her art portfolio slung over one shoulder. She was quite a gifted painter. Her miniature still lifes were amazingly luminous.

"Callie, are you okay living here?"

"What do you mean by that?" Callie possessed a voice that was, well, nasal. She sounded a lot like a spacey high-school girl. Looked like one, too, for that matter. She was twenty but she could easily pass for sixteen. Barely five feet tall with long, straight blond hair, chubby chipmunk cheeks and big gray eyes. Mitch doubted she weighed over a hundred pounds. She hid her slender figure inside an oversized, paint-splattered T-shirt and baggy jeans.

"I mean that Winston is getting worse. Has he ever? . . ."

"Not to worry, Mitch. He's totally harmless."

"Plus it smells awful inside of that house. Maybe we should find you somewhere else to stay."

"No way. I'm totally cool here. My room has an incredible view of the water. And the girls let me fling paint half the night out on their sun porch. I can put on an old bikini—or not—and just let it fly. Which, like, totally keeps me sane. Because once you walk in the door of the academy everything you do has to *represent*. I have a great set-up here, honest. Besides, when Winston's lucid he's really very insightful about my work. He was a marvelous draftsman. Um, okay, maybe sometimes I . . ." Callie hesitated, her lower lip clamped between her teeth. "I *do* get the feeling he's, you know, watching me when I'm flinging paint. From outside the window, I mean. But that could just be my imagination. And, hey, if it makes him happy to stand out there eyeballing my tush, it's no big. Besides, I have an open invite to crash with June on board the *Calliope* any time."

Callie had been romantically involved with June Bond for a

couple of months. Thanks to him, she'd landed a cushy part-time gig as the Bond Girl on those inane *"Just ask Justy"* commercials that ran day and night on local TV.

"Can I give you a lift to school? We can throw your bike in back."

Callie shrugged her narrow shoulders. "Why not?"

He hoisted her bike into the back of the Studey and made room for her on the front seat. She got in next to him and Mitch eased the truck down the long, rutted gravel drive. He offered her a donut. Callie declined. He helped himself to one. "How's June doing?"

"He's fine," she answered as Mitch inched out into the traffic snarl on Turkey Neck. "Except he doesn't want to sell cars anymore. Never did, if you ask me. He's just been trying to please his father. As if."

"What does he really want to do?"

"Sail the *Calliope* down to the Florida Keys. His dream is to work on sailboats there full-time. Restore them and sell them for a profit. It's something he's real good at, Mitch. The *Calliope* was an absolute wreck when he bought her. Now she's a thing of beauty. He . . . sort of wants me to sail down there with him," Callie added with a casual toss of her hair.

"And when would you do that?"

"This weekend."

Mitch shot a startled look at her. "That's a bit sudden, isn't it?"

"It's totally sudden. He just dropped it on me last night. He really, really wants the two of us to get away from this place."

"Are you saying he wants you to quit the Dorset Academy?"

"Yes."

"Are you going to?"

"I don't know. I haven't decided."

"I don't get it, Callie. What's the big rush?"

"Don't ask me. He's just real unhappy here."

"Are things okay between June and his dad?"

"As okay as they ever are. Justy rides him awful hard."

"And how about between *you* and Justy?"

She rolled her eyes. "Oh, puh-leese. Not you, too. Everyone figures that because I'm so sucky in those commercials that I *must* be doing him. Darlene, the last Bond girl? She totally was. I hear Bonita caught the two of them getting busy on the sofa in the customer lounge. An epic screechfest went down. Next thing anybody knew there was a sudden opening for a Bond girl." Callie changed her mind and reached for a powdered donut, munching on it as they broke free of the traffic on Turkey Neck and started cruising up Old Shore Road toward the Historic District. "Justy gave me the job as a favor to June. He knows I really need the money to help cover my tuition. Although he still owes me like a thousand bucks from the last spots we filmed. Mitch, I swear he's never put a move on me. Not that he'd ever get anywhere. I mean, God, he's fifty-five years old. He smells like *cheese*."

"Do you get along okay with Bonita?"

"I guess. She's not really my kind of person. She's a total taker. She broke up Justy's marriage to June's mom, you know."

"Justy had a little something to do with that."

"June thinks Bonita took advantage of him. Justy tries to come across as all take-charge but he's really just a horny, clueless trog who drinks too much. Bonita sized him up right away and moved in for the kill. Or so June thinks. He doesn't like her very much."

"You say Justy owes you money. What's up with that?"

"I think he's having cash flow problems. People aren't buying cars like they used to. There was nobody around the place last time I was there."

"Do you think that's why June is suddenly so anxious to leave—because Bond's Auto Mall is circling the drain?"

"Mitch, I really wish I knew. But I don't." Callie sighed woefully. "Are you going to eat that last donut?"

CHAPTER 3

"I MAY NOT BE a football star but I have rights, too," proclaimed Stewart Plotka, who was holding an impromptu news conference on the shoulder of the road just outside Tyrone Grantham's driveway. The camera crews practically engulfed him. "I'm here for some justice. And I'm staying here until I get it."

Plotka was short, tubby and on the whiny side. As photo-op proof of how grievously he'd been injured by Da Beast he wore a highly theatrical black eye patch over his left eye and a splint around his right hand. Picture the world's shlumpiest pirate and that was Stewart Plotka. The man looked about as dashing as a baked apple standing out there in the hot sun in his sweat-stained knit shirt and rumpled Dockers. His slickly tailored power lawyer, Andrea Halperin, towered over him in her stiletto heels.

Des stood there watching them, fuming. She was pissed at herself for letting Bob Paffin move her around. Not that the old weasel had left her a way out. He knew how to get ugly when he needed to. And, with a rich resident like Justy Bond climbing up his ass, he needed to.

"I have a right to be here," Plotka went on. The news crews were pretty much blocking the entire road now. The trooper on traffic detail—a big, empty uniform—had lost control of the situation. "And I'm staying here until Tyrone Grantham owns up to what he did to Katie O'Brien."

Des strolled on over and said, "I hope you don't mean *here* here, Mr. Plotka. Because you're impeding the flow of traffic."

"Mr. Plotka has a legal right to speak," asserted Andrea Halperin, who had sleek auburn hair and an intensely self-important air about her. "We're on public property."

"And I work for the public. I'm Resident Trooper Desiree Mitry and I'm informing you that you are creating a safety hazard. Please move along."

"My client is not going anywhere. He has taken up residence at the Saybrook Point Inn and he intends to show up here each and every day until Mr. Tyrone Grantham owns up to what he's done."

"I said please move along." Des kept her voice calm for the cameras. If she wasn't careful it could bottom out on her and she could come across like Barry White on a bad hair day. "Move along."

Andrea Halperin knew how to get her client on TV. She also knew when to cut and run. She steered Plotka toward a black Mercedes that was double-parked on the shoulder of the road. They climbed in and sped away, Andrea behind the wheel. The media throng promptly began shouting questions at Des. She ignored them as she strode toward the front gate. A tall, impassive blond trooper stood guard there.

"Hey, Oly," Des said, smiling at him. Trooper Olsen was a pro who didn't get all weird around her because she was a she. "What are you supposed to be doing?"

"Nothing," he replied.

"Nothing?"

"Orders straight from the top."

"I'm going in."

"Are they expecting you?"

"They are if they're watching CNN."

He pushed a button on the inside of the gatepost. The gate

swung open and Des started her way up the long, winding gravel driveway toward the house. The Grantham place had been built during the boom years of the nineties. It resembled a cluster of giant glass Kleenex boxes, some laid out lengthwise, others standing on end. A pair of Cadillac Escalades—one black, one white—was parked out front, along with a silver Range Rover, a blue Porsche 911 Carrera convertible and a tan Lexus SC 430 two-seater. Also a Dodge minivan and a beat-up old Ford pickup. All of the vehicles had New York plates except for the pickup, which had Texas plates.

Des rang the bell.

The door was opened by a lanky, way long young black man in a loose-fitting T-shirt and swim trunks. He was long enough to be a baller—six-feet-eight or nine, easy—and sported a retro-eighties high-top fade, a hairstyle she hadn't known was staging a come-back. "Yo, lookie here, we got us Resident Trooper Des-aye-ray Mitry!" he exclaimed, flashing her a playful grin. "Ain't nobody messes with you, sister. When you say move along you *mean* move along. I'm Big Tee's cousin Clarence. Clarence Bellows. But since you and me's about to fall in love just call me Cee, awright?"

It was bright and sunny inside the glass house. From the entry hall Des could see floor-to-ceiling river views. Hear a television blaring. Also hear someone playing jazz chords on a piano. Someone who could really play.

Clarence stood there with his hands on his hips, admiring her from head to toe. "Aren't you the cutest thing with your big hat? Girl, you have got to come back when you're not packing heat."

"That will be quite enough, Cee." A much smaller black man wearing gold-framed glasses appeared next to Clarence in the entry hall. "Resident Trooper Mitry did not come here to lip with you. Pleased to meet you, Trooper. I'm Rondell Grantham. Tyrone is my brother. Half-brother, to be precise. We share the same mother.

Neither of us ever knew who our father was. Nor did she. I'm three years younger than Tyrone."

"*And* a midget," Clarence pointed out.

Not a midget, but Rondell Grantham stood no more than five-feet-eight and was so compactly built Des doubted he weighed more than a buck-forty. He wore a white oxford cloth dress shirt, tan gabardine slacks and polished brown Ferragamo loafers. His hair was trimmed high and tight. "I was informed that Dorset's resident trooper was a highly competent young woman of color," he said to her. "I've been looking forward to meeting you. We all have."

Now a broad shadow fell across the entry hall and the famous Tyrone Grantham stood before her in a tank top and gym shorts, his heavy lidded eyes watchful and curious. The warrior athlete wasn't nearly as tall as his cousin Clarence. He stood a mere six-feet-three. But he was as wide across as three grown men and it was all muscle. His gleaming shaved head didn't sit atop his bulging neck so much as it receded into it. His biceps were the size of boulders. His thighs were as big around as an average man's torso. Tattoos of snarling lions, tigers and attack dogs covered practically every inch of skin that Des could see. So did the battle scars of his brutal profession. His broad, flat nose had been broken countless times. His face scratched and gouged. Jagged surgical scars adorned both knees and both shoulders. His huge knuckles were battered and the index finger of his left hand stuck out at an odd angle.

Tyrone Grantham was an utterly savage-looking man. Yet he seemed totally relaxed and at ease. "Glad to know you, Trooper," he said, a boyish smile creasing his face. "Did you meet my little brother, Rondell? I'll bet he didn't tell you he has a graduate degree in business from Wharton. He isn't one to brag. I can't tell you how proud I am of him. When we were coming up I looked out for him. Now he looks out for me. Right, little man?"

Rondell gazed up at his brother worshipfully. "That's right, big man."

"Damned right. Little brother manages my investments and various ventures. I'm presently expanding into the music business. We've installed a recording studio right here in the house. Cee's a sound engineer with skills. We got us some big plans. Hey, what are we standing out here for? Come on in."

There was an immense fieldstone fireplace in the glass living room and a sunken seating area of white leather sofas. A very pretty, very pregnant young black woman was plopped on one of the sofas watching CNN on a sixty-inch flat screen TV—a live report on what was going on right now outside this very house. Which was, Des decided, a tiny bit surreal. The focal point of the living room was the hugest home aquarium she'd ever seen. Half a dozen pale gray sharks were swimming around in a water world of brightly colored coral reef.

"It's two thousand gallons," Tyrone said, following her gaze. "Saw a tank just like it one night at a club in Tribeca and said I've got to have me one. An outfit in the city designs them, installs them, everything. Those are black tip reef sharks you're looking at. I can watch them for hours. Always want to make sure you have six. It's all about team. Fewer than six and they prey on each other. More than six and you've got a jailbreak. Turn off that TV, will you, Cee? We have a guest. Trooper Mitry, say hello to my lovely wife, Jamella."

Jamella eyed Des with a gaze that was anything but friendly. It was guarded, streetwise and extremely protective of who and what was hers. "Hey," she said.

"Glad to know you," said Des, who'd read all about Da Beast's twenty-three-year-old bride. Jamella Jameson was a professional dancer out of Houston who'd toured with Beyoncé before she'd snagged the NFL's biggest, baddest star. She was a natural beauty with smooth skin and sculpted lips. Her strong jaw and high hard cheekbones gave her a distinctly Native American look. She wore her hair long and braided. The maternity shift she wore was an unusual, brightly patterned patchwork design that was quite lovely.

Tyrone settled himself on the sofa next to Jamella and took her slim hand in his big, battered one. "Sit, sit, Trooper. Can I get you anything to drink? You hungry? Moms just got back from the store. She can fix you anything."

"I'm good, thanks." Des perched on the edge of a sofa, big hat on her knee. Somewhere in the house someone was still playing a piano.

Rondell sat directly across from her, watching her alertly. Clarence sprawled his long self out next to him.

"Take your big feet off my sofa," Jamella scolded him.

He obeyed her at once. "Sorry."

"Let me take a wild guess," Tyrone said to Des. "The powers that be sent you here to tell me to behave myself, am I right?"

"No, you are not."

He frowned at her. "Then what are you doing here?"

"Trying to head off trouble."

"You can't," he stated flatly. "Trouble's going to find you. It always finds me. Like that clown Plotka out there. The man's nothing but a lying shakedown artist looking for a cheap payday."

"Our attorney calls it nothing more than civil extortion," Rondell said. "A thorough criminal investigation was conducted. Tyrone was cleared of any and all criminal assault charges."

"Damned right," Tyrone agreed. "Plotka intruded on my private space, okay? Came up to me in that Dave & Buster's when I was having lunch with Jamella after practice. Started claiming that I done this and that to his fiancée. Who, I swear, I've never met in my life. He got very abusive. His language was inappropriate. It's a family restaurant. Our fans bring their young kids there. He was way out of line. Jamella can tell you."

She nodded. "He called my man ghetto trash. And me a skanky ho."

"He got in my face," Tyrone continued. "I simply tried to excuse him from my face. Did I put my hand on his chest? Yes. Did I shove him? No. The man slipped and fell. Did he suffer any injuries as a result of falling? No. I guarantee you he has a perfectly healthy eyeball under that patch he's sporting."

"That so-called doctor of his is a quack," Rondell said. "When an independent physician examines Mr. Plotka as part of the civil proceedings the man's injuries will be revealed as utterly bogus. That's why we're refusing to settle with him. He won't get one nickel out of us."

"But the damage is already done," Tyrone said regretfully. "The Players Union wanted me to fight my suspension. I'm accepting my punishment. Never should have put my hand on the bastard. A man my size has to learn how to control himself. Mind you, that's easier said than done. I don't know how to dial down. I get paid to *never* dial down."

"But he's learning how," Jamella pointed out. "When we're together he's just a gentle teddy bear. And he has never once put his hands on me without it being about our love for each other. The Tyrone Grantham I know is a good man."

"And I intend to be a good father to our baby. I haven't been to my other babies. Truth? I don't even know what it means to be a father."

"But he's going to learn that, too," Jamella said. "That's what this time off is all about—learning."

"It's been a wake-up call for me, no question. I let my family down, my teammates down. I miss the game like you wouldn't believe. But everything happens for a reason. This is my opportunity to change how I go about my business. I'm all done being bad Hercules. I'm not looking to get in any more fights. Not looking to rip any more pub. No more trash talking . . ."

"I make sure he drinks his glass of shut up every day," Jamella said.

"No more clubbing. No more partying. No more drama. That's why I rented out my place in Glen Cove and moved us here. It's quiet here and that suits me just fine. I'm happy. My priorities are straight now. We'll have us our baby. And I'll walk the walk. Represent my family the right way."

"What about the way you play the game?" Des asked him. "Aren't you afraid Da Beast will lose his edge?"

"Da Beast is never afraid. Next season I'll be a stronger, more dependable leader." He studied her from across the coffee table. The piano that someone was playing fell silent. There was only the gentle gurgle of the shark tank now. "So why *are* you here?"

"To inform you that you've got some rich neighbors who are used to getting their way."

He let out a laugh. "Hey, I know that. Justy Bond, right? I haven't met him. Only know him from the pissed-off letters and phone messages he keeps leaving me. But it would appear he has himself a problem with a brother taking up residence next door. I pay him no mind. I'm not looking for trouble. Or attention. That's why I said no to the reality show they wanted me to film."

"We had *two* offers," Rondell put in proudly. "Firm offers."

"That whole media circus out front is Plotka's doing, not mine.

I'm strictly looking for peace and quiet, like I said. No muss, no fuss. And for damned sure no parties."

"That's probably a wise thing," Des said.

"You telling us we can't have a few friends over?" Clarence demanded.

"I'm not 'telling' you anything. Just advising you to be smart. Otherwise, I can guarantee you that we'll have a situation. You know how to reach me if there's trouble. How do I reach you?"

"I'll give you our unlisted number." Rondell reached for a notepad and pen on the coffee table and wrote it down for her.

Tyrone shook his shaved head. "These folks out here are terrified of me. I'm their worst nightmare. *Your* worst nightmare, too, right, girl?"

Des shoved her heavy horn-rims up her nose. "I don't think I understand."

"Sure you do. You're one of those nice, polite girls. Did your homework every night. Stayed away from bad boys like me. Where'd you go to college?"

"West Point."

He raised his eyebrows, impressed. "You saw action?"

"I saw action."

"The real kind, too. Not a game like I play, hunh?"

"It was no game," Des said, hearing footsteps approach them on the hardwood floor.

Rondell's face lit up. "Resident Trooper Mitry, this is Jamella's sister Kinitra."

"Hey," Kinitra said shyly. She was seventeen, maybe eighteen, and real cute in a baby-faced, dimply sort of way. Big, doe eyes. A soft young mouth. Actually, her face looked soft all over, as if it were constructed out of marshmallows. Kinitra wore her orange-streaked hair in a short, punky updo. She was petite, no more than five-feet-four, but she had a lovely, curvy figure. The brightly patterned top and shorts she had on were of the same patchwork design as her older sister's shift.

"You ain't *heard* singing until you've heard this little girl," Clarence informed Des.

Rondell continued to glow in the girl's presence. It was plain to Des that little brother was ga-ga over little sister. Des wondered if it was mutual.

"She's not just a sister with a set of pipes," Tyrone pointed out. "She hears a song one time and she can sit down at the piano and play the whole thing by ear. Been that way since she was, what, ten?"

"Younger. Five, six years old." Jamella smiled at her. "My baby girl's a prodigy."

"Stop it," Kinitra demurred as she sat down next to her. "You're embarrassing me."

"Don't be bashful," Tyrone said to her. "Be proud. Trooper Mitry, this little girl is going to be the next Rihanna. Except with class and decency. No photos of her naked titties on the web. And no thug's *ever* beating the crap out of her. We're taking our time and doing it proper. She's only eighteen. A fresh young sister from Houston. But she is going to be huge. Tell her, little brother."

Rondell nodded his head enthusiastically. "She has an incredibly diverse repertoire—hip-hop, jazz, blues, folk. What's critical now is how we fuse all of those flavors together. We intend to craft her sound *before* we present her to a label so as to retain full creative control."

"And her career will be a family enterprise all the way," Tyrone explained. "I have the resources to launch her. She's why I installed a recording studio in the west wing. Cee knows everything there is to know about sound mixing. Rondell will manage the business end. And Jamella is choreographing her whole image—her dance moves, what she wears."

"I'm designing a clothing line for her," Jamella said. "Similar to what we have on now. I made these. They're inspired by our mother's Bahamian ancestry. Mama passed two years ago. It'll be our way of honoring her."

"I like the look," Des said admiringly.

Jamella arched an eyebrow at her. "Do you really?"

"Absolutely. I'd wear it. It's not as if I always go around in a uniform."

"I'd like to see you in a bikini," Clarence said.

"Oh, shut up, Cee," Jamella snapped.

"Put on her demo for the trooper to hear," Tyrone told him. "That old Joan Baez song. The one Bob Dylan wrote."

"Do you *have* to?" Kinitra protested.

"Get used to it, girl," Tyrone said to her. "People all around the world are going to be listening to you soon."

Clarence reached for a remote control device on the coffee table and powered up the house's sound system. Des heard a bluesy piano with a bit of a hip-hop beat. And then she heard Kinitra singing "Love Is Just a Four-Letter Word," the folk hit from the sixties that had showcased Baez's amazing vocal range. Kinitra's own range was equally astonishing. The girl could soar way up there into Minnie Riperton territory. And she didn't just have range. Her voice was so angelic, so achingly beautiful that the hairs on the back of Des's neck stood up.

When the song was over Clarence flicked the system off, smiling hugely. They were all smiling. It was something magical. This bashful young girl who couldn't take her big brown eyes off the floor had *it*.

"She's the real thing, am I right?" Tyrone asked Des.

"Yes, you are."

"Hell, yes." He squeezed his wife's hand and said, "How do you feel, baby? Can I get you some orange juice?"

"That sounds good."

"I'm on it. You just hang right here with your girl. Come on, trooper. I'll show you around."

Tyrone led Des back toward the entry hall, Clarence and Rondell tagging along. He had a bodybuilder's rolling gait, arms out wide to his sides. And he limped slightly on his surgically repaired knees.

"Do they give you trouble?" she asked him.

"Nothing I can't handle."

"No pain, no gain?"

"No pain, no *pay*. Our bedrooms are up those stairs right there. Except for Cee's. He's down there in the east wing. This here's our home theater," he pointed out as they passed a plush screening room. Next door to it was the recording studio. The piano was in there. "And this here's my game room." He paused so Des could check it out. The game room had a pool table, poker table and a half-dozen old-school arcade games. His many trophies and awards were crowded into a floor-to-ceiling glass case that filled an entire wall. "That there's Rondell's office," he said, continuing down the hallway past a closed door. "And this here's my weight room." Training center was more like it. Not just free weights but Nautilus machines, treadmills, stair climbers and exercise bikes. "I work out here every day with Cee. He used to start at small forward for Clemson until his scholarship was revoked due to an unfortunate misunderstanding."

Clarence's jaw muscles tightened but, for once, he had nothing to say—joking or otherwise. Des made a mental note to run a criminal background check on him as soon as she got near a computer.

"I'm taking it easy right now. Giving my body a chance to repair itself. Two hours of lifting in the morning. Two hours of cardio after lunch."

"That's your idea of easy?" Des asked.

"The game doesn't get any easier after you turn thirty. I've been watching my carb intake, too. Eating a lot of chicken and fish. Kitchen's down this way."

It was a commercial-sized kitchen with a six-burner Viking range, two ovens and the biggest refrigerator Des had seen in anyone's home in her life. It was very sunny in the kitchen. A set of French doors opened out onto the patio, swimming pool and pool house. Des could also see the dock where his cigarette boat, *Da Beast,* was tied up.

A mountainous gray-haired woman was putting groceries away in the walk-in pantry. She wore a lavender fleece sweat suit, sneakers and somewhere between six and eight chins.

Tyrone smiled at her. "Hey, Moms. You made it back from the store."

"That I did, praise the Lord," she replied, wheezing slightly. She needed to lose at least seventy-five pounds. Take off a hundred and she'd still qualify as meaty.

"This here's Trooper Mitry. Came to say hello."

"Pleased to meet you, Mrs. Grantham."

"It's Chantal, honey," she said to Des warmly. Chantal Grantham had attracted a great deal of attention after her son was selected in the first round of the NFL draft. The lady was a recovering crack whore who had totally neglected her two young boys until she found God and fought her way back from the gates of hell. "Skinny thing, ain't she?"

"I think she's cute," said Clarence. "We'll have to get her out on *Da Beast*."

Tyrone nodded in agreement. "You like boats, Trooper Mitry? I took Moms out one time but she won't go again."

"*Never* again," Chantal said emphatically. "You bounced me up and down so hard I swear I lacerated a kidney."

"Well, *I* ain't going out either if Rondell's behind the wheel again." Clarence mimicked a bug-eyed Rondell gripping a steering wheel tightly in the ten until two position, swiveling sharply left, right, left, whipping his hands back and forth spasmodically. "He almost flipped us, I swear."

"I was merely familiarizing myself with the boat's handling capabilities," little Rondell said defensively.

"You was merely freaking out!" Clarence laughed.

Des heard footsteps on the stairs that were next to the kitchen door. A barefoot girl in her late teens or early twenties came tromping down. She was a heavy, homely girl. Moon-faced, pimply and dull-eyed.

"This here's Monique," Chantal informed Des. "Daughter of a dear friend of mine who passed last year. I look out for her now. Monique's not well suited to being on her own." She tapped her own forehead to indicate that Monique was intellectually challenged. "But she's a good girl. Helps me around the house. Keeps me company. It works out well for both of us." Chantal smiled at her. "Monique, what were you doing up in your room?"

"Nuthin' much, Chantal."

"We need to finish stocking that pantry, hon."

"Yes, Chantal."

Clarence stepped in front of the girl and began to tickle her playfully. "*Hey*, Monique."

She giggled. "*Hey*, Cee."

"Leave her alone, Cee," Chantal ordered him.

"I'm just funning with her." Clarence tickled the girl some more. "She don't mind, do you, Monique?"

Des heard a strange noise next to her. Turned to discover it was the sound of Tyrone Grantham breathing in and out very hard and very fast. A vein was throbbing in his forehead. "Don't you disrespect my mother!" he roared at Clarence, his eyes bulging with fury. "Don't *ever* do that!"

In all of her years of law enforcement Des had never seen a man flare so hot so fast.

Clarence backed down at once, cowed by fear. "I-I didn't mean nothing, cuz. Sorry."

"Don't apologize to *me*! Apologize to *Moms*!"

"Sure, sure . . ." Clarence moistened his lips with his tongue. "Sorry, Moms."

"It's okay, Clarence," she assured him.

And with that Tyrone relaxed instantly. Seemingly, the man was an emotional roller coaster. His gaze fell on Des now. He seemed to be measuring her. "You have family?"

"I'm an only child. My mom lives in Georgia. My dad's with me right now. He just had some surgery."

He processed her answer carefully, nodding his shaved head. "You're taking care of him?"

"Just until he gets back on his feet."

"That says a lot about you. Your folks must be real proud of you."

"I'm proud of both of my sons," Chantal pointed out. "They've come *so* far. You got yourself a man, Trooper Mitry?"

"Of course she does, Moms. She goes with that movie critic's on the TV all of the time. Jewish guy with those funny eyebrows."

"Wait, she *who*?" Clarence was aghast. "Why you want to be doing that for when there's a fine available brother right here?"

Tyrone let out a laugh. "Give it up, Cee. She's too smart for you."

The patio door opened now and a middle-aged black man stood there gaping at Des in horror. Or, more specifically, at her uniform. He was quick to recover, grinning as he strolled on in. But he was too late. Des already smelled yard on him.

"Trooper Mitry, this here's my father-in-law, Calvin Jameson," Tyrone said. "He came up from Houston as soon as Jamella got pregnant. Lived with us in Glen Cove over the summer. Now he's staying out in the pool house."

"Pleased to meet you, miss," said Calvin, who was in his late forties or early fifties. Hard to tell exactly because he dyed his hair an inky black. And wore a half-jar of pomade in it. He was a bit of a peacock. The sports shirt and slacks he had on were loud and louder. His cowboy boots were snakeskin. He was not very tall. And he was for sure not very fit. His gut hung way out over the waistband. He fetched himself a can of Bud from the fridge, popped it open and took a long drink, smacking his lips. "You get my smokes, Chantal?"

"Get your own damned smokes," she responded, her face tightening.

"Chantal, why you all of the time got to be busting on me?"

"Because you're no good freeloading trash. Don't do nothing all day but sit around drinking beer and watching porn."

Calvin shook his head at her. "Can't we just get along?"

"I don't get along with punks."

"I'm no punk. I'm a grown man with two grown daughters."

"You're still a punk." Chantal turned her attention back to Des. "I hope you'll watch out for my Tyrone. The people don't like him, you know."

"Which people?" Des asked her.

"I worry about him day and night. Pray to the good Lord that no harm will come to him."

Des glanced at Tyrone. "Have there been any incidents or threats I should know about?"

"Not a thing," Rondell interjected. "We're fine."

"Moms is just being Moms," Tyrone agreed. "Pay no attention."

"No, *pay* attention! I ain't no crazy person. I know what I know." Chantal reached over and clutched Des by the wrist. She had a powerful grip. "I have nightmares every night. Keep dreaming that something awful's about to happen."

"Lighten up, Moms," Tyrone said. "You're freaking everybody out."

"Do you keep any weapons in your home?" Des asked him.

"I have a Glock 19 for my personal protection. It's the preferred pistol of the NYPD. I've got a permit for it."

"In Connecticut?"

His face dropped. "New York. Why, is that a problem?"

"Now that you've established your residency here you'll want to swing by Dorset Town Hall and apply for a local pistol permit. Once you get that you can apply for one from the state—if you want to be in complete compliance, I mean."

"Oh, he does," Rondell assured her. "Absolutely."

"Are there any other weapons around?"

"No, ma'am," said Clarence, who would not go down in history as one of the world's great liars.

Chantal still had not let go of Des's wrist. Des's fingers were getting numb. "*Promise* me you'll watch out for my boy!"

"There won't be any trouble, Mrs. Grantham. Not if I have anything to say about it." Des smiled at her reassuringly. "And it just so happens that I do."

CHAPTER 4

BOND'S AUTO MALL, THE state's highest volume General Motors dealership—*"Just ask Justy!"*—was a mammoth cluster of airplane hangar-sized showrooms surrounded by acres and acres of sleek, shiny new cars and trucks. Mitch felt like a member of the Joad family when he pulled in there in his old Studey. Everywhere he looked rows of digital-age rides were gleaming in the Indian Summer sun. American rides, Japanese, German, Swedish—you could find pretty much anything at Bond's Auto Mall.

Except for customers. Mitch didn't see a living soul anywhere.

His cell phone rang as he was parking.

"Hey, hey, Boo Boo!" a familiar voice hollered in his ear. "I tried you at home. You weren't there."

"Yeah, I'm out running errands, Pop. What's going on?"

"Wanted to let you know we're all set to head out there tomorrow. I'm picking up our rental car this afternoon."

"Why don't you just take the train out? I can pick you up at the station and drive you to your bed and breakfast."

"Nah, we like to come and go as we please. Do you mind if we get an early start in the morning? I'd like to beat the traffic."

"Not a problem. I'm always up early." Mitch reached across the seat for the open bag of Utz potato chips and stuffed a generous handful in his mouth. "How did your appointments go?"

"My what?"

"You said you had appointments."

His father fell silent. Which was *not* like him. "We can talk about it when we get there. We . . . have a lot to talk about."

"Sure thing, Pop," Mitch responded, feeling his chest tighten as he hung up. *Grapefruit-sized tumor.* There was now zero doubt in his mind that he'd be hearing those words tomorrow. The only question was which one of them had it.

He calmed himself, or tried, and went looking for June Bond. Tried two different showrooms but couldn't locate anyone. Not only were there no customers but every salesman's cubicle was empty, too. Mitch was beginning to think he'd wandered into an old episode of *The Twilight Zone* when he finally spotted a young janitor vacuuming the office rugs in the third showroom he tried. As Mitch approached him he realized that the young janitor was June.

The heir to Bond's Auto Mall was quick to notice him. It was awful hard to miss another warm body in that barren wasteland. June shut off the vacuum and loped across the showroom toward Mitch, looking super-preppy in his polo shirt, khakis and Top-Siders. "Hey, good to see you, bro," he exclaimed. "I'm afraid I have to do a little bit of everything around here these days. People just aren't buying cars. Plus this isn't your father's GM, Mitch. We're staring at a future without Saturn, Olds, Pontiac *and* Hummer. We've shrunk our full-time sales and office staff, laid off mechanics. We used to have a custodial crew come in every night to tidy up. Now guess who we have?"

"That would be you?"

"Ka-ching." June was acting very upbeat about it. And yet, Mitch noticed, he had dark worry circles under his eyes. "What can I do for you? Don't tell me you're finally giving up on your Studey."

"Not a chance," Mitch said as June's father, Justy, came strutting into the showroom from the service department. He went into a glassed-in office, sat behind the desk and got busy on the telephone, watching the two of them intently through the glass. "I ran into Callie this morning. She seemed kind of upset."

June eyed him curiously. "She sent you here?"

"Callie has no idea I'm here."

"Then why are you?"

"Because she told me you want to take off on the *Calliope* right away. And want her to quit the academy and come with you. And that it's all real sudden and urgent and she doesn't know why."

June ran a hand through his mop of hair, swallowing. "It's not something I can talk to her about."

"Why not?"

"Because she won't understand. Listen, I can talk to you, right? You won't go running back to Callie with every word I say, will you?"

"Whatever you tell me stays between us. Scout's honor."

June glanced over in the direction of his father's office. "We'd better make this look like a work thing." He fished around in the pocket of his khakis for a set of keys. "Come on, let's take a Silverado out for a test drive." He led Mitch out the door and across an acre of pavement toward a row of huge, shiny new Chevy pickups. "If you actually *are* interested in a new truck we're practically giving them away right now. Factory incentives up the wazoo."

"I'm pretty attached to my Studey."

"Sure, I understand. Can't say I blame you."

"Not exactly Mister Hard Sell, are you?"

"I'm not Mister *Sell*, period. I hate trying to convince people to buy something that they truly don't need. At least half of our new car and truck sales are to customers who already own perfectly serviceable vehicles. But thanks to Madison Avenue they get it into their heads that they need, need, need to trade up. It's totally insane."

"You'd better not let your dad hear you talk like that. You're spouting pure blasphemy."

"Believe me, I've done much worse." June came to a halt before a shiny blue behemoth. "He's watching us through the showroom window right now. Pretend you're interested in my spiel, okay? This here's your new Silverado 2500 HD. It's got a choice of a Duramax 6.6 liter turbo-diesel or your standard 360 horsepower Vortec 6.0 liter V-8. It has a six-speed automatic transmission, four-wheel anti-lock brakes, air bags . . ."

"Nice color," Mitch offered encouragingly. It was all he could think of.

"That's the Imperial Blue metallic finish. The interior's light titanium with dark titanium accents." June swung the driver's door open for him. "Hop in."

Mitch climbed in behind the wheel. The cab's interior was as cushy and carpeted as somebody's living room. And the wood-trimmed dashboard was so loaded with high-tech controls that it made his bare bones Studey look like a museum piece.

"You've got cup holders here, here, here and here," June said, climbing in next to him. "This right here controls your air conditioning. . . ."

"Wow, it has air conditioning?"

"And this is your heat. . . ."

"Wow, it has heat?"

"This particular model has an MP3-compatible CD player, XM radio, a USB port, Bluetooth and the OnStar Safe and Sound plan."

"June, this truck is better equipped than my house."

"If you opt for the crew cab you can just roll out your sleeping bag in the backseat and you're home." June's face fell. "God, I truly suck at this, don't I?"

"You're doing fine. But it helps if you believe in the product you're selling."

"I couldn't agree more." He handed Mitch the keys. "Let's ride."

Mitch started the engine and steered them out of the Auto Mall in quiet, air-conditioned comfort. The truck drove like a luxury sedan. He couldn't imagine taking it to the town dump with a load of brush.

"My dad will do anything to make a sale," June informed him. "He has no scruples, no conscience and *no* patience with me. He thinks I'm soft."

"And what do *you* think?"

"That I like to fix up old sailboats. I think I can make a living at it if I move someplace where people sail all year round."

"Someplace that also happens to be far from your dad?"

"Well, yeah. That, too."

Mitch took the on-ramp to Route 9 and punched the accelerator. The truck was so powerful that he was cruising the highway at eighty before he realized it. A far cry from his Studey, which started to shake, rattle and roll if he tried to push it past fifty-five. He eased off the gas and said, "What happened, June?"

"Something truly horrible," June confessed miserably. "Callie . . . stays over with me a lot, okay? That's one thing my dad's cool about. He doesn't mind her spending the night. Sometimes, she stays until morning. Sometimes, she goes home after I fall asleep and paints for hours. A few nights ago we had the place to ourselves for the evening. Dad and Bonita were at the club with some friends getting drunk. I picked up a pizza. We smoked a joint, watched some totally lame movie and—"

"Wait, which totally lame movie?"

"Uh, *Pineapple Express* with Seth Rogen and James Franco."

"You're telling me you were stoned and yet you still didn't find it funny?"

"Not really. Why does that even matter?"

"It doesn't. You're just in my wheelhouse is all. Go on. . . ."

"We started, you know, getting busy on the sofa. Then went up to my room and made love. I dozed off after that. I don't know how many hours later it was when Callie woke me up to make love again. She was totally on fire. And pretty soon I was, too. It had never, ever been like that with us before. We'd always been real gentle and loving. This was just *wild*. And it was all over so fast that, well, it didn't hit me until it was too late."

"What didn't, June?"

"That she felt all wrong, smelled all wrong. I turned on the bedside light and it was *Bonita* who was naked in bed with me, her big blue eyes gleaming . . ." He shot a guilty look at Mitch. "Has anything like that ever happened to you?"

"You mean waking up inside of the wrong woman? No, I've been Jewish my whole life. Not to mention a very light sleeper. You're telling me you honestly couldn't tell the difference between the two of them?"

June let out a distraught sigh. "Maybe I did know. Maybe I was just beyond the point of caring. It's not something I want to think about too much. But I can't sugarcoat it, Mitch. I had freaky sex with my stepmother. I-I jumped out of bed, totally wigged out. Bonita was, like, 'Chill out, hon, we're cool.' She was real drunk. And unbelievably horny. Told me my dad hasn't been able to get it up for months. Not since they took away his Hummer franchise."

"So there *is* a connection."

"Bonita *thanked* me, Mitch. She said she can't step out on him because people would find out. It's awful hard to hide an affair in Dorset."

"It's impossible," said Mitch, whose own relationship with Des had become hot news all over town before either of them knew what hit them.

"Next morning I couldn't look my dad in the eye. Or Bonita. And for damned sure not Callie, who is such a genuine, sensitive person. She'll never understand. I figure our relationship's toast if she finds out. I moved out of my room and onto the *Calliope* that day so I wouldn't be right down the hall from Bonita. Callie had a late class that night. Didn't come over. I locked the *Calliope* down good and tight and went to bed early. I thought I'd be safe out there. I was wrong. At three o'clock in the morning Bonita's out on deck pounding on the hatch cover and calling out my name. I let her in so she wouldn't wake up my dad. Right away she was all over me again. I stopped her. I said that what happened last night was never, ever going to happen again. Bonita is . . . gorgeous. And she can be real persuasive. I totally wanted her again even though I knew it was wrong. I wanted her so bad that I went nuts and shoved her the hell off me. She cracked her head on the corner of a bookcase. Then she started screaming at me so loud she woke up my dad. Lights came on all over the house. She ran back inside and intercepted him. Made up some lame story about hitting her head in the kitchen. Told him she'd been awake because she was afraid there'd be a drive-by shooting next door. Just a bunch of paranoid, racist crap. But he totally bought it because he's wired that way." June broke off, swallowing. "This can't go on, Mitch. Any day now the crazy bitch will lose it and tell him what really happened. I humiliated her. You don't do that to Bonita. And she'll mess up my thing with Callie for sure. I totally love that girl. I want to spend the rest of my life with her. But we've got to get out of this place right away or it'll destroy us. Destroy Bonita, too."

"Destroy her how?"

"My dad will beat the crap out of her. He used to beat up my mom. That's why she left him."

"I thought Bonita split them apart."

"Everyone does. But my mom told me their marriage was over long before Bonita came along—because of his temper. He has no control over himself, Mitch. Like father, like son."

Mitch kept his eyes on the road. "You're not your father, June."

"Yeah, I am," he said bitterly. "Deep down inside I'm no good. I want to do what's right. Go far, far away with Callie. I just don't know if it'll ever be the same between us after this. People who love each other don't keep secrets. But what am I supposed to tell her—that my stepmother sort of raped me and that I sort of went along with it because she's a real bunny in the sack?"

"Yeah, I don't think I'd phrase it quite that way."

"Mitch, you've been married. You know women better than I do. Will you give me an honest answer if I ask you something?"

"I'll certainly try."

"What would you do right now if you were me?"

"So what *would* you do?"

"Me? I'd grab Callie and sail the hell out of that nuthouse as fast as the wind would take me."

"But that's running away, doughboy."

"You bet your sweet *tuchos* it is."

The sky over Long Island Sound was bathed in a pinkish glow as they walked Big Sister's narrow beach together at sunset. The air was still insanely warm for late October. According to the Weather Channel's ace storm tracker, Jim Cantore, a storm front would bring thunderstorms tomorrow night along with much colder temperatures. For now, it felt like August as they strolled along barefoot in shorts and T-shirts, sipping Bass Ales and holding hands. Mitch relished these precious moments with his lady love. And he never took them—or her—for granted.

There was a decommissioned lighthouse out on Big Sister, the second tallest in New England. Forty or so acres of woods. And four houses besides Mitch's antique post-and-beam caretaker's cottage— all of them belonging to the Peck family. It was the Pecks who'd founded Dorset back in the 1600s. A rickety wooden causeway connected the private island to the mainland at the Peck's Point Nature Preserve.

"So is that what you told June to do?" Des asked him.

"No, I'd never tell some young guy to quit the family business and take off. Who am I to tell him that? Although it's pretty clear that he does need to get out from under his father's—"

"Wife?"

"I was going to say thumb. But if you want to talk dirty . . ."

"I don't."

"Are you sure about that?"

"Positive. Move it along, mister."

"He asked me if I thought he should tell Callie. I said that when the time was right to tell her, he'd know. And he would tell her. He'd want to because they'd be a serious, committed couple by then and he'd want her to know everything. I'm not sure whether that was sound, mature advice or just something I picked up from watching *Gidget Goes Hawaiian*. But it was the best I could do. Hell, I'm driving along with the guy in this shiny new truck and he drops this on me. Do you think I need a new truck?"

"She'll never understand. She'll forgive him—*maybe*. But never understand."

Mitch glanced over at her as she strode along next to him, her smooth skin glowing in the pink sunset. "What would you have told him?"

"I have no idea. And you don't need a new truck. You already have the world's greatest truck."

"It doesn't have air conditioning."

"Open a window."

"It doesn't have heat."

"Wear a jacket."

"It won't go faster than fifty-five."

"Good. You shouldn't."

"Yeah, that's kind of what I thought."

Des sipped her beer and said, "I thought I sensed something between June and Bonita this morning. The way she looked at him. And the way he *didn't* look at her. I can't believe she actually played the race card just to cover her skanky ass. She's a thoroughly reprehensible person. And Justy's no dreamboat either."

"He used to beat up on June's mom, according to June. It's only a matter of time before he starts in on Bonita—if he hasn't already."

"Really nice bunch of people. It's a heartwarming story."

"Welcome to Dorset, where life is beautiful all of the time."

"Do you believe June's version of the story?"

"Which part?"

"The part where he woke up inside of another woman and didn't know it. Because *you'd* know if you were making love to someone and it wasn't me, wouldn't you? I'd sure know if it wasn't you."

"Well, that's not a fair comparison. You've grown accustomed to incredibly high standards in terms of technique, attention to detail, girth . . . Okay, ow, that hurt."

"I'm serious, Mitch. Do you believe him?"

"No, I don't. I believe he's spinning the truth about what happened so that he can live with himself. 'This is the West, sir. When the legend becomes fact, print the legend.'" On her blank stare, he explained, "That's from *The Man Who Shot Liberty Valance*, a very good picture John Ford made toward the end of his career. Lee Marvin slays in it."

"Do you realize that sometimes I have no idea what you're talking about?"

"But sometimes you do. How cool is that?"

"Justy and Bob Paffin persuaded me to pay a 'courtesy' call on our newest, blackest resident this morning."

"Oh, yeah? What's Da Beast really like?"

"There's no short answer to that. He's bright, self-aware and intuitive. He has a sense of humor. But he can go rage monster almost instantly—and then thirty seconds later be totally calm again."

"Are we talking steroids here?"

"Real? I have no idea. I just know it's hard to tell who Tyrone Grantham is from one minute to the next. Maybe that's how Tyrone likes it. He dictates the flow by keeping the people around him off balance. He has an extended family staying there. Some very decent people. His younger brother, Rondell, has an MBA from Wharton. His wife, Jamella, is nobody's fool. And her kid sister, Kinitra, has a set of pipes on her like you wouldn't believe. The girl's a major singing talent. But I ran a check on his cousin Clarence, who fancies himself a recording engineer, and it turns out he got kicked out of Clemson for stealing stereos from dorm rooms. Not only lost his basketball scholarship but got sentenced to a hundred hours of community service plus a year of probation. And the girls' father, Calvin, has spent half of his adult life in lock-up down in Houston. You name it, Calvin's done it—car theft, armed assault, pimping, dealing. It was the girls' mother who raised them. She worked as a cashier at a Walmart. Got shot to death in the parking lot two years ago. The shooter was never apprehended. And the girls have been on their own ever since. When Jamella took up with the famous Tyrone Grantham, Calvin suddenly resurfaced. Tyrone's letting him stay there with them, but he's a punk, as the boys' mother, Chantal, so

66

eloquently put it. And she would know. Back home in South Central L.A. she was picked up a gazillion times for prostitution and drug possession."

The sky was turning from pink to violet. The darkness came fast this late in the year.

"Stewart Plotka was out front trying to drum up publicity for his lawsuit," Des went on as they started back toward Mitch's cottage. "Just for the hell of it I phoned the Nassau County P.D. detective who investigated that Dave & Buster's fracas. He told me they declined to pursue criminal charges against Tyrone because the waitresses and customers all backed up what Tyrone and Jamella said—which was that Plotka approached their table and started shouting and screaming at Tyrone. When Tyrone stood up, Plotka went into a tizzy and tripped over a chair. Plotka claims he broke his eyeglasses when he fell and suffered severe eye and hand injuries. But no one saw that happen. No ambulance was called to the scene. And Plotka's 'doctor' lost his license to practice medicine in the state of New York five years ago. What he has is a license to practice chiropractic medicine in Nevada. Where *I* could get a license to practice. The Nassau P.D. detective thinks the man's just looking for a payday. That lawyer of his, Andrea Halperin, is famous for squeezing go-away money out of celebrities."

"You're saying Plotka's a creep who has no case and yet the NFL suspended Tyrone Grantham anyway. They were just looking for an excuse, weren't they?"

Des nodded. "They're tired of his act."

"So am I. When I was growing up in New York City in the eighties, I had three huge sports heroes—Dwight Gooden, Darryl Strawberry and Lawrence Taylor. All three of them turned out to be drugged-out bums. I was utterly crushed. Never, ever got over it. Kids need heroes who they can count on. Not that professional athletes *are* heroes. But you have to be older before you can recognize who the real heroes in this world are."

"Such as? . . ."

"My dad. He showed up every single day at Boys and Girls High to teach those kids algebra. Not a lot of them made it. But some of them did. And it was because he was *there*. And then he came home every night and was *there* for me. He never ditched my mom for a younger babe. He paid his bills on time. That's my idea of a hero—my dad. Your dad, too, don't you think?"

Her only response was taut silence.

"How *is* your dad?"

"Well, I almost blew his head off this morning."

"Accidentally or on purpose?"

"Don't even go there. He'd driving me nuts. He haunts my hallways all night long. He's gloomy, listless . . ." She glanced at her watch. "At this very minute I guarantee you he's sitting in my living room with his jacket on staring at a rerun of *NCIS* for about the fifteenth time."

"Okay, I'll grant you he's no Mr. Sardonicus."

"Mister who?"

"Wait, are you telling me you've never seen *Mr. Sardonicus* with Oscar Homolka? It's a William Castle shlocko classic. I can't believe you've never seen *Mr. Sardonicus* with Oscar Homolka. That settles it—this year's Halloween viewing will be highlighted by a special midnight screening of *Mr. Sardonicus* with Oscar Homolka."

"Are you really, truly into this movie or do you just like saying the name Oscar Homolka?"

"Both," he confessed. "Why is it that I can't lie to you?"

"Because you know I'll shoot you if you do."

"Right, right. I knew there was a good reason."

They took the narrow sandy path back toward his snug little antique cottage. As they neared the house, Quirt, Mitch's lean outdoor hunter, darted across the garden and collided headfirst with Mitch's shin. Just the cat's way of telling Mitch he was hungry. Mitch let him inside and Quirt headed straight for the kibble bowl. Clemmie, who rarely ventured out, was taking a power nap in her easy chair.

The little house had exposed chestnut posts and beams, a stone fireplace and oak plank floors. It was basically just one big room—with windows that looked out at the water in three different directions. There was a kitchen and a bathroom. A sleeping loft that was up a steep, narrow staircase. He'd furnished the place with whatever he could find. The moth-eaten loveseat and easy chairs had been in his neighbor's barn. The coffee table was an ancient rowboat with an old storm window over it. His desk a mahogany door that he'd dragged home from the dump and set atop sawhorses. Mitch's sky blue Fender Stratocaster and monster stack of amps took up one corner of the living room. Books and DVDs were piled pretty much everywhere else.

He put some old Sam and Dave on the stereo and asked Des what she felt like having for dinner.

"Don't bother making anything for me. I'm really not hungry."

"Well, that's just tough. You're going to eat. I don't like the way you're losing weight again. You have almost no boobage."

"Mitch, I never have any boobage."

"And just take a look at your booty, will you?"

"Why, what's wrong with my booty?"

"Not a thing—I just like looking at it," he said, grinning at her. "Hey, I know, I could run over to McGee's and get two chili cheeseburgers and a couple of orders of spiral fries. Also something for you."

She shook her head at him. "Doughboy, you haven't stuffed your pie hole this way in ages."

"I don't know what you mean."

"I mean you have powdered donut residue all over your T-shirt. And that grease around your fingernails has Utz potato chips written all over it."

"That'll teach me to fall for a trained investigator."

"What is this?" she demanded. "Are you getting antsy about me meeting your folks?"

"Not at all. They'll adore you. How could they not?"

"I just hope my father won't be a total drag."

"Don't even worry about it. My dad can get anyone to lighten up. He's amazing that way." Mitch went in the kitchen and started poking around. "I have a loaf of day-old ciabatta and some stinky Hooligan cheese. What would you say to a grilled cheese and bacon sandwich with slices of my late-season tomatoes? There's also a half-bottle of that amusing Cote-du-Rhone. Deal?"

"Deal," she agreed. "For our starter course grab the wine and two glasses and I'll meet you up in the sleeping loft. We can do some scientific research on whether we recognize each other in the dark. If you have any trouble I'll be the one who's naked under the covers."

"Be right there," he said eagerly, fetching two glasses from the cupboard.

For the record, Mitch had no trouble recognizing her in the dark.

Later on, his growling stomach insisted on being fed. Des was dozing contentedly next to him. It was the most relaxed she'd been since the Deacon moved in. Mitch slipped out of bed quietly and tiptoed down to the kitchen, where he heated up his Lodge cast iron skillet and laid some thick slices of bacon in it to cook.

When his phone rang he grabbed it on the first ring, hoping it didn't wake her.

"Oh, Mitch, thank God you're there!" It was Lila Joshua, the more fluttery of the two sisters. "I have been trying to call you for nearly thirty minutes but an automated recording kept telling me they could not complete my call as dialed. An operator *finally* got through for me."

"Did you remember to use the area code, Lila?" The phone company now required Dorseteers to dial the 860 area code even for local calls. It wasn't an easy habit to get into, especially for older, wiftier residents.

"I-I may have forgotten," she confessed. "It so happens I'm just a bit—"

"Here, give that to me . . ." Now he heard a more assertive voice on the other end of the line. "Is that you, Mitch?"

"What can I do for you, Luanne?"

"It's Winston. He's taken off again. I turned my back for one second and he was out the door and gone. I tried to go after him but you would not believe how fast he can scoot. And it's terribly dark out."

Now Mitch heard Des's cell phone ring up in the sleeping loft. She answered it right away.

"Luanne, do you have any idea where Winston was heading?" he asked.

"That's the part that has us a bit alarmed. Just before he darted out of the door he, well, he said he really wanted to go 'bite some colored ass.'"

"Uh-oh . . ."

CHAPTER 5

WHEN HER CELL RANG she snatched it off the nightstand and said, "This is Resident Trooper Mitry." It was nearly ten-thirty, according to her watch.

"Young lady, you need to get over here *right* now," a familiar male voice thundered at her.

"What seems to be the problem, Mr. Bond?"

"He has an out-of-control dance party or rave or whatever they call it going on over there. *Hundreds* of them are swarming the neighborhood . . ." *Them.* "They're screaming like banshees and—and playing their thug music so loud it's shaking my whole house. I *demand* that you do something."

"I'll be right over."

Des had just swung her size twelve-and-half AA bare feet to the floor when her cell rang again. This time it was the 911 dispatcher. A call had just come in from Mr. Rondell Grantham requesting an ambulance to treat the victim of an "incident" at the Grantham residence. Little brother hadn't asked for state police assistance but it was automatic for Des to be called. She hurried down the stairs for her uniform and discovered Mitch throwing on a T-shirt and shorts. "You going somewhere, boyfriend?"

"Winston has wandered off again. The Joshua sisters are afraid he may have headed over to Tyrone Grantham's." He watched her jump into her uniform. "And you?"

"They're having a party. And there's been an incident of some kind."

Mitch frowned at her. "Des, you don't suppose? . . ."

"I don't suppose anything yet." She was fully dressed in less than two minutes. Her West Point training. "But you'll never get in the gate on your own. I'm flooring it there. Can you keep up with me?"

"You betcha. Mind you, if I had a brand new Silverado with the 360-horsepower Vortec—"

"Mitch, you don't need a new a truck."

"Be right behind you, Master Sergeant."

She went outside to her cruiser, jumped in and pushed it across the rickety causeway. Mitch stayed right behind her on the dirt road that twisted through the Nature Preserve, but once she made it onto the smooth pavement of Old Shore Road and floored it, he fell back a bit, his vintage sepia-toned headlights growing weaker in her rearview mirror. When she turned onto Turkey Neck and ran into the hot mess there, he caught up with her again.

Dozens and dozens of parked cars were crowded onto shoulders of the narrow road. Des spotted plenty of New York license plates, not to mention New Jersey and Rhode Island. Partiers were coming and going on foot right down the middle of the street. Boisterous groups of young guys, joshing and laughing. Couples walking hand in hand. All of them black. *Them.* She had to hit her siren to get through, Mitch snug on her tail. The media mob, when she managed to get near the Grantham place, seemed even bigger than before. The bright lights of the news cameras lit up the driveway out front like a red carpet movie premiere. People were lined up at the gate trying to get in. Big, impassive Trooper Olsen was turning them away.

"Hey, Des," he said when she pulled up at the gate. "The Jewett girls got here two seconds ago." Marge and Mary Jewett ran Dorset's volunteer ambulance service.

"What happened, Oly?"

"Fist fight between a couple of partiers, I hear. I was just on my way back to check it out."

"You can stay here. I'm on it."

"It was supposed to be a small party, Des. Clarence had a very short guest list. He left the father-in-law, Calvin, up here to make sure no one else slipped in. Because I told him flat out—I'm a state trooper, not your doorman. Well, you know how it goes with parties. Word gets out and everyone just starts showing up. Good old Calvin let in pretty much anyone who had a pretty girl with him. I've got it on lockdown now."

Des looked around at the media crowd. "Any sign of Plotka?"

"Him I haven't seen, thank God."

She jerked a thumb back in Mitch's direction. "He's with me."

She eased down the gravel driveway with Mitch on her tail and pulled up behind the Dorset volunteer ambulance van, hearing the music loud and clear. Jay-Z and Alicia Keys were singing "Empire State of Mind." Not exactly her idea of "thug" music but what did she know? Mitch pulled up behind her and got out.

"If Winston's here, you hustle him home and don't look back," she said briskly as they started around the house toward the pool. "Just clear out, got it?"

"Got it."

At least a hundred partiers were enjoying the warm night air, the swimming pool and each other. They were dancing to the music. Splashing around in the water in their bathing suits. Shrieking, laughing, having a great time. And why not? They were kicking it at the mansion of an NFL superstar. There was a long table

74

loaded with food, an open bar and more than a trace of reefer smoke in the air. A DJ was working the music. Lights were on inside the house, upstairs and down, but the party seemed to be confined to the outdoors.

Des didn't spot either of the Grantham brothers or Jameson sisters. She did see Calvin floating in the pool on an inflatable chaise, his man boobs sagging, beer gut hanging out. Des could have gone her whole life without seeing Calvin Jameson in swim trunks. She went directly to the DJ and ran a finger across her throat. He cut the music at once. A chorus of boos met the silence until the partiers noticed her uniform. Then they fell silent, too.

The Jewett sisters were crouched over a lounge chair by the pool house with a cluster of guests gathered around them. It was Winston Lash who Marge and Mary were attending to. The old fellow was stretched out there, in a pair of striped PJs and bedroom slippers, bleeding from his nose and mouth. Marge was packing his nostrils with gauze while Mary pressed an ice pack against his upper lip and blood-soaked handlebar moustache.

Standing nearby, sobbing and carrying on, was a deeply upset twenty-something sister who was wearing a gold string bikini and a lot of exotic war paint. She was amply built. Her full breasts and even fuller booty were pretty much exploding out of that little bikini.

Clarence was standing there, too, seething with anger. Two burly young guys were trying to settle him down. At least half a dozen partiers had whipped out their cell phones and were sending streaming video of it all to their friends.

"Evening, girls," Des said to Marge and Mary, ultra-mindful of the camera phones. Bystanders routinely produced them at crime scenes these days and there wasn't a thing she could do about it— other than go about her business the right way. "How's Mr. Lash?"

75

"He's responsive, which is good," Marge answered.

"What the hell happened to him?" Mitch wanted to know.

"He got punched in the face by that giant over there," Mary said, meaning Clarence. "The back of Winston's head hit the pavement pretty hard but he never lost consciousness, according to the witnesses. His pupils are reactive to light. He's not complaining of dizziness or ringing in his ears or nausea. Mind you, he's normally a tad confused due to his dementia but we don't believe he suffered a concussion. Just a bloody nose and a cut lip."

"What's your name?" Des asked the girl in the bikini.

"Asia," she responded, sniffling.

"Your full name, please."

"What you be needing my full name for?"

"If I'm going to file an incident report then I have to have your name, your address . . ."

"Why you be needing to file an incident report?" Asia turned plaintively to Clarence. "Why she be needing to file a—?"

"Why don't you just tell me what happened," Des said to her patiently.

Before Asia could do that, Rondell came rushing across the pool area toward them, looking like a middle-aged businessman in his button-down shirt and tailored slacks. The first thing little brother did was plead with everyone to put away their phones. They grudgingly complied. Then he approached Des, forcing an uneasy smile onto his face. "I appreciate you attending to this matter personally, Trooper Mitry."

"Actually, I'm responding to a neighbor's complaint about your music."

"I apologize for that. Didn't realize it was so loud. As you can see, there has been an unfortunate altercation of a physical nature.

It is my hope that we can alleviate this situation with a minimum of public blowback."

"That all depends on what happened, Rondell. Where's your brother?"

"Tyrone doesn't care for parties anymore. He's been upstairs in the master suite all evening watching a movie with Jamella."

"Which movie?" Mitch inquired.

"I'm not sure." Rondell frowned at him. "Why do you ask?"

"Well, was it an action picture or a chick flick or—?"

"Excuse me, *who* are you?"

"He's with me," Des said. "Mitch? . . ."

"Sorry, my bad. Go ahead."

"Jamella happens to be seven months pregnant, as you know. She doesn't care for parties either. And Kinitra never hangs around with this sort. Nor do I." Rondell glanced around at the crowd with keen-eyed disapproval. "I've been crunching numbers in my office. Kinitra's been working on a new composition on her piano."

"If all of you hate parties what are these people doing here?"

"Clarence invited them. It's his party. My brother's not even around, as you can see for yourself."

"It's Tyrone's house, Rondell. That makes it his party."

Rondell moved closer to her, lowering his voice. "Is there any way you can square this with the media?"

"That's not my concern right now. Just give me some breathing room, okay?" Des turned her attention back to Asia. "Tell me what happened."

"I was just . . ." Asia trailed off, fanning her face with her fingers to calm herself. Her nails were at least an inch long and painted purple and white. "I-I was dancing with Clarence. And that filthy old man, he came over to me and he-he . . ."

"He bit her on the booty!" Clarence blurted out. "That crazy man got down on his hands and knees and he bit her like some kind of a-a animal. So I let him have it."

Des shook her head. "You're telling me that big bad you punched out a seventy-two-year-old dementia patient?"

"He *attacked* my girl," Clarence said defensively. "He's some kind of sex offender."

"He has a medical condition," Mitch said.

"Medical condition my ass!" Clarence huffed.

"No, *my* ass!" Asia sobbed. "Will I need to get, like, a shot?"

"Here, hon, let me see . . ." Madge knelt behind her to examine her butt cheek. "No, he didn't break the skin. It doesn't even show. You're fine."

Mary had Winston up on his feet now and was walking him around.

"How did he get in?" Des wondered. "The estate's fenced all the way around. There's a trooper on the gate. How did he just waltz in here in his PJs?"

"I couldn't say," Rondell answered. "But I assure you we will undertake a thorough security review first thing in the morning."

Des heard hushed, reverent oohs and ahhs now as Tyrone Grantham made his way through the crowd toward them, ignoring the partiers one and all. He showed no interest in the pretty girls in their bikinis. Or in the guys who were patting him on the back and capturing live footage of him with their phones. Only in the altercation. His hooded eyes flicked from Des over to Winston, then to the Jewett girls, Clarence and Asia before they returned to Des. "Who's the old man?" he asked her in a low voice. "And why is he bleeding?"

"He's Winston Lash, your next door neighbor. Clarence punched him."

Tyrone grimaced. "Why you be wanting to do that, Cee?"

"He tried to bite my girl Asia here," Clarence explained.

"Winston doesn't know what he's doing," Mitch spoke up. "He has a medical condition."

Tyrone narrowed his gaze at Mitch before he turned back to Clarence and said, "I told you to keep it low profile. I also told you to collect their phones at the door. Don't you get what'll happen now? This'll go viral." He looked around at all of the partiers. "And you said a *few* friends."

"That's all I invited, I swear," Clarence insisted. "A dozen folks. It was Calvin who let all of these others in. I left him on the gate with the guest list."

"Yeah, that was a real smart play." Tyrone's eyes located his father-in-law, who was chatting up a pair of tipsy young babes as he floated there in the pool. "We'll talk about this later, Cee."

"I swear I didn't invite all of these people."

"And *I* said we'll talk about it later." Tyrone looked at Mitch again. "What sort of a medical condition?"

"He has frontotemporal dementia. It's a degenerative disease of the frontal lobe of the brain that causes him to do sexually inappropriate things. He doesn't know he's doing them."

"Are you his doctor?"

"No, I'm a movie critic."

"Mitch is with me," Des explained.

Tyrone thawed slightly. "Oh, sure, you're Mitch Berger. Glad to know you, man." He stuck out a gigantic fist and held it there until Mitch bumped knucks with him. "I saw you on TV a while back dumping all over the new James Cameron movie."

"Yeah, that sounds like me."

"I didn't agree but I admire your passion." Tyrone stared at Winston intently. "I've got no beef with any man who has dementia.

I've met retired players who had their bell rung so many times they barely know their own names. Can't drive a car. Can't feed their families. Breaks my heart." He rubbed his chin thoughtfully. "You say he lives next door?"

Mitch pointed toward the Joshua place. "Right over there."

"How'd he get in here?"

"We'll endeavor to ascertain that in the morning," Rondell promised.

Tyrone moved over toward Winston, who was seated in a chair now holding the ice pack to his mouth. "I want to apologize for what happened, sir. It was an unfortunate misunderstanding. I'm Tyrone Grantham, your new neighbor."

Winston removed the icepack and said, "My, you're a big one, aren't you?"

"Big enough. Can I help you get home or maybe send for someone?"

"That would be me," Mitch said.

"He's a friend of yours?"

"Yes, he is."

Winston noticed Mitch standing there and waved to him. "Hey, Brubaker, is this a party or is this a party?"

Mitch gave him two thumbs up. "Winston lives with his late wife's two sisters," he told Tyrone. "They're having a hard time of it. I make deliveries three times a week from the Food Pantry."

Tyrone's eyes widened. "Real?"

"Real."

"I thought this was a rich town."

"You thought wrong."

"Man, you push right back, don't you? You're all right. Figured you would be. Otherwise our resident trooper wouldn't be wasting her time on you." Tyrone turned to his little brother and said, "Ask Moms to pay a call on them tomorrow, okay? Maybe take them a mess of her fried chicken and potato salad. Tell her to make a whole lot. And *you* are going over there with her," he informed Clarence. "Those ladies need anything done—a light bulb changed, brush cleared, carpet vacuumed—you're doing it for them, hear?"

"I don't vacuum carpets," Clarence said indignantly.

"Yeah, you do," Tyrone assured him.

"Okay, whatever," he conceded. "But we still got us a situation here. This old man sexually assaulted Asia. He should be arrested."

"What do you think about that?" Tyrone asked Des.

"We can go that route. But if I charge Mr. Lash then I'll have to charge Clarence, too."

"With what?" Clarence demanded.

"You criminally assaulted him."

"I was defending my girl!"

"You cold-cocked a helpless old man, Clarence," Des pointed out. "And if you pursue this, you *will* get the attention of the media— especially given your criminal record."

Clarence's eyes widened. "How do you know about that?"

"It's my business to know."

"Maybe you ought to let it slide, Cee," Tyrone suggested.

"No maybe about it," Rondell put in firmly. "We do *not* need more negative attention."

Des said, "Actually, it's not up to you gentlemen to decide. Asia is the alleged victim here."

"That's right, girl," Asia said, nodding her head up and down. "And there ain't no 'alleged' about it. He bit me."

"Do you wish to file a criminal assault charge against him?"

Asia hesitated, peering over at Winston. "My grandmoms has

Alzheimer's. She don't even know where she is half the time. I don't want to break bad with some sick old man. That's just wrong. Can we forget the whole thing?"

"Yes, we can. We'll call it a minor disagreement. Clarence, if you and Mr. Lash will shake hands on it, I'll be on my way."

"I'm not shaking that pervert's hand," Clarence grumbled.

"Yeah, you are," Tyrone assured him.

Reluctantly, Clarence went over to Winston. "Hey, I'm sorry, awright?"

Winston grinned up at him. "My, you're a tall one, aren't you?"

"Just shake my damned hand, will you, old man?"

The two of them shook hands.

Des asked the Jewett girls if Winston was okay to go home now.

"He's fine," Marge said.

"I'll take it from here," Mitch said, starting toward him.

"Anything else we can do for you, Trooper Mitry?" Tyrone asked.

"Yes, there is." Des glanced at her watch. "While we were standing here having all of this fun, the clock just ran out. Pull the plug for me, will you? This party is history."

CHAPTER 6

THE OLD COOT BOLTED on him just as they were about to climb into Mitch's pickup. Took off across the lawn and went crashing into the woods that separated the Grantham place from the Joshua estate.

"Winston, where are you going?" Mitch cried out as he sprinted after him.

"Home!" hollered Winston, who could scoot along pretty fast for someone in his bedroom slippers. Especially considering that Clarence had just gone Tarantino on him. "Lila gets all weepy if I stay out too late. She was some kind of beauty in her day. But who wants an old broad when there's so many young ones and so little time. Know what I mean?"

"Not really, but that's okay." Mitch caught up with him, grabbing him by the arm. "You can't get home this way. They put up a chain-link fence, remember?"

"Of course I remember. How do you think I got here?" Winston yanked his arm free, feinted left and went right, speeding past Mitch. He had wicked playground moves. Possibly, a leash was in order. "Boy, that was some party," he cackled gleefully from the wooded darkness. "Why, there were more bare-assed colored girls—"

"Women of color."

"In the same place at the same time than I can shake my stick at."

Mitch groped his way along in the moonlit darkness, avoiding the trees and boulders as best he could. "Are you feeling okay, Winston?"

"Never better," replied Winston, who seemed to know exactly where he was heading. "Why does everyone keep asking me that?"

"Because you just got punched in the mouth."

"Dear, sweet Asia. I must come back and see her in the morning."

"I don't think that's a good idea."

"But we bonded. I felt a connection."

"Your teeth bonded with her ass. I'd hardly call that a connection."

"Shows how much you know. Women *cherish* a man who isn't afraid to show his feelings. My God, there is something so intoxicating about tender young flesh. Nothing else like it on God's green earth. *He* knows that."

"Who does, God?"

"*God?* Who's talking about *God?* I meant my good buddy. We're a lot alike, you know. Have very similar tastes."

Mitch let that one slide on by. He wasn't sure if imaginary playmates were part of Winston's illness or not. He only knew that the old guy was starting to drive him loco. "Winston, we'd better go back to my truck now."

"What for?"

"Because we're lost in the woods in the dark."

"Are not." Winston came to a halt, breathing heavily. "There's the big boulder, see?"

Mitch could barely make out a huge boulder looming before them. The eight-foot chain-link fence was just beyond it. "So? . . ."

"So that's where the hole is." Winston felt around for a moment. Then, with a cry of delight, he got down on his hands and knees and scurried through the fence like a little boy. "Are you coming?"

Mitch knelt there and discovered that a three-foot-square section of the fence had been neatly cut away. "Did you make this hole?" he asked as he followed Winston through it.

"Not me," Winston replied.

"How long has it been here?"

"Wouldn't know. I just found it yesterday."

Mitch pondered this. The street outside of Tyrone Grantham's house was swarming with photographers—any one of whom could fetch major bucks for candid shots of him relaxing poolside with Jamella. Or, better yet, with some hot, topless babe who *wasn't* Jamella. Would one of those creeps cut a hole in the fence and try to sneak onto his property? You bet.

As they neared the clearing at the edge of the woods Mitch could see lights in the windows of the old Joshua mansion. And floodlights were on out back. Callie was stretched out in a lawn chair on the patio. She was so lost in thought that she didn't seem to notice their arrival.

But Luanne and Lila sure did. The two of them rushed to the kitchen door, utterly distraught.

"Winnie, *what* happened to your mouth?" Lila cried out.

"He got punched," Mitch informed them.

"Who would do such a rotten thing?" Luanne demanded.

"One of your new neighbors took offense at his behavior."

"But Winnie's not well," Lila protested.

"He understands that now. It's all been ironed out."

Lila examined Winston's bloodied face, clucking over him. "Come, let's get you cleaned up." She took him by the hand and led him upstairs.

Luanne remained with Mitch in the kitchen, which still smelled nasty even though he'd unclogged that drain. Some form of rodent must have died in a cupboard somewhere. The trick would be finding it. Sounded like a job custom made for cousin Clarence.

"What did Winnie do?" Luanne demanded, hands on her hips.

"Took a bite out of a young lady's behind. Or tried to."

"Dear, dear. Mitch, I'm so sorry we had to drag you out into the night this way."

"No problem. That's what neighbors are for. Speaking of which, your new neighbors will be paying you a visit tomorrow."

"You mean that football star?"

"His mother and his cousin Clarence. They'd like to meet you. And Clarence is real sorry about what happened."

"Well, isn't that sweet of them. It will be nice to have callers. And now, if you'll please excuse me, I'd better go help Lila."

"Luanne, have you seen Winston with a pair of wire cutters recently?"

She stared at him blankly. "Did you say wire cutters?"

"I did. Do you own a pair? I seem to have misplaced mine."

"The toolbox is out in the mudroom. Help yourself," Luanne said, starting down the hallway toward the stairs.

The mudroom was off the kitchen. Mitch found a rusty toolbox on a shelf next to assorted mud-caked winter boots. It contained the usual household tools—including a pair of wire cutters. They were right on top, in fact. He stared at them before he closed the toolbox and went back out onto the patio.

"Hey," he called to Callie.

"Hey," she responded, stretched out there in a baggy T-shirt and jeans.

He sank gingerly into an ancient director's chair, positive it would give way under him. But it held. "I test drove a new Silverado today."

"I didn't know you were shopping for a truck."

"I'm not."

Her big gray eyes searched his face carefully. "What did you find out?"

"That June sucks as a car salesman."

"He hates it, Mitch. And his dad bullies him nonstop. That's why he's absolutely determined to set sail for the Keys as soon as humanly possible. Do you think I should go along or not?"

"Callie, I can't answer that one for you. I do think June will be happier if he strikes out on his own. He's stewing in his own juices right now." Not to mention Bonita's. "But you two have only been together for a couple of months. And you've dreamt about coming to the Dorset Academy for years. You're living out your dream here. You'll be giving that up if you go away with him."

"I know that." She sighed. "But I want to be with him. I can't imagine *not* being with him. And what's more important than love? It's the only thing that really lasts, isn't it?"

Mitch didn't go anywhere near that. He'd loved and lost Maisie to ovarian cancer. Loved and lost Des to her ex-husband Brandon. True, he did have Des back now. But for how long? Love didn't last. Nothing lasted. All you could truly count on was the moment that you were living in right now. "Christmas break is just a few weeks away. You could finish out the semester, then fly down there and meet up with him."

"I don't have that kind of money."

"I can loan you the plane fare."

"I wouldn't be able to pay you back for ages."

"So that'll be my Christmas present to you. Just think about it, okay? Who knows, by then you may not feel the same way about each other."

She looked at him suspiciously. "Is June seeing somebody else?"

"Why would you ask me that?"

"Because he's been acting so strange the past few days. Like he's, I don't know, all torn up emotionally."

"You should talk to each other about it. That's what couples do."

"You're right, I guess." She shrugged her narrow shoulders helplessly. "I mean, whatever."

Mitch said good night to Callie and headed back into the woods toward the hole in the fence, wondering if he should have told her everything. But it wasn't his business to tell her about June and Bonita. That was up to June, wasn't it?

Well, wasn't it?

He found the hole easily enough but took a wrong turn somewhere in the woods on the other side and came out by Tyrone Grantham's swimming pool instead of his driveway. The party was over. Everyone was gone—except for an enormous middle-aged black woman and chubby young black girl who were gathering up all of the plastic cups and paper plates and stuffing them into a trash barrel. The smell of perfume lingered in the air. Someone's yellow bikini top was floating in the pool.

"What do *you* want?" the woman demanded, glowering at him. "You some kind of a reporter?"

"I was seeing Mr. Lash home. Just came back to get my truck. I'm a friend of the resident trooper. Are you Mrs. Grantham?"

She nodded her head. "Chantal. I know you from the TV, don't I? You're that movie critic with the funny eyebrows."

"That's me, all right. Except there's nothing funny about my—"

"This here's Monique."

"Hello there, Monique."

"Hi," she responded distantly, her gaze fastened on the pavement.

"That bunch of no good leeches had *no* business here," Chantal fumed as she tossed more trash in the barrel. "It was that old fool Calvin let 'em in. Hoping one of those girls would get so high she'd spend the night with him. I worked the streets, okay? I know what men are really like. Even you so-called respectable men. You're all sick. And weak. Can't control your evil impulses. *We're* the strong ones. The good Lord knows that."

"Yes, ma'am."

"Don't 'ma'am' me," she barked at him. "My Tyrone's a good boy. He tries to do the right thing. But he's had to fend for himself and Rondell ever since he was a child. I wasn't there for him then. Now I am. So you go home and leave us alone, hear? Just go home."

She answered her cell phone on the first ring. Always did.

"Did I wake you up?"

"No, I just climbed into bed."

"What's the Deacon up to?" he asked, fetching a Bass Ale from his fridge. Quirt was nose down in the kibble bowl enjoying a late night happy meal.

"Watching a rerun of *NCIS*, what else?"

"Is he wearing his jacket in the house?"

"He is. I was thinking I might burn it when goes to bed—except I swear he never does. You get Winston home okay?"

"I did. Someone cut a hole in the fence between the two properties. That's how he got in."

"Did Winston do it?"

"He says not. I did find wire cutters in his toolbox, but my money's on a tabloid scuzzball."

"I'd believe that. I'll tell the Granthams in the morning. Thanks for the heads up."

"Da Beast was a lot nicer than I was expecting him to be. I kind of liked him, I must confess."

"He can be very likeable. He can also change gears uber-fast."

"So shall we talk menu for tomorrow night?"

"Serve whatever you want, Mitch. I won't be eating a single bite."

"That's my girl. Have I told you recently how adorable you are?"

"I'm not feeling very adorable right now."

"Beg to differ, thinny."

"Sleep tight, doughboy."

His stomach was rumbling. He'd never managed to eat any dinner. He cooked himself up those grilled cheese and bacon sandwiches he'd been starting to make and devoured both sandwiches while he trolled on his computer.

Sure enough, twenty-seven seconds of shaky video-phone footage of the heavyweight Clarence Bellows-Winston Lash bout was already up and streaming on a high-traffic celebrity gossip site, which was calling it a "rumble" between a member of Da Beast's "crew" and "an unidentified, pajama-clad man." Mitch couldn't believe how far the goalposts of the news business had shifted. Editors used to wait until they had an actual story before they ran the visuals. Now the raw video *was* the story. By morning it would go viral, which did Tyrone Grantham no good. Then again, his cousin Clarence hadn't done him any favors either.

Mitch washed up in the kitchen, but was still way too wired to sleep, so he opened another Bass and put on *Anywhere, Anytime, Anyplace*, a circa-1949 recording by John Lee Hooker and his Coast To Coast Blues Band. He powered up his monster stack, grabbed his sky blue Stratocaster and sat in on "Come Back Baby," laying down his riffs behind John Lee's low, seductive growl, bare toes wrapped around his wah-wah pedal as he reached for it, found it, *felt* it.

It was nearly three by the time Mitch climbed up to his sleeping loft and burrowed under the covers. He was asleep instantly. And swore his head had barely hit the pillow when his phone started ringing and ringing on the nightstand.

He groped for it, groaning. "Hello? . . ."

"Rise and shine, Boo-Boo! Everybody out of the sack!" His father sounded up as a pup. Always did. "Hey, I didn't wake you, did I? You said you get up early."

"I-I do, but . . ." He let out a huge yawn, blinking. "Pop, it's still dark out. What time is it?"

"Five-thirty."

"Are you getting ready to leave the city?"

"Nope. We're here."

"*Where* here?"

"At the foot of your causeway. But we can't get out to the island. There's a barricade blocking our way. You have to hit a buzzer or something?"

"Yeah, I do."

"So hit it already, will you?"

"Wait, you're *here?*" Mitch's brain was still not quite firing on all its cylinders. In fact, he thought the chances were good that he was actually still asleep. "What time did you leave the city?"

"We set the alarm for two-fifteen. Had our coffee and All-Bran, locked up your apartment good and snug and were out the door by three o'clock sharp. Are you going to raise this barricade or what?"

"Sure, sure. Right away . . ." Mitch staggered downstairs and hit the buzzer by the front door, his bleary eyes still swollen half-shut. He threw on a T-shirt and shorts and ran a hand through his mop of curls. Flicked on the porch light. Sure enough, they were pulling up in the driveway in a rented Ford Focus.

He went out into the muggy pre-dawn warmth and hugged and kissed them both. It had been nearly a year since they'd made it up from Vero Beach.

"Is Desiree here?" Chet demanded to know. "It's fine by us if she is. You don't have to hide her in a closet. We're all grown ups."

"She's home with her dad. He's recuperating from bypass surgery, remember? And I don't have any closets."

91

"What'd he say?" Chet was hard of hearing but refused to acknowledge it. Just talked really loud. Pretty soon everyone else was, too.

"He said he doesn't have any closets," Ruth told him.

"What's that supposed to mean? *Everyone* has closets."

"We can't wait to meet her, sweetheart."

"Yeah, when are we going to meet her, Boo-Boo?"

"Tonight. We're all having dinner here. And . . . could you do me a huge favor and not call me Boo-Boo in front of Des? I'll never hear the end of it."

"But I've called you Boo-Boo your whole life."

"I know this, Pop."

"And Maisie never minded that I called you . . . ouch!" Chet yelped as Ruth's elbow collided with his ribs. "Okay, son, if that's how you want it." His eyes fell on Mitch's Studey. "Hey, your truck is sa-weet. What year is it?"

"A '56."

"Sa-weet. I haven't seen one of those babies in years. Can we take it out for a spin? Come on, let's take it out for a spin."

"Pop, are you high on greenies or something?"

"He's just excited," explained Ruth. "We're happy to see you."

"Likewise. Come on in. I'll make us some coffee. And when the sun comes up I can show you around the island. Then I'll take you to your bed and breakfast. Sorry I can't put you up here, but it's real tiny, as you'll see."

They followed him inside, gazing around as he flicked on the lights.

"Man oh Manischewitz, this place is straight out of an American history book," Chet exclaimed. "Did George Washington sleep here?"

"Actually, he slept on Sour Cherry Lane before he crossed the Connecticut River. It was a ferry landing in those days."

"No closets, Ruthie. He wasn't kidding."

"Of course he wasn't kidding."

Mitch got his first good look at his parents now—and their appearance alarmed him. They weren't ancient. His dad was sixty-four, his mom a year younger. Yet both of them had . . . *shrunk*. His dad had always proclaimed himself to be six feet tall on the button. Yet Mitch towered over him, even barefoot. Chet had always been stocky, too. But he'd been on such a strict diet to bring down his cholesterol and blood pressure numbers that he actually looked gaunt. He wore his salmon-colored Florida slacks *way* up near his armpits. The lines in his face were deeper. His salt-and-pepper hair was more salt than pepper. He was still his same old peppy self. Mister Go-Go-Go. But he came off less like Chet Berger and more like Jiminy Cricket.

Was it *he* who had the grapefruit-sized tumor?

Or was it his mom—who had turned into one of those stooped little white-haired ladies that Mitch always offered his seat to on the subway. Ruth wore a pair of reading glasses on a chain around her neck. Once a librarian always a librarian. She had on a floral-patterned blouse, pink slacks and a pair of those bone-colored walking shoes that are the official footwear of AARP members who reside in the Sunshine State. Mitch's mom was a shy, sensitive woman. But very direct. She said what she meant—just did so in a much quieter voice than his dad. Then again, Bobcat Goldwaith was quieter than his dad.

Was it *she* who had the grapefruit-sized tumor?

"You're looking well, sweetheart. And I'm glad you let your eyebrows grow back. You reminded me of—"

"Joan Crawford, I know."

"I was going to say Robert Taylor."

"Wow, there's a name you never hear anymore. He was such a huge star in his day. Yet he's totally vanished into the celluloid haze—along with the likes of John Hodiak, Farley Granger and Elliott Gould."

Chet made a face. "Don't mention that bum Elliott Gould around me."

"Why, what's wrong with? . . ." Mitch noticed the dreamy look on Ruth's face. "Oops, I forgot. He was your chief competition for Mom's heart."

"My entire adult life I've had him hanging over me," Chet grumbled. "She even watched that stupid *Friends* on TV because every once in a while he'd turn up as Ross and Monica's father. He's a fat old man now, you know."

"He is not," Ruth objected. "And I could say a few words about your girlfriend Sharon Gless, mister. So behave yourself."

By now the sun was rising up out of the Sound. Mitch went into the kitchen and put the coffee on, groping around in the cupboard under the sink for his reserve box of Cocoa Puffs. He helped himself to a starved handful out of the box, cursing himself for not having bought more donuts yesterday. It had been appallingly shortsighted of him.

Clemmie sauntered into the kitchen and had some kibble.

"Since when are you into cats?" Chet wanted to know.

"Des rescues feral strays."

Clemmie padded out into the living room, sniffed at Mitch's folks and elected to go back up to bed. Another rough day at the office.

When the coffee was ready, Mitch filled three mugs and asked his folks if they wanted to check out Big Sister while they drank it.

They did. He led them down the path toward the lighthouse and the narrow strip of beach. There was a soft early-morning haze hanging over the tranquil water. A great blue heron was having breakfast at the water's edge. It took flight in the direction of the river. Mitch could hear the flapping of its wings.

"This is just lovely, sweetheart," Ruth said as they strolled along. "It's the sort of a place that you dream about."

"I still can't believe I actually live here. I keep waiting for someone to notice me and yell, 'Hey, you with the curly hair—get the hell off our island!'"

"I was hoping for real autumn weather," Chet groused. "The McCoy."

"Soon, Pop. We're supposed to get a storm tonight." Mitch took a sip of his coffee and said, "Okay, give it to me straight—which one of you is dying?"

His parents exchanged a confused look.

"Dying?" Chet repeated dumbly.

"Is it you or is it Mom? Tell me everything right now. I mean it."

Chet shook his head. "What in the heck are you talking about?"

"I'm talking about all of those 'appointments' that you had in the city. I'm talking about you showing up here in the middle of the night."

"We like to beat the rush hour traffic."

"Pop, you practically caught up with *last night's* rush hour traffic. I know you two. Something's up."

"Nothing's up. Everything's sa-weet."

"And will you *please* stop saying that? You're driving me ka-rayzee."

"Everything's fine, sweetheart," Ruth assured him. "We're both fine."

"Oh, yeah? Then what's going on?"

95

"Lots of stuff," Chet said. "We're 'happening' people."

"Pop, I swear . . ."

"We'll discuss it tonight, okay? First, we want to meet Desiree. You can understand that, can't you?"

"Not really."

"Sure you can." Chet squinted at the beach up ahead of them. "What's that lying in the sand—is it a seal?"

It lay a hundred feet ahead of them at the edge of the water. It was dark-skinned and shiny. But it was no seal. It was a young black woman. She appeared to be naked. She also appeared to be dead.

Mitch dashed toward her with his father in hot pursuit. She lay facedown in the sand. She was not naked. Her thin, sleeveless undershirt and panties were just so plastered to her wet skin that they were see-through. The undershirt had been torn in several places. Mitch turned her over. She was freezing cold to the touch—the air was warm but the water in the Sound wasn't. She was a teenager, no more than eighteen. A beautiful girl with a voluptuous figure. Her knees were badly scraped. There were fresh bruises around her wrists and throat. Also atop her thighs. Someone had gotten rough with her.

"Here, let me . . ." Chet had been a lifeguard at Jones Beach in his youth. He fell to his knees, wiped the caked sand from her face and stuck his ear to her mouth, listening closely. "She's alive but she's barely breathing." He performed mouth-to-mouth on her, then listened once again, shaking his head. "She's full of water. Got to get it out of her." He flipped the girl back over onto her stomach, turned her head to one side and pressed firmly against her back with both hands. She coughed up some seawater. He pressed again. More water came up. "Mitch, I'm going to stay with her. You run back to the house and call an ambulance, okay? And bring back plenty of blankets." He turned her back over and tried more mouth-to-mouth on her. "Hurry, son. We don't have a lot of time."

The girl coughed once again—except this time she abruptly regained consciousness, her big brown eyes gazing up at them wildly. "Don't make me go back there!" she cried out. *"Please* don't make me go back there!" Then she passed out and stayed out.

CHAPTER 7

By the time Des got out to the island Marge and Mary Jewett had already loaded the girl into the back of their EMT van in Mitch's driveway. Mitch was standing there with an adorable little sun-browned couple who were instantly identifiable as his parents. Mitch had his mother's dense curly hair and busy little rabbit nose. And his father's bright, probing eyes. Happily, Mitch did not share his father's fashion sense. Mr. Berger's salmon-colored slacks were yanked up so high it was a wonder the man could swallow.

"Morning, Des," Marge said wearily as Des climbed out of her cruiser.

"Back at you. Feels like I just saw you ladies ten minutes ago."

"It *was* ten minutes ago," Mary said.

Des hopped into the van with the girl, acutely aware of Mitch's parents watching her. "What have we got here?"

"Collateral damage from that party, we're figuring," Mary said. "Meet Jane Doe."

Jane Doe was an African-American in her teens. She had an oxygen mask over her face and an IV tube in her forearm. She was swaddled in blankets.

"The Bergers got most of the water out of her," Mary said. "Her lungs sound pretty clear now. We're oxygenating her and giving her fluids for dehydration. Her blood pressure's a little low but she's stable and conscious—although she won't tell us who she is or what happened to her."

"All she has on is her underwear," Marge said, lowering her voice. "Her panties are intact but her T-shirt's torn. She has fresh bruises on her thighs and around her wrists and throat. Her knees are all scraped up, too. We've phoned ahead to Shoreline Clinic for a SANE." Meaning a Sexual Assault Nurse Examiner.

Mary bent down and removed the oxygen mask from the girl's face. "How are you doing, hon?"

"Fine," she answered hoarsely. She didn't look fine. Panicky was more like it.

"Would you like to tell us your name now?"

"I can do that," Des said, studying the girl with great concern. "It's Kinitra Jameson. Her older sister, Jamella, is married to Tyrone Grantham." Des crouched down close to her. "What happened, Kinitra?"

Kinitra wouldn't say. She just shook her head.

"Were you out on a boat? Did someone attack you? How did you get all of those bruises?"

Kinitra shook her head again, then started to cry—huge, wrenching sobs.

Des turned to Marge and said, "Get her up to the clinic. I'll be along after I speak to the Bergers."

"And you'll notify next of kin?"

"That, too," Des said as she climbed out.

"Lucky you."

"Yeah, I'm just lucky all over."

Mary pulled the rear doors shut from the inside as Marge got behind the wheel. The van started its way back toward the causeway.

Des strode toward the Bergers, her pulse quickening.

Mitch was grinning at her in a most unfamiliar way. He looked as if his upper lip had been Krazy Glued to his top teeth. "I guess this is the moment we've all been waiting for," he said, his voice soaring at least an octave higher than usual. "Ruth and Chet Berger, I'd like you to meet the one and only Desiree Mitry."

"This is a real pleasure, Desiree," Chet said effusively. "Mitch has told us so much about you. Except he *didn't* tell us you were so beautiful."

"Or so tall," Ruth said, gazing up, up at her.

"It's the hat," said Des, who suddenly felt as if her own top lip had been glued to her teeth.

"Is that poor girl going to make it?" Chet asked.

"She'll be okay."

"I marked the spot where we found her," Mitch said. "Want to see it?"

"Is there anything to see?"

"Not really."

"Then it can wait. I need to contact her family now."

"So you've got an I.D. on her?"

"I know her. She's Tyrone Grantham's sister in law."

His face dropped. "Uh-oh . . ."

"Uh-oh is right." Des turned back to his parents and said, "This is really not how I planned to meet you folks. And now I'm afraid I have to run."

"Do what you have to do, Desiree," Chet said. "Besides, the best way to get to know someone is to watch them at work. Not at some artificial dinner party."

"Which we will, in fact, be having later on," Mitch pointed out. "Artifice and all. But you're absolutely right, Pop. It so happens that the two of us met because of her work. Dinner came much, much later. First, she had to make sure I wasn't a murderer."

Chet's eyes widened. "You thought Boo-Boo was a murderer?"

Des blinked at him. "I'm sorry, what did you just—?"

"Nothing," Mitch blurted out. "He didn't say anything."

"Really? Because it sounded like . . . did he just call you—?"

"Pop, I begged you."

"No, no. I like it large, Boo-Boo. And for the record, Chet, I never thought he was a murderer. Wouldn't have brought him Baby Spice if I did."

"Who's Baby Spice?" demanded Chet, who had some volume control issues. Talked a bit on the loud side. Maybe it was the pants.

"From the Spice Girls," Ruth said to him. "That English singing group, remember? One of them's married to David Beckham. The one with those huge, fake boobs."

Chet shook his head. "Who's David Beckham?"

"The soccer player."

"He has huge, fake boobs?"

"No, *she* does."

"Who does?"

"Des was referring to Clemmie. Her name used to be Baby Spice." Now Mitch's voice had a semi-adolescent edge to it. The poor man was growing younger by the minute. Before long his testicles would be retreating back up into his pelvis. "I'll be right back," he said to them, steering Des across the driveway toward her cruiser. "You saw all of those bruises?"

"I saw them."

"When she came to, she said, 'Please don't make me go back there.' She seemed really, really terrified."

"I'll take down your formal witness statement later. Your folks, too. Will they be okay?"

"Are you kidding? They spent their entire working lives in the New York City public school system. They've seen shootings, knifings—don't worry about them."

Des looked out at the water. "I'm all turned around. Where's the Grantham house from here?"

"A mile or so that way." He pointed up river. "The river current sends all sorts of debris our way. Tree limbs, plastic bottles—everything washes up here. She's lucky she did. Otherwise she would have drifted out into the open Sound. Then again, maybe that's what she wanted to do."

"You mean commit suicide?"

"Why else would she go for a swim in the middle of the night—in her underwear?"

"Could be some guy was getting rough with her. She jumped in the water to get away from him but the current was too strong and she couldn't get back."

"That plays," he conceded. "Especially if she was drunk or high. There *was* a party there last night."

Des shoved her heavy horn-rimmed glasses up her nose and said, "I don't like this."

"I wouldn't either if I were you."

She waved good-bye to Mitch's parents, got in her Crown Vic and drove back across the causeway, stopping when she reached the Nature Preserve. She'd input Tyrone Grantham's unlisted home number in her cell phone. Chantal answered the phone, sounding sleepy and grumpy.

"Sorry to disturb you so early, Chantal. It's Resident Trooper Mitry. Is Jamella awake yet?"

"She been up since dawn with her morning sickness. Poor thing hasn't gone a day without vomiting since she got pregnant. You need her?"

"Yes, I do."

"I'll go get her."

Des gazed out across the undulating green meadows of the Nature Preserve, cherishing this fleeting moment of serenity.

"Hello? . . ." Jamella's voice sounded guarded.

"It's Resident Trooper Mitry, Jamella. I'm calling about Kinitra."

"She's asleep in bed. You want me to wake her? Chantal could have done that for you."

"Kinitra's not in her room. I'm afraid she's being taken by ambulance to Shoreline Clinic."

Jamella let out a gasp. "She's *what*?"

"A resident of Big Sister Island just found her washed up on the beach there. She nearly drowned, but she appears to be okay."

"Oh my lord! . . ."

Des heard noises in the background. And a man's voice demanding, "What's going on?"

"Tyrone, they're taking my baby sister to the hospital! Trooper Mitry, are y-you still there?"

"I'm here. But I'm afraid I have more bad news. She's pretty bruised up. It's possible that she may have been sexually assaulted."

"Are you telling me one of those punks at Clarence's party *raped* her?"

"*Who* raped her?" Tyrone hollered in the background.

"Oh, my sweet girl," Jamella sobbed. "Where's this place you're taking her to? No, wait. Baby, you talk to her. I can't. I just can't."

"This here's Tyrone," he said angrily. "Where do we go?"

"Shoreline Clinic on Route 153 between Westbrook and Essex."

"Will you be there?"

"I'm on my way right now. Tyrone, you need to find Kinitra's wallet with her driver's license and other forms of I.D. Bring it with you, okay?"

"Is this an insurance thing? Because I got her covered no matter how much it costs."

"It's not an insurance thing. It's an age of consent thing. They need to verify that she's eighteen."

"Why's that?"

"They'll explain everything to you when you get there."

Shoreline Clinic was a small, highly efficient emergency response facility affiliated with Middlesex Hospital up in Middletown. Des accessed the emergency room directly from the driveway through the ambulance doors and found herself in a bustling bullpen of nurse's and doctor's stations. The examining and treatment rooms formed a big U around the bullpen.

The Jewett girls had come and gone by the time she got there. Kinitra was being examined by a doctor. The door to her room was closed. Des, who was several hours shy of sleep, fetched herself a cup of coffee from the nurses' lounge. Sipping the coffee gratefully, she returned to the E.R. and peeked through the glass door to the admitting desk and waiting area. Tyrone and Jamella were seated out there with Rondell, all three of them looking tight-lipped and grim. There were only a few other people out there at this early hour. By nine o'clock the place would be mobbed.

The door to Kinitra's room opened now and the SANE, a chubby young redhead, came out clutching the results of the CT100 Sex Crimes Kit—Kinitra's T-shirt and panties, the vaginal swabs, all trace and biological samples and photographic evidence. Every item was bagged and tagged separately. She led Des over to the nearest counter so that Des could sign for it, thereby maintaining the chain of custody.

"Dr. Tashima will be out in a minute," the young nurse informed her before she went bustling off.

Des used that minute to lock the evidence bags in the trunk of her cruiser. When she returned Dr. Cindie Tashima was coming out of Kinitra's room, closing the door softly behind her. Des had worked with Cindie on numerous occasions. She was a Harvard-trained Japanese-American whose parents had been born in an internment camp in Utah during the Second World War.

Right now, she had a very unhappy look on her face. "The Jewett girls told me to expect you."

"How is she?"

"Stable, comfortable and lucid. Also quite adamant that she wasn't raped last night. I advised her to consent to a rape kit anyway just for her personal safety. She consented even though she swore it wouldn't show anything. And it didn't."

"Her being in the water like she was would wash away all of the evidence, wouldn't it?"

"That's a 'yes' as to someone else's pubic hair. And a 'no' as to semen. There should still be traces of it in her vagina even after two hours in the water. But we found nothing when we swabbed her."

"Say he wore a condom."

"We found no fresh internal or external vaginal abrasions. Kinitra wasn't raped." Cindie let her breath out slowly. "Not last night, anyhow."

Des frowned at her. "What's that supposed to mean?"

"It means that I found extensive scarring. Someone has been sexually abusing this young woman for months. I'm talking about repeated, forcible vaginal and anal penetration."

"Damn, this just keeps getting better and better."

"Oh, I'm just getting warmed up," Cindie warned her. "Kinitra's also pregnant. Eight weeks along, I'd say."

"Did she know about it?"

"She knew. Took a home pregnancy test."

"Does her sister know?"

"Would that be Jamella?"

"Yes."

"The answer is no. She's been keeping it from her. Afraid she'll go nuts. Not exactly mature behavior but Kinitra *is* a teenager. And Jamella is the mother figure in her life, I gather."

"You gather right. Exactly what does Kinitra say has been going on?"

"She told me that she's been in a consensual relationship with a young man and that they happen to enjoy rough sex."

"Do you believe her?"

"No, I do not. But her sister provided us with valid I.D. that verifies Kinitra is eighteen and, therefore, an adult under the law. If she says she and her boyfriend like it rough then that's how it is. What happens next is entirely up to her. She would *not* grant me consent to discuss her condition with members of her family. If I do I'll be violating her privacy under the HIPPA laws. You and I can discuss it because this is a potential criminal investigation. Or I should say was. If she keeps insisting that no crime took place . . ."

"Then no crime took place. And I'm out of here. Cindie, she had to know what your exam would turn up. Why did she agree to it?"

"My opinion? It was a cry for help. But don't ask me from whom or what because I truly don't know."

"Well, how is she explaining the events of last night? How did she end up half-drowned on Big Sister Island?"

"She's refusing to say a word about it. The subject's off limits. I did take blood samples for the presence of alcohol and drugs in her system. If nothing else, we'll be able to determine if she was high. I should have those results back from the lab in a few minutes."

"Are we looking at a suicide attempt here?"

"We could be. Or she may have been trying to terminate. An acute physical trauma such as a near drowning can trigger a miscarriage—although it didn't in her case. The fetus is fine."

"How about the identity of this boyfriend of hers?"

"Won't say a word about him either. Otherwise, she's a regular chatterbox."

"You can do a fetal DNA test at this stage, can't you?"

"Absolutely. We can determine paternity with no risk to the mother or the baby. But she has to agree to it. We can't compel her. Not even if a crime took place. And she refuses to acknowledge that one has."

"Does she know that her family's outside?"

Cindie nodded. "Doesn't want to see them."

"Not even her sister?"

"Especially her sister."

Des opened the door to the small, windowless examining room and went in, Cindie trailing close behind her. Kinitra was sitting up in bed drinking from a Styrofoam cup of what appeared to be a hot tea. Her hair was wrapped in a towel. Her fresh-scrubbed face gleamed in the overhead lights. She looked thirteen.

"Hi, Trooper Mitry." Sounded thirteen, too. Her voice was all sing-songy and girlish. "Sorry to put you to so much trouble."

"No trouble at all. It's my job. But Dr. Cindie told me you don't want to see your sister. How come?"

Kinitra lowered her big brown eyes. "She'll be mad at me."

"No, she won't. Jamella loves you. She's worried sick about you."

Kinitra thought it over, her lower lip stuck out. "Who else is out there?"

"Tyrone and Rondell."

"Well, I *don't* want to see them. But I guess it's okay for Jamella to come in."

"Is it okay if Dr. Cindie talks to her about your medical condition?"

Kinitra shrugged. "If she wants to."

Cindie riffled through the forms that were attached to her clipboard. "I need your autograph to that effect right here."

Kinitra took the pen from her and signed it.

Des told her she'd be right back with Jamella. Then she and Cindie left the room, closing the door behind them.

"Cindie, how long will you be keeping her here?"

"After a near drowning we like to keep them under observation for six to eight hours, then have them come back the next day to be reexamined. There's a risk they can develop a lung infection."

"I need you to do better than that."

"Better as in? . . ."

"I want her out of that house for a day or two. It's an iffy situation there. An extended family of in-laws and hangers-on. A party atmosphere. Can you admit her overnight to Middlesex for, say, a psych evaluation?"

Before Cindie could respond, there was a disturbance outside the glass door at the admitting desk. Tyrone had gotten tired of waiting around. He was hollering, screaming and generally acting as if he wanted to hit someone. Little Rondell was trying to calm him down while Jamella pleaded with the woman at the desk.

Cindie watched them, her brow furrowing. "That big one in the orange T-shirt is Tyrone Grantham, isn't it? The pro football player who's always beating the crap out of people?"

"He's married to Jamella. The pint-sized one's his kid brother Rondell."

"Am I seeing things or is Jamella pregnant, too?"

"Seven months."

Cindie promptly got busy at a computer. "I'm going to admit Kinitra to Middlesex for that psych evaluation."

"I owe you one, Cindie. And you'll fill Jamella in?"

"You bet. That's why they pay me the big bucks."

Des opened the glass door and motioned to Jamella. "You want to see Dr. Tashima. She's right over there."

"Oh, thank God!" Jamella came waddling into the E.R. in a loose-fitting yellow shift and gold sandals, clutching a Prada handbag.

"Yo, what about us?" Tyrone demanded angrily.

"Please remain out here for now."

"No way!" he roared, barging his way through the doorway.

Des put her hand up against his massive chest and stopped him, lowering her voice. "Tyrone, Kinitra is very upset right now. She wants to be with her sister. Just let this process unfold, okay? I'll call you when it's time."

"To hell with that! I want to know what's happening *right now*!"

The folks in the waiting area were missing none of this. Tyrone Grantham was huge. He was black. And he was famous. Already, their cell phones were starting to come out. In three more seconds there would be video of this whole incident. Then the media would get into it—and Kinitra's privacy would be lost.

"Okay, fine," Des sighed. "Come with me."

"That's more like it. Come on, little man. We're going in."

The Grantham brothers followed her into the E.R. Jamella was huddled with Cindie, shaking her head in disbelief.

Des found a small, vacant examining room and ushered Tyrone and Rondell inside. "Wait right here, okay?"

"What the hell's this?" Tyrone demanded.

"The V.I.P. lounge. If you create a scene out there I can guarantee you it will be the lead story on *SportsCenter* tonight. Is that what you want for Kinitra?"

"No, we do not," answered Rondell, who looked totally distraught.

"Is Clarence waiting outside in your car?"

"He's still in the rack," Tyrone replied. "Up all night with that Asia."

"How about Calvin?"

"Naw, he never stirs before noon. There's nobody out in the car."

"Did any media people follow you here?"

Tyrone shook his shaved head. "Too early for them. We're good."

"Thank you for your consideration, Trooper Mitry," Rondell said. "We'll be right here when you're ready for us."

By now Jamella had gotten the full dose of bad news about her kid sister. The tears were streaming down her face. "She's . . . *how* many weeks?"

"Eight," Cindie informed her.

"I-I don't believe this. She's never even had a serious boyfriend. It must be a mistake."

"It's no mistake."

A lab technician approached Cindie with a computer printout.

Cindie studied it for a moment before she said, "No trace of alcohol or drugs in Kinitra's blood. She was clean last night."

"Of course she was," Jamella huffed. "My sister's no party skank. She's a serious artist."

Des put her hand on Jamella's shoulder. "I'd like for the three of us to have a talk together. Do you think you can keep it together in there?"

Jamella breathed in and out. "I'll try. But who *did* this to her?"

"That's what I want to find out."

Des led her into Kinitra's room, closing the door behind them.

Jamella rushed toward her and gave her a hug, her eyes widening at the sight of those bruises around Kinitra's throat. "Hey, baby," she said gently.

"Hey, I'm really, really sorry about all of this."

"No, I'm the one who's sorry. I let you down."

"How did you let me down? You didn't let me down."

"Trooper Mitry wants to ask us some questions, okay?"

"Questions?" Kinitra had a puzzled expression on her face. "What about?"

Jamella settled into a chair, her fists clenched, eyes fixed on the floor.

Des leaned against the closed door with her arms crossed. "About what happened to you."

"I *don't* want to talk about it."

Jamella gave her a hard stare. "You have to talk about it."

"No, I don't. And don't look at me that way."

"What way?"

"Like you think I'm some kind of ho."

Jamella's face tightened. "I don't think that, baby."

"And *stop* calling me 'baby.' I'm all grown up."

"Okay, okay. Just . . . chill out for me, will you? I got Tyrone out there about ready to kill somebody. I'm sitting here, size huge, trying to wrap my mind around what in the hell has happened a-and I got you all of a sudden giving me an attitude like I never, ever . . . Just, p-please . . ." Jamella broke off with a sob. Des went over to the sink and got her a tissue. "Sorry, it's my danged hormones. I cry *all* of the time." She dabbed at her eyes, sniffling. "Just tell us what happened, okay?"

"It's private," Kinitra snapped.

"Girl, there's nothing *private* about some dog *raping* you!"

"Why don't we back this up a little bit?" Des suggested, keeping her voice low. "How long have you two been living with Tyrone?"

Jamella stiffened. "Why, what's *he* got to do with this?"

"Not a thing, as far as I know. I'm just trying to get a sense of your situation. Walk me through the past, say, twelve months."

"Twelve months is like a whole lifetime ago," she said. "Kinitra and I were still living in the same apartment in Houston where Moms raised us. I met Tyrone when his team flew down to play the Texans last season. He came to the club where I danced and did choreography. I waited tables and slung drinks, too. Whatever it took to keep a roof over our heads. Not just me, either. Kinitra busted her booty every day after school at Walmart. Anyhow, he asked me for my number. We started texting back and forth. And then we started seeing each other," she recalled, warming to the memory. "When I got my chance to tour with Beyoncé he'd pop up wherever I was on the road. Or if I was home he'd fly down to Houston and we'd hang. I knew his reputation. And I'm real careful about who I get involved with. I told him from the start that I have my sister to look out for, my career. I am a serious person. Demonstrate to me that you are serious or go home. And he did. He *respected* me. After six months or so he asked me to move in with him in Glen Cove. It's near where the team practices. A lot of his teammates have places there. I said to him, I have a sister, remember? He told me to bring her along. I said, I am not going to uproot her unless we're talking about marriage. And that's when he showed me *this*." She held out her left hand so Des could admire her huge diamond engagement ring.

"The two of us came north and moved into his place last February, I think it was. There was still snow on the ground. Within a few weeks I was pregnant. We got married in July. Tyrone really wanted our popsy to be there to give me away. I told him Popsy hadn't been a part of our lives for a long, long time—because he was either in jail or because Moms wouldn't have anything to do with him. Popsy's no angel. Not that he's a mean or bad person. He tries to do the right thing. He's just weak. Lacks will power, you know? Tyrone hired someone down in Houston who found him living in a homeless shelter. Tyrone flew him to New York for the wedding and he's been with us ever since. It's worked out real good for him. He and Chantal fight like crazy, but that's family, right?"

Des looked at Kinitra and said, "So Tyrone has been pretty nice to you?"

"He's been real nice. Wants to produce me and everything."

"How about Rondell? Has he been nice to you?"

"I guess."

"Do you have feelings for Rondell?"

"Get out! He's a total Urkel."

"How about Clarence?"

"Cee's a pest but he's harmless." Jamella glanced at her kid sister. "Right?"

Kinitra nodded. "And kind of lame. He keeps saying he's a sound engineer but I know more about the studio than he does."

"After the commissioner suspended Tyrone," Jamella went on, "we decided it would be a good idea to get away from his teammates and all of their friends. A lot of them are no-good punks from the neighborhood, if you ask me. So we ended up in Dorset."

"Which brings us to last night," Des said to Kinitra.

"I already told you," she responded crossly. "I've got nothing to say."

"Did you go to Clarence's party?"

"Hell, no!" Jamella answered. "I don't let her near those sort of people."

Des looked at Jamella and said, "Please let her answer for her-self, okay?"

"Fine. Whatever, you say."

"I was working at my piano on some things," Kinitra allowed grudgingly. "Until Clarence got in that fight and all hell broke loose. Things settled down after a while but I felt, I don't know, kind of wired. So I had myself some wine."

"You had some *what?*" Jamella demanded.

"Wine," she repeated hotly. "Do you have a problem or something?"

"*I* do," Des said. "Dr. Cindie just told us that there was no trace of alcohol in your system."

"I can't help what her test said. It's wrong. I also smoked some reefer."

"Okay, now I *know* you're lying," Jamella said angrily. "You've never been near weed in your life. Who are you protecting?"

"Nobody!"

"This is bull. I am *not* going to listen to this."

"Where did you get the reefer?" Des asked her.

"Found it in an ashtray out on the patio."

"What were you doing out there?" Jamella wanted to know.

"I went outside for a few minutes, okay?"

"Who with?"

"Nobody!"

"Don't you lie to me! Did that no good Cee get you high?"

"No!"

"So you got high by yourself?" Des asked her.

"That's right. I got high by myself. A-And it was real warm out so I decided to take a swim."

Des nodded. "Makes sense. You didn't bother with a bathing suit?"

"What for? It was late. No one else was around. Plus I was high, like I said. That's how I scraped my knees. I tripped on some rocks on my way down there. The water felt great. But I was *so* high that I swam out too far, I guess, because I got caught in the current. I swam and I swam but I couldn't get back to shore. I was lucky I found my way to that island."

"Yes, you were."

"Girl, were you trying to kill yourself out there?"

"Don't be silly."

"Look at me," Jamella ordered her. "*Were* you?"

"No, I was not trying to kill myself."

"You mentioned those scrapes on your knees," Des said. "How about the bruises around your wrists and throat? How did you get those?"

"I figured from when they did the CPR on me or whatever."

"The folks who found you told me that the bruises were there *before* they called 911."

"They're wrong."

"They also told me you came to for a second and cried out, 'Please don't make me go back there!'"

Kinitra lowered her eyes, swallowing. "I really don't remember that. I must have been delirious."

"Okay, I've heard enough of your bull," Jamella blustered at her. "Tell us who attacked you right goddamned now. Was it the same dog who got you pregnant or was it someone else?"

Kinitra reached for the Styrofoam cup of tea on the bedside table and took a sip. She wouldn't say.

Des said, "You told Dr. Cindie that you took a home pregnancy test."

She nodded. "A few weeks ago."

"And you don't tell me?" Jamella cried out.

"How could I? I knew you'd freak. Just like you are right now."

"Because I'm your sister and I love you! What is this, are you trying to punish me or something?"

"Why is this about you? Why does *everything* have to be about you?"

"Ladies, let's try to lower our voices, okay?"

"You tell her to stop lying to me, and I'll lower my damned voice!"

"Kinitra, are you planning to have this child?"

"Not if I have anything to say about it," Jamella put in.

"Which you *don't!*"

"Girl, what about your musical career?"

Kinitra shrugged. "Stuff happens."

"But you have a gift. You have dreams."

"Those are your dreams, not mine."

"They're *what?*"

"Does the baby's father know that you're pregnant?" Des asked.

"No."

"Is he the same man who attacked you last night?"

"I *wasn't* attacked. How many times do I have to tell you?"

Jamella said, "Your doctor told me they can give you a paternity test. I want you to have that."

Kinitra stuck out her chin. "No way. And you can't make me. This is *my* thing."

"Is it true that you're presently in a consensual relationship?" Des asked her.

"That's right. But don't ask me his name because I'm not going to tell you."

"Why's that?"

"Because it's personal."

"She's lying again," Jamella said. "She hasn't had a boyfriend since she was thirteen."

Kinitra let out a harsh laugh. "Like you'd know."

Des said, "Dr. Cindie found signs of forcible vaginal and anal penetration when she examined you. You have all kinds of scarring down there. Care to talk about it?"

"That's just how we roll."

"So you like it rough?"

Kinitra smirked at her. "The rougher the better."

"More lies," Jamella said, fuming. "Girl, who are you trying to protect?"

Kinitra sighed wearily. "I don't want to talk about this anymore. What's the point? You don't believe me anyway."

"Okay, if that's how you want it," Des said. Clearly, the girl wasn't going to give up anything else. Not with her sister present.

"Can I take her home now?" Jamella asked.

"I'm afraid not. She's being transferred to Middlesex Hospital for overnight observation."

"What for? She's fine. Aren't you, baby?"

"It's okay, I don't mind," Kinitra said offhandedly.

Which totally flabbergasted Jamella. "Wait, you're good with that?"

"Well, yeah. I mean, if the doctor thinks I should."

She stared at her kid sister long and hard. "Okay, if that's what you want."

Des led her back out into the E.R., closing the door behind them.

"I swear, I don't even know who that person is." Jamella's voice sounded hollow. She was badly shaken. "It's like she's turned into somebody else. Lord, what *happened* to her?"

Tyrone came charging across the E.R. toward them with Rondell on his heels. "What in the hell is going on?" he demanded to know. "The doctor won't tell me. The nurses won't tell me. I swear, if I don't get some answers I am going to tear someone's head off!"

Jamella let out a sob. "Some punk raped my baby sister and got her pregnant, that's what. She's going on eight weeks already."

Rondell let out a gasp. "Oh, my God. . . ."

That vein in Tyrone's forehead was beginning to throb. Then he let out a lion's roar of pure rage and drove his giant fist through the door of the supply closet next to Kinitra's room.

Everyone in the E.R. stopped what they were doing and stared at him. It wasn't every day that the Incredible Hulk showed up in their work space.

The security guard who was on duty next to the ambulance doors rushed over and said, "Sir, I'll have to ask you to control yourself."

Not a chance—Da Beast was loose. He picked the guard up and hurled him bodily against the wall. The man crumpled to the floor, dazed.

"*No,* Tyrone!" Jamella cried out.

Now a pair of husky young orderlies rushed over and attempted to subdue him. Good luck with that. Tyrone sent one orderly flying across a nurse's desk and kicked the other's legs out from under him. Then, his massive chest heaving, Tyrone whirled and—discovered that his forehead was flush up against the nose of Des's SIG-Sauer. He froze instantly.

"Are you listening, Tyrone?" Des kept her voice quiet as she stood there holding her weapon to his head.

"I-I'm listening," he panted.

"Dr. Cindie has her hand on the telephone at this very moment. If she has to call for back up, you will be looking at the business end of a criminal assault investigation—not to mention a lifetime ban from the NFL. Do you understand what I'm saying? Nod your head if you do. I won't shoot you."

Slowly, he nodded his head up and down. "Is that what you want?" Now he shook his head.

"You've got a pregnant wife standing here who has just gotten the shock of her life. Jamella is freaking out right now, okay? She needs for you to be a husband to her."

"The trooper's right, big man," Rondell spoke up nervously. "You don't want to be upsetting Jamella. Think about your baby."

Tyrone steadied himself. His breathing returned to normal. The crazed look in his eyes faded away. "You're right. You're totally right. I'm okay now," he told Des. "And I'm sorry." He went over to the security guard and helped him to his feet. "Hey, man, I'm real sorry. I just got some bad news is all. Are you hurt? You need anything?"

The guard grunted that he was fine. So did the orderlies after Tyrone had helped them up, apologizing profusely. Everyone seemed to be fine. No harm, no foul. Des holstered her weapon. The E.R. returned to normal.

Tyrone put an arm around Jamella, his brow furrowing with concern. "You okay?"

"No, I am not okay," she answered in a small voice. "My baby girl was attacked last night."

"By who?"

"She won't say."

"Well, was it the same guy who got her pregnant?"

"She won't say, Tyrone."

Rondell shook his head in disbelief. "Such a sweet, innocent girl. Who would want to hurt her?"

Tyrone looked at Des. "You don't suppose this is about me, do you?"

"I don't suppose anything at this point. What are you suggesting?"

"Some bastard trying to hit me where it hurts. Like that sleaze Plotka."

"There's no way he could get onto our property," Rondell reminded him. "We've got that fence all around."

"Actually, you do have a security problem," Des informed them. "I intended to phone you about it this morning. There's a hole in your fence between you and the Joshuas. Mitch discovered it last night when he was escorting Mr. Lash home."

Rondell frowned at her. "You're suggesting that someone could have snuck onto our property last night through this hole?"

"Not *someone*," Tyrone said tightly. "Plotka."

"But how did he get into our house?" Rondell wondered. "We have a security system. I checked it personally before I went to sleep."

Jamella said, "Maybe she went out for a swim like she told us. Maybe the bastard was out there waiting for her."

"She wasn't taking any swim when I went to bed," Rondell countered. "She was in the recording studio."

"What time was that?" Des asked him.

"I was in my office until well after one o'clock. I couldn't sleep after all of that commotion."

"How about you two?" she asked Tyrone and Jamella.

Tyrone said, "We were asleep by twelve, weren't we, baby?"

"I know *I* was," she said. "I'm just so tired all of the time."

Des mulled this over. "Even if it was Stewart Plotka—and I'm not saying it was—he wasn't anywhere near Kinitra eight weeks ago, was he?"

"Could be he was," Tyrone argued. "He did hang out at that Dave & Buster's where him and me got into it. She was there with us a bunch of times. And it's not far from my place in Glen Cove."

"He lives in Forest Hills, Queens," Rondell added. "That isn't far from Glen Cove either."

"Are you going to talk to that bastard?" Tyrone demanded. "Because if you don't, I will."

"We'll talk to him," Des said. "Keep your distance, understand?"

Rondell said, "I'm slightly confused about something. Can't the doctors simply administer a DNA test to determine who the father is?"

"Yes, they can," Des affirmed. "But only if Kinitra consents to it. And she's refusing. She won't even acknowledge that a crime has taken place. Says she's been in a consensual relationship."

"She hasn't got any man," Tyrone shot back. "Just her music."

"That's what I told the trooper," Jamella said. "There's nobody."

Des looked at Rondell. "How about you? You spend a lot of time around Kinitra. Seem pretty fond of her."

Little brother cleared his throat uncomfortably. "Of course I'm fond of her. She's like a sister to me."

"And how about Clarence?"

"Cee knows I'd break his fool neck if he touched her." Tyrone glowered at Des. "And don't you be looking at me. I'm a happily married man, not some animal."

Des said, "Someone has been sexually assaulting that girl repeatedly for weeks, maybe months. It's my belief, despite what she told us, that she was assaulted again last night. I believe she had reason to fear for her life. And I believe she's still afraid. Therefore, I'm going to request the assistance of the Major Crime Squad."

Jamella looked at her searchingly. "Will your people figure out who did this to my sister?"

"They're very good at what they do. They'll get to the bottom of this." Des mustered a reassuring smile. "Whatever this is."

CHAPTER 8

"Sa-weet room!"

"Real glad you like it, Pop."

Mitch had made sure he booked Chet and Ruth into the Admiral Bramble room of the Frederick House, which had a canopy bed, a private bath with a claw-footed tub and a terrific view of the Lieutenant River. It was the same room that Mitch had stayed in when he'd first shown up in Dorset—highly reluctantly, if he remembered right—on a weekend getaway assignment for his newspaper's travel section. He'd barely gone out of his apartment in those brutal months after Maisie died, let alone traveled anywhere. Lacy, his editor, had thought he needed a wake-up call. Lacy was very clever that way.

"It's a charming room, sweetheart," Ruth said brightly, gazing around at the antique furniture.

"Sa-weet!" Chet exclaimed.

His father would, Mitch felt certain, totally freak if he knew just how much sa-weet cost per night in Dorset. But Mitch had also made sure that his father would never see the tab.

"Get yourselves settled in, okay?" he suggested. "Come on back out to the island whenever you're ready. We'll have drinks and a bite to eat. It'll be fun." Was it his imagination or had his voice started changing back to his pre-Bar Mitzvah falsetto? He was definitely sporting two fresh zits on his forehead. But, hey, his parents were not making this easy for him. They were stubbornly refusing to spill one word about those "appointments" of theirs in the City. Chet had said they'd talk about it tonight and he'd meant it. The man had always been maddening as hell that way. "And I'm real sorry about this morning," Mitch added. "Finding a half-dead girl on the beach isn't really a typical way to start your day out here. Well, actually it *is*, come to think of it. But Dorset's really a very nice place—once you get used to the fact that everyone's a bit funny in the head."

He left them there and piloted his Studey through the Big Branch Road shopping district toward The Works, his mind on that beautiful, terrified young girl whom they'd rescued on the beach. If they hadn't stumbled upon Kinitra Jameson, she would be dead right now. Was that what she'd wanted? To do herself in? Des had phoned from the clinic with ample reason why. Someone had been brutalizing the poor girl up, down and sideways. *And* gotten her pregnant.

The Works was a European-style food hall located in what had once been a huge red-brick piano works on the banks of the Connecticut River. There were food stalls that sold locally grown produce and farm-fresh eggs. There was a coffee bar that stayed open until late at night. A juice bar that sold fruit smoothies. A butcher, a fishmonger, a deli counter, a kick-ass bakery. Out in the center of the food hall there were tables and chairs where people could hang out over a cup of coffee or meet for a sandwich.

Mitch's first stop was the bakery, where he bought two dozen chocolate biscotti. One dozen was for tonight's dessert, the other to devour right goddamned now. Next he intended to buy a slab o' salmon to throw on the grill. Dinner was going to be real simple and healthy. The Deacon was on a heart-smart eating regimen. Chet was watching his cholesterol and blood pressure. And Des was on her trendy Connecticut Gold Coast Clenched Stomach Diet.

As he was crossing the food hall Mitch encountered Stewart Plotka seated at a table having lunch with his turbocharged power lawyer, Andrea Halperin. Plotka was plump, soft-shouldered and boneless. Gave the impression of being constructed entirely out of blubber. And that black eye patch of his really wasn't working for him. Moshe Dayan the man wasn't. His eye and hand injuries didn't seem to be hurting his appetite. He was attacking a foot-long shrimp salad hero, potato chips and a chocolate milk shake. Andrea was nursing a black coffee.

"Mitchell Berger, am I right?" she said, showing him her nice white teeth. Andrea was in her late thirties and, unlike her client, lean and taut. Her pinstriped suit was impeccably tailored. Her white blouse was silk. Her pearls were real. She had chicly styled hair, full red lips and terrific legs. Quite a sexy package if you were partial to greedy, soulless predators. "Join us, won't you please?"

"Sorry, I really have to get to work," Mitch said as her client continued to devour his lunch like a feral four-year-old. The man was spraying shrimp, mayo and shredded lettuce everywhere.

Andrea reached over and dabbed at Plotka's mouth with a napkin. Mitch wondered if they were sleeping together. He doubted it. Plotka wasn't exactly in her league. "Just for a moment, Mitchell. It's quite important."

Reluctantly, he sat down with them.

She sipped her coffee and said, "I miss your reviews on television. You were *the* best thing about the midday news. Was it a contractual thing?"

"No, it was more of a self-image thing."

"Are you sure? Because if it's about money, I'm the girl who can get it for you. Just turn me loose."

"I'm not a talking head, that's all."

"But you were so *good* at it. Funny, charming, even a bit sexy, if you don't mind me saying so. A lot of my friends had crushes on you."

"I'm happy doing what I'm doing. I didn't like being on TV."

She let out a laugh. "Who does?" Like any top-flight lawyer, NBA point guard or professional assassin, Andrea Halperin could pivot on a dime. "It's merely a way to get what you want."

"Like what?" Mitch asked.

"Like restitution," Plotka answered around a mouthful of shrimp salad. "Take me for a sec, okay? I had a beautiful future with a beautiful girl all lined up. Now I've got squat. My Katie's never been the same since Tyrone Grantham attacked her. She has crying jags like you wouldn't believe. Plus her dumb-assed shrink got her so hooked on happy-happy pills that she had to go into rehab." He paused to take a loud slurp of his shake. "When I saw Grantham at Dave & Buster's that day I was just trying to explain it to him. I wanted him to understand what he'd done to my nice girl. A nursing student. An angel of mercy. He came at me like a wild animal. Now I have permanent retinal damage plus tendon and ligament damage in my wrist."

"And what's happened to Katie?"

"Katie is down in Boca Raton at the present time," Andrea answered delicately. "Her mother isn't well. Katie's been taking care of her and trying to get her own life back together. She hasn't had an easy time of it, emotionally or financially. Stewart is well aware of that. He fully intends to share the proceeds with her when we reach a financial settlement with Mr. Grantham. And we *will* reach a settlement."

"Did she graduate from nursing school?"

"Katie hopes to resume her nursing studies very soon," Andrea replied. "But her family obligations have made that impossible. She's currently working as a dancer at a gentlemen's club in Boca."

Mitch blinked at her. "She's a stripper?"

"It's a perfectly respectable way for a single woman to earn a living, Mitchell. The club is very high-end. And just because Katie happens to be earning her living that way now doesn't mean she was 'asking for it' three years ago from Tryone Grantham. In fact, I'm surprised you even went there."

"I didn't. You did. Still, I'm amazed that the tabloids aren't all over it."

"Don't be. It's cost me dearly to keep it under wraps. My favor bank is practically belly up."

"So why tell me?"

"Because I want you to know that I'm being totally straight. I'll never shade the truth with you, Mitchell. I won't even try. The truth is I advised Katie against working there. I told her that in these sorts of cases appearances are crucial."

"And what did she tell you?"

"I can't repeat it. My mother told me to never use such words in public."

"I find that hard to believe."

"That I don't use naughty language in public?"

"That you had a mother."

Andrea threw back her head and laughed. "You are *so* funny. We have to get you back on TV."

Mitch looked over at Plotka. "And how do *you* earn your living now?"

"Well, I can't work with computers anymore," he answered bitterly. "I have a disability. Besides, I don't have time. I'm too busy trying to get justice. It's taking *forever.*"

"Justice requires patience," Andrea lectured him. "Look how long it took to bring the Nazi war criminals to trial at Nuremberg."

"Please don't ever do that again," Mitch said to her.

"Do what, Mitchell?"

"Mention the Holocaust and this case in the same breath."

"Before that bastard came along," Plotka said angrily, "Katie and me were planning a June wedding. I had a good job. I was putting down a deposit on a house in Mineola. Now look at me."

"I'm trying to," Mitch responded. "But it's really hard. That eye patch is just so totally *Pirates of the Caribbean*. Seriously, all you need is a peg leg and a parrot on your shoulder. Can you say 'Aaarggh? . . .' Can you?"

"Shut the hell up," Plotka growled at him.

"Andrea, you said this was important? . . ."

"Yes, it is. We need to talk about what really happened at the Grantham house last night." She was all business now. "I've seen the video of the dust-up between cousin Clarence and that feeble old man. The whole world has. But the whole world doesn't know why it happened. Or whether Tyrone Grantham was or was not in the middle of it. No one in the family is talking, naturally. And the resident trooper has written it off as a minor misunderstanding."

"So? . . ."

"So a little birdie told me that you and she showed up at the front gate together." Andrea arched a sculpted eyebrow at him. "It's not exactly a secret around these parts that you two are friends with privileges. I thought you might speak to her on my behalf."

"And say what?"

"That I'm someone who can help her if she'll help me. All I'm asking for is a little cooperation."

"You mean information."

"I've done my homework, Mitchell. I know that Desiree Mitry wasn't always a lowly resident trooper. A high-profile case such as this one could put her career right back on the fast track. The lime-light has a way of doing that."

"A bit of advice, counselor. That argument didn't work when Robert Vaughn tried it on Steve McQueen in *Bullitt* and it won't work now with you and Resident Trooper Mitry. Besides, you're no Robert Vaughn."

"Okay, I have no idea what you just said."

"And you never will. How cool is that?"

"I need someone on the inside, Mitchell."

"Sorry, I can't help you."

"You can't or you won't?"

"Okay, I won't."

"Fair enough," she said easily. "But it might interest you to know that we intend to produce irrefutable evidence this afternoon."

"Evidence of? . . ."

"Direct, intimate sexual contact between Katie O'Brien and Tyrone Grantham. We'll be holding a press conference outside his gate in a short while. I'm timing it so that ESPN can make it their top story on *NFL Live*." Andrea Halperin smiled at him savagely. "Stay tuned, Mitchell. This is about to get extremely down and dirty."

CHAPTER 9

"It's good to see you again, Miss Thing."

"Right back at you, *Lieutenant* Snipes."

"Cut that *Lieutenant* bull."

"I'm so proud of you, Yolie."

"I couldn't have done it without you, girl."

"Yes, you could. And you did."

Des and Detective Lieutenant Yolanda Snipes of the Major Crime Squad were catching up outside the entrance to Middlesex Hospital while Yolie's sergeant parked their car. They'd shown up there at Des's request from the Central District headquarters in Meriden. It was not an official request. It was Des reaching out to a friend who happened to be so smart, tough and good that she'd finally blasted her way through the concrete ceiling and made lieutenant. Her promotion, as Des saw it, was way overdue. But it hadn't been easy for Yolie Snipes. She was half-black, half-Cuban and all pit bull—an intimidating, fearless hard-charger who did not play well with others. She stood five-foot-nine barefoot and was into power lifting. The sleeveless knit top she had on showed off her tattooed guns.

"How's the Deacon doing?" she asked Des.

"Better every day." Which was entirely true . . . from the neck down.

"And your boy, Mitch?"

"Actually, he's the reason why you're here. Our sexual assault victim washed up on his island. If she is a victim. That's up in the air right now."

"What's she saying went down?"

"She isn't saying."

"Well, who's the complainant?"

"There isn't a complainant."

Yolie looked at Des doubtfully. "Girl . . ."

"Just hear my thing, okay?"

"No prob, I can do that," Yolie said as her female sergeant came marching across the parking lot toward them, arms pumping, fists clenched.

They'd given her a pint-sized young brunette to break in. She was a feisty-looking little thing in a shiny black pants suit who had the sort of sculpted big hair that Des thought went out with leg warmers and Pat Benatar. Her boobage was big, too, and she wasn't shy about displaying it. The top three buttons of her tight red blouse were unbuttoned to reveal cavernous cleavage.

"What's the deal, Loo?" she demanded, her chin stuck out at them.

"Master Sergeant Des Mitry, kindly give it up for Sergeant Toni Tedone," Yolie said with a grin on her face. "She's Rico's younger cousin."

Des's eyes widened. "No way."

"Totally way," Yolie said, nodding.

Rico "Soave" Tedone had been Des's semi-bright weasel of a sergeant back when she was a homicide lieutenant on Major Crimes. Until, that is, she blew up her career—with a not-so-generous assist from Rico—and got demoted to resident trooper. When Rico made lieutenant he was assigned Sergeant Yolie Snipes. Now Yolie was a lieutenant and Rico was living large on the state's Organized Crime Task Force, strictly because he was a Tedone and therefore hard-wired into the Waterbury Mafia—the Italian-American clan of brothers, uncles, cousins and in-laws who pretty much ran the Connecticut state police. The Brass City boys were a force within the force. And there were so damned many of them that, well, Des supposed it was inevitable one of them would turn out to be a she.

"Rico is *all* up in my face about you," Toni informed Des. "I'm supposed to watch how you walk, talk, work the room. I was, like, do I have to follow her into the bathroom and watch how she takes a crap, too? And he's, like, just pay attention, okay? And I'm, like, you think I suffer from A.D.D. or something? And he's like, whatever."

Des waited for her to come up for air. She was definitely a Tedone—raring to go, chippy, knew it all. "Pleased to meet you, Toni. How long have you two ladies been partnered up?"

Yolie glanced at her watch. "Two days, three hours and seventeen minutes. So who've we got here, girl?"

"A sweet, innocent, eighteen-year-old girl named Kinitra Jameson."

"No one who's eighteen is innocent," Toni shot back. "Trust me, I went to Catholic schools my whole life."

"Kinitra washed up on Big Sister early this morning in her underwear, half drowned. She had bruises around her throat and wrists and she was terrified. She's a talented young singer who's been living in one of the waterfront mansions on Turkey Neck with her big sister Jamella—who is married to Tyrone Grantham."

Yolie's eyes widened. "Okay, this just got a lot more interesting."

"Tyrone's cousin, Clarence, threw a big party at the mansion last night. Kinitra claims she got high on wine and weed, took herself a midnight dip and accidentally got swept up in the river current. But her doctor at Shoreline Clinic found no trace of alcohol or drugs in her blood. The rape kit results were negative but the doctor did find scarring from repeated, forcible vaginal and anal penetration. Kinitra's also eight weeks pregnant. Jamella went nuts when she found out. Says the girl's never had so much as a boyfriend."

Yolie peered at Des. "And what's Kinitra saying?"

"That she's in a consensual relationship and they like it rough."

"Which you don't believe?"

"No, I do not. Someone's been raping this girl, Yolie. Someone who either lives in the mansion or has access to it. I think she jumped in that water last night to get away from him—and then decided to try on suicide for size. They're keeping her here overnight for a psych evaluation. Slipped her in under the media radar. Nobody knows she's here. Her family would like to keep it that way."

Toni raised her hand. "Can I ask something, Loo?"

"Put your damned hand down, will you? This ain't no classroom. What is it you want to ask?"

"Who's the complainant?"

"There isn't one."

"Then what are we doing here?"

"Responding to a resident trooper's request for assistance."

"But we're the Major Crime Squad and, hello, no crime's been committed."

"Des thinks otherwise. Sometimes you have to come at things a little sideways."

Toni shook her big hair. "But how do we write it up?"

"We don't. Not yet, anyhow. And we stick together. We don't go running our mouths about this to our cousins and uncles over Sunday dinner, got it?"

"I don't have Sunday dinner with them anymore," Toni said defensively. "I'm tired of them trying to fix me up with every wop cop in Connecticut who's single and under thirty. Like I want to hang with someone who's exactly like me. I mean, I'd go completely nuts."

"Let's go talk to the girl," Yolie said, starting toward the door with Des.

"What's my role here?" Toni asked, scampering along behind them.

"Listen and learn," Yolie answered between gritted teeth.

"Okay, I can do that."

Kinitra had a private room on a high floor with a view of the Connecticut River. Her orange-streaked up-do was combed out and she wore some grape-colored gloss on her plump young lips. Jamella was seated in a chair next to her bed leafing through a fashion magazine. She'd brought Kinitra a whole stack of them. Also her iPod, which Kinitra was listening to when Des arrived in the doorway with Yolie and Toni.

Kinitra removed her earbuds and smiled. "Hey, Trooper Mitry," she said in that sing-songy little-girl voice of hers.

Des asked Jamella to step out into the hallway for a moment. Jamella hoisted her huge self out of the chair and joined them. After Des had made the introductions, she said, "We'd like to talk to your sister alone, if you don't mind."

Jamella's eyes narrowed. "You think you might get more out of her if I'm not around. Is that it?"

"We might. It's certainly worth a try."

She hesitated. "How do I know you won't try to bully her?"

"Because we don't work that way," Yolie said.

"That's my baby sister in there. I'm trusting you. Don't make me sorry."

"We won't," Des promised her.

"I'll be in the waiting area," Jamella said, waddling off down the hall.

"God, I love those," Toni said, watching her go. "I wonder who made them."

"Made what?" Yolie demanded.

"Her gold sandals."

"Keep your eye on the ball, Sergeant!"

They went in the room, closing the door behind them.

Kinitra looked at the three of them a bit warily. "Where's Jamella?"

"She'll be back soon," Des said. "These are my friends Yolie and Toni from the Major Crime Squad. They'd like to talk to you some more about what happened."

"You don't want to wait for Jamella to come back?"

"It's just going to be us, okay?" Des kept her voice gentle. "And whatever you tell us stays with us. We won't repeat a word of it to her if you don't want us to. You're an adult. So we're treating you like one, understand? Now how about you tell us what really happened last night."

She rolled her big brown eyes. "*Nothing* happened. I already told you."

"The evidence tells us otherwise. So just talk to us, okay? We know you're afraid. That's why we're here. You can count on us to protect you. And we'll make sure he gets what's coming to him."

Kinitra's hand went to her bruised throat, fingering it gingerly. For a brief moment she seemed genuinely frightened and ready to spill. But then the moment passed and she lowered her hand to her lap and said nothing.

Yolie started in now. "Des told me you're carrying your boyfriend's baby."

"So? . . ."

"So is he the one who attacked you last night?"

"I wasn't attacked. I already told her that."

"Girl, we do this for a living. Stop disrespecting us, will you?" She blinked at Yolie. "I don't know what you want from me."

"For starters, why don't you tell us about your boyfriend?"

"What's the deal—you won't go away until I do?"

Yolie crossed her big arms in front of her chest. "Pretty much."

"Well, okay," Kinitra said defeatedly. "But if you repeat one word of this to my sister I'll swear you made it up. There was . . . this boy in Glen Cove over the summer. That's where we were living before Tyrone got suspended. A whole bunch of his teammates lived in the same neighborhood. It was really fun. Somebody was always having a barbeque or showing a movie. Raymond Harris, who plays strong safety, lived right next door. And a boyhood friend of his named Lonnie came to stay with him for a few days. Lonnie Berryman. He plays linebacker for the University of Georgia. He's a junior this year. Big and strong and *so* cute. The first time he smiled at me, I swear, all of the breath just went right out of my body. I played him some of my music. He liked it. He liked me. And one thing led to another. You know how that goes. Jamella has this idea that I'm some kind of virgin. I'm not. Boys like me. And I like them. Lonnie . . . he was definitely a little rough. But I'm cool with that. He also liked to do certain things that some girls don't like. But I'm cool with that, too, if I really like the guy. And I really liked Lonnie."

"Let me make sure I'm hearing you," Yolie said. "You had consensual vaginal and anal sex with Lonnie. He got rough with you but you didn't mind. And he's the father of your baby."

Kinitra nodded her head vigorously. "That's right."

"Why didn't he wear a condom?"

"He doesn't like to. He says they diminish his pleasure."

"Why didn't you insist? I haven't known you for very long but you don't seem like a total idiot."

"Stuff happens," she answered with a shrug.

"It most certainly does. And where's Lonnie at now?"

"Back down in Athens playing ball. He was just visiting Raymond for a few days, like I said."

"Does he know you're pregnant?"

"No."

"Why haven't you told him?"

"We hooked up is all. No promises."

"Do you do that a lot?" demanded Toni, who'd apparently had her fill of listening and learning.

"Do what?" Kinitra asked, frowning at her.

"Get skanky with guys who you barely know."

"I like to have fun. And why are *you* being so nasty?"

"I'm just trying to figure you out."

"Well, talk nicer to me or I'm going to make you leave."

Yolie shot a chilly look at Toni, who promptly backed off. Then Yolie softened her gaze at Kinitra and said, "Let's talk about that party last night."

"I've got nothing to tell you. I didn't go. Just stayed inside and worked on my music all evening. Little brother Rondell was right across the hall in his office until he went up to bed. By then the party was over and everyone had gone home. But I was totally wired, like I told Trooper Mitry. So I drank me some wine. And smoked some reefer I found out on the patio."

"You had no trace of alcohol or drugs in your system," Des reminded her.

"I can't help what some stupid test says. I'm telling you I got wasted, okay? Then I went for a swim and got swept up in the current."

"What about those wraparound bruises you've got?" Yolie asked.

"Talk to the people who revived me on the beach."

"I have," Des said. "They told me you had those when they found you."

"And you believe them?"

"Why shouldn't I?"

"Because they're just covering their booties. That little old man put his hands *all* over me. That much I remember."

"That little old man happens to be my fiancé's father."

"Sounds like you're the one who has the problem, not me."

Des gazed at Kinitra Jameson sternly, wondering how many hurtful lies she was prepared to tell. Who was she *so* afraid of? "Do you wish to lodge a sexual assault complaint against him?"

"No, I'll let it go *if* you don't tell Jamella about Lonnie." She hesitated, lowering her eyes. "Will you be talking to him?"

Yolie frowned. "Why are you asking?"

"Because if you do, tell him I said 'hi,' okay? Not 'hi' like I'm missing him. Just 'hi' like from a friend." She sounded like a twelve-year-old passing messages in class. "Know what I mean?"

"We'll play it just right," Toni promised her, girl to girl.

Kinitra smiled at her. "I like you much better now."

"I think we're all done here," Yolie said. "Thank you, Kinitra."

She reached for her iPod earbuds. "Sure thing."

They went back out into the hall, closing the door behind them.

"What do you think now?" Yolie asked Des.

"I think she was play acting. I didn't believe a single word that came out of her mouth."

"Me neither," Toni agreed. "She was spinning a total schoolgirl fantasy. I know she's pregnant, Loo. I get that. But, trust me, that is a full-time practicing virgin in there. Plus she's *way* immature. My fourteen-year-old sister is more grown up than she is. Your average college horn dog would know that in less than thirty seconds and hit on some other girl. Especially a big-time football star like this Lonnie Berryman is supposed to be. Guys like that do not waste their time on dreamy little teeny-weenies. They don't have to."

Yolie nodded. "Agreed. So let's say she was raped . . ."

"Oh, she was definitely raped," Des said.

"Are we looking at two different men or did the same man who got her pregnant two months ago in Glen Cove come after her again last night?"

"Two different men is so much more of a long shot," argued Toni, who Des was starting to think had some game. She was definitely smarter than her cousin Rico. Then again, so was a rutabaga. "If it's different men then that would make her a full-time hurt-me machine."

"I've seen it happen," Yolie countered. "Especially with cutesy girlie-girl types like her. There's a certain breed of guy who loves to pound the crap out of that. Des, what do you think?"

"I think you'd better smile," Des answered as Jamella waddled down the hallway toward them, her sandals clacking on the polished floor.

"Did you find out anything?" she asked, her brow creasing with concern.

"Your sister told us she was in a consensual relationship this summer," Yolie answered.

Jamella flared instantly. "Who with? Did she give you his name?"

Yolie nodded. "In confidence."

"What is *that* supposed to mean?"

"It means she chooses to keep his identity private. And we're obligated to respect that."

"This is crap," she fumed. "Was it Clarence? Because he'll hit anything that moves. I swear, if he touched my baby girl, I will cut his—"

"She didn't name Clarence," Des told her.

"Then who *did* she name?"

"We'll keep you posted," Yolie said. "Just be patient, okay?"

"Don't you tell me to be patient! Somebody *attacked* my baby sister!"

"And we will find out what happened," Yolie said calmly.

"You'd better," warned Jamella. "Because if you don't, then Tyrone will—and heads will get busted. Trust me, you do *not* want to go there." She turned her back on them and went in Kinitra's room, shutting the door behind her.

They rode the elevator down to the cafeteria in silence. Shared the ride for two floors with an orderly who was transporting an old, old man in a wheelchair. The old, old man was hooked up to an IV. Looked as if he had about a week to live. Des had to avert her eyes. She hated hospitals.

Down in the cafeteria the three of them got coffees and found a table.

"So what's your professional opinion?" Yolie asked her new sergeant. "Is there a case here?"

Toni took a nail file out of a jacket pocket and went to work on her fingernails with controlled fury. "Oh, absolutely, Loo."

"And who are you liking for it?"

"The man himself. It's so totally obvious. Tyrone Grantham's wife is massively pregnant. Her hot little sister's available. And he has a history of getting rough with women. Naturally, Kinitra's terrified to say anything. So she made up that story about Lonnie in the hope that we'd back off and let it drop. Tyrone Grantham has been raping her, no question. I say we go right at him."

"The man's an NFL superstar," Yolie pointed out.

Toni's eyes gleamed eagerly. "And if we nail his balls to the wall, it'll be huge."

A Tedone to the bone, Des reflected. They were pub sluts one and all.

"Slow it down," Yolie cautioned her. "There are a lot of other possibilities. And even if it *is* Da Beast, we still have Kinitra's privacy to respect."

"Sure thing, Loo," Toni said, working that nail file back and forth, her big breasts jiggling inside her unbuttoned blouse. It was downright dizzying.

Des sipped her coffee and said, "Lonnie Berryman ought to be easy enough to run down. Assuming he exists, that is."

"True that," Yolie acknowledged. "Sergeant, go back to the headmaster's house and see if you can find the man through the University of Georgia Athletic Department. If he's real then get him on the phone and hear what he has to say. Who knows, maybe we'll get freaky lucky."

Toni frowned. "Freaky lucky as in? . . ."

"As in maybe he's been visiting his good friend Raymond Harris in Glen Cove these past few days. And maybe he was at that party last night. If so, have the Glen Cove P.D. pick him up and hold him."

"On it, Loo. Anything else?"

"We need a guest list."

"Talk to Clarence," Des advised. "It was by invite only—until the girls' father, Calvin, let in pretty much anyone who showed up with a hottie. That's what Trooper Olsen told me. He was on the gate to keep the media at bay. Clarence and Calvin both have priors, by the way. Got their sheets in my ride."

"Reach out to the media people," Yolie told Toni. "The tabloid outlets won't cooperate but the local TV news channels will. You need a look at their footage of who went in and out. Run the license plates of anybody and everybody who was parked nearby. And if you're able to download a photo of this Lonnie, run it past Trooper Olsen. Maybe he'll remember seeing him."

"You got it, Loo. Is he cute?"

"Is *who* cute?"

"Trooper Olsen."

Yolie glared at her. "I'm sorry, did I just wander into a slumber party?"

"Come on, it's just us girls. Can't we vibe? My sisters are married. My cousins are married. They're into babies. I'm into violent crimes."

"That's the job. If you don't like it, get out now."

"I love it, Loo. But I'm a first-of. There's never, ever been a Tedone woman doing what I'm doing. I have no one to talk to. Sure, my cousin Rico counsels me—"

"Um, okay, this is scary on so many different levels," Des said.

"What do you mean by that?" Toni wondered, filing, filing.

"Oh, nothing. I used to be the one who counseled him. You saying that makes me feel old, that's all."

"He really admires you. Thinks you're the smartest person he ever worked with." Toni glanced at Yolie and said, "You he's just plain afraid of."

Yolie watched Toni file her nails. "Do you *have* to do that right now?"

"It helps me think."

"It's driving me crazy."

Toni made a face. "Whatever. I'm going outside for a shmoke. Feel free to talk about me behind my back." She got up and marched out of the cafeteria.

Yolie heaved a sigh. "I fantasized for years about making lieutenant. I finally make it. And what do they do? They give me a Tedone with ta-tas."

"Yeah, I noticed them. Couldn't help it."

"They call her Toni the Tiger at the headmaster's house. I'm supposed to be seasoning her."

"She's not a complete idiot."

"Not a slacker either," Yolie had to admit. "She does the donkey work and then some. What, you think I should go easier on her?"

"No, no. Do what you have to do. Although you could talk to her about that blouse."

Yolie let out a laugh. "You hate the Brass City mob even more than I do. Are you getting soft on me?"

"Not a chance. But I know what it's like to be a woman on this job."

"And I don't?"

"She's one of us, Yolie."

"She's not one of us. She's a Tedone."

"Sure, sure. Whatever you say."

Yolie sipped her coffee in brooding silence for a moment. "*Something* has been happening to that little cutie upstairs. That doesn't mean we can build a case out of it. But I'm with you. I'll chalk it up as a teaching tool if my captain reams me. Who else should we be looking at?"

"Tyrone likes Stewart Plotka for it."

"The cat who's suing him for that Dave & Buster's beat down?"

Des nodded. "Plotka claims that Tyrone raped his girlfriend, Katie. Could be that raping Kinitra is his idea of payback. He *is* a sniveling creep. And he's been grabbing pub outside the Grantham place lately. *And* we found a hole in Tyrone's brand new fence. Plotka could have snuck in last night and attacked her. It does play. You'll want to establish his whereabouts down to the minute. He and his high-priced lawyer have rooms at the Saybrook Point Inn."

"Who else?"

"Tyrone has had problems with his next door neighbor, Justy Bond."

"As in 'Just Ask Justy?'"

"That's him. He has been nothing but pissed off ever since Tyrone moved in. Hates his fence, his dock, his boat, his music . . ."

"Let me guess—his pigment, too?"

Des smiled at her. "There's definite animosity there. I'm also hearing that Justy beats up on his women. His son, June, keeps a sailboat tied up at Justy's dock. Sleeps out on the thing. Maybe June heard something down there last night. I can sound him out. Or stay out of it. Whatever you want."

"Girl, I'm partnered with a rug rat. What do *you* think I want?"

Des also told her about the beating that Clarence had given Winston Lash for biting Asia's booty. And how it was Winston who'd tipped off Mitch to the hole in the fence.

"Let's hear more about this Winston. Could *he* be our attacker?"

"He's a seventy-two-year-old dementia patient. Kinitra's on the small side but she's still a strong, healthy girl. She could have handled him."

"You sure about that?"

"I'm not sure about anything," Des replied. "Except that Toni isn't wrong. Tyrone himself has to be considered the prime suspect. It fits his profile."

Yolie studied Des across the table. "You like him for it or not?"

"That all depends on which *him* you're talking about. He told me he's trying to change his badass ways. And he's plenty persuasive— right up until he loses his temper. Once that happens anything's possible."

"Who else lives there with him?"

"Rondell, his kid brother. He takes care of the man's financial affairs. Also worships the ground Kinitra walks on."

"Maybe he's been doing more than worship it. He have a sheet, too?"

"No, Rondell's a real straight arrow. Has an MBA from Wharton. Plus he's on the twerpy side. The boys' mother, Chantal, lives there, too. She's a former working girl and crackhead. Heavily into the Lord now. Or doing a pretty fair imitation of it. A slow girl named Monique helps her around the place. That's everybody."

Toni returned to their table now, reeking of cigarette smoke.

Yolie glanced up at her. "Ready to get some honest work done now, Sergeant?"

"You bet, Loo."

"Then let's ride. Oh, and, sergeant? . . ."

"Yeah, Loo?"

"Button your damned blouse up, will you? This is the Major Crime Squad, not Hooters."

CHAPTER 10

MITCH HAD ALREADY DEVOURED his fourth biscotti by the time he turned off Old Shore Road and started his way through the Nature Preserve. Pressured. He was feeling unusually pressured. He absolutely had to send his Halloween Scare-a-Palooza column off to Lacy this afternoon. And clean his house from top to bottom for tonight's quasi-monumental dinner party. And go for a three-mile run so as to work off the truly alarming number of calories he'd been mainlining over the past seventy-two hours. And try on every single pair of pants he owned so as to determine if any of them were creeping northward toward his armpits. Plus he felt an overwhelming urge to take a long, hot shower after his little chat with Stewart Plotka and Andrea Halperin. He was positive that Plotka had spit shrimp salad on him. Andrea? She'd just made him feel soiled.

As Mitch neared the barricade to the Big Sister causeway, he came upon a gleaming blue Porsche Carrera convertible parked there with its top down. Rondell Grantham stood leaning against it, neatly dressed in a white button-down shirt and tan slacks. He was a very serious, professional-looking little guy—aside from the half-empty fifth of Grey Goose vodka he was chug-a-lugging. He seemed to have been weeping. His eyes were red and swollen behind his gold-framed spectacles.

"Can I help you?" Mitch asked him through the Studey's open window.

"Yes, sir, you can," he answered thickly. Wasted. Rondell was totally wasted. "Are you . . . Mr. Berger?"

"I am."

"I am sorry to bother you but my family has suffered a terrible experience. My brother's wife . . . Her sister washed up on your beach."

"I know. I'm the one who found her. And I know *you*, Rondell. We met last night at the party. I was with Resident Trooper Mitry. I escorted Mr. Lash home, remember?"

Rondell peered at him, his gaze unfocused. "Of course. Please forgive me. I'm a little . . . upset." He took a big gulp of the vodka, holding the bottle out to Mitch. "Care for some?"

"No, thanks. It's a little early for me."

"I hardly ever drink. Maybe a glass of champagne at New Year's."

"Rondell, was that bottle full when you started in on it?"

"Yes, I believe it was. I opened it. Needed a drink." He took another gulp, wavering as he stood there. "Has Resident Trooper Mitry . . . told you anything?"

"I know Kinitra's pregnant, if that's what you mean."

Rondell let out a grief-stricken sob. "Who would *do* such a thing to her?"

"Rondell, would you like to come out for a cup of coffee?"

"Actually, I was wondering . . . I would very much like to see the spot where you found her."

"What for?"

"Because I almost lost her. Want to see where she was found. That make any sense?"

"Sure, it does. I'll be happy to show you. Nice car you have, by the way."

"Thank you. It was a birthday present from my brother."

"Why don't you leave it here? We can take my truck, okay?"

Rondell was certainly an agreeable drunk. He opened the Studey's passenger door and climbed right in, bottle in hand. "This truck is very much an antique type of truck, is it not?"

"It is an antique type of truck, yes."

"Most interesting."

"Glad you think so."

Mitch steered it across the wooden causeway and pulled up outside his cottage.

Rondell squinted at it through the windshield. "This is very much an antique type of house, too. Rather modest in scale. I thought it would be much grander."

"It's plenty big enough for me. I live by myself."

"Really? I personally have never lived by myself. Wouldn't even know how. I've always lived with my brother. Or a-a succession of college roommates. None of them liked me very much. Do you like me, Mitch?"

"Sure, I like you fine. Why wouldn't I?"

"Because most people do not. They consider me to be a drippy, dweeby sort of individual. I never spent much time with my roommates. I was always at the library studying. I had to be. I couldn't let Tyrone find out my secret." He drank down some more vodka, hiccoughing slightly. "Would you like to know my secret?"

"Okay."

"I'm not very smart."

"Who are you kidding? You don't get an MBA from Wharton by being a dummy."

"No, listen to what I'm saying. *Listen.* The others were *so* much smarter. I had to play catch up at the library every single night. Cram and cram and . . ." Rondell noticed the groceries that were piled on the seat between them. "You do your own cooking?"

"I do."

"You're an accomplished type of person, aren't you?"

"Yes, I'm what they call a renaissance schlub."

Rondell blinked at him. "May I see the inside of your home?"

"Absolutely."

Mitch stowed the dinner groceries in the fridge while Rondell flopped down on the love seat with his vodka bottle, gazing around at the living room.

"Very nice home, Mitch," he observed.

"Just do me a favor and don't call it sa-weet."

"Wasn't going to. I would be very happy in such a house. It's exceedingly atmospheric. You play the guitar?"

"I make some noise."

"Kinitra plays the piano."

"Yes, I know."

Rondell set the bottle down sharply on the coffee table. "I would like to see where you found her."

Mitch led him down the path toward the beach. Rondell walked slowly and carefully, one foot in front of the other as if he were on a tightrope. It was still warm and muggy out. The sky was a hazy summer sky. And yet Mitch could feel a slight change in the air. A breeze was starting to pick up. A few sailboats were out there trying to catch hold of it.

Rondell peered out at them. "Tyrone has a cigarette boat."

"I've seen it. And heard it."

"I hate the thing. It's so childish."

"We're all children inside."

"Very true, Mitch. You are a profoundly deep individual."

"That's me, all right. I was voted North America's Deepest Critic at the Cannes Film Festival last year."

"Were you really?"

"That was a joke, Rondell."

He nodded sagely. "Another reason why nobody likes me—I have no sense of humor whatsoever."

"I can give you some homework if you want. A thorough grounding in the films of Preston Sturges ought to help. Plus a steady diet of Abbott and Costello, The Three Stooges, Daffy Duck . . . Tell you what, I'll put together a list."

"I would appreciate that very much."

Mitch had left an orange safety cone where they'd found her. The tide had gone out since then. The cone stood well back from the water's edge.

As he approached the cone Rondell began to cry. He fell to his knees and flattened his hands against the sand, holding them there as if he were trying to soak up Kinitra's aura. "She . . . was naked when you found her?"

"She had on a white sleeveless T-shirt and panties."

"But you could see through them."

"Well, yeah. They were soaking wet."

He looked up at Mitch accusingly. "You saw her private bits."

"I'm not the only one who did."

"Shut your filthy mouth!" Rondell staggered to his feet and threw a wild roundhouse right at Mitch, who ducked it easily and stuck out his leg, tripping him. Rondell sat down hard on the sand, gulped and then proceeded to gaack up that bottle of Grey Goose along with, seemingly, everything he'd eaten in the past three days.

"Feel better now?" Mitch asked him when he was all done.

"I suppose," he replied weakly, kicking sand over the mess.

"I wasn't disrespecting her, Rondell. All I meant was that my parents were with me when I found her. They saw her, too. So did the Jewett girls."

"I understand. Absolutely, totally my mistake. I apologize. Would you care to hug it out?"

"Not necessary. We're good."

"I love her so much that it hurts," he confessed. "It physically hurts, Mitch. Right here in my chest. Kinitra's my angel. You should hear her sing. You should be around her. She's . . . so beautiful. All I ever dream about is the day we will be together."

"Does she feel the same way about you?"

Rondell shook his head. "Not yet. She still thinks of me as someone who's too serious for her. Bordering on dull. My brother keeps telling me to lighten up around her. Be more casual. He's even taken to buying me hipper clothes. Tell me, is there something wrong with what I'm wearing?"

"I don't think so."

"Thank you."

"You're welcome."

Rondell sat there on the sand, hugging his knees to his chest. "I realize she's not going to fall for someone like me at this particular stage of her life. She's about to become a huge singing star. She wants a handsome movie actor or professional athlete, not a glorified accountant. And I'm okay with that for now. I'll be proud to manage her career for her. Keep her finances in order so she won't get robbed blind like so many young performers do. And, over time, my hope is that she will eventually see me the same way I see her. I'm patient. I can wait for years if I have to. Because, for me, there's no one else." He let out a forlorn sigh. "My brother thinks I'm a fool. He's had hundreds of women. Possibly even thousands. They literally throw themselves in his path at clubs, at parties, wherever he goes. Mind you, that was before he met Jamella. Now he has to toe the line. She makes sure he does. Watches his every move. Believe me, you do not want to piss that one off."

"How about Clarence?"

Rondell looked at Mitch blankly. "What about him?"

"Does he think you're a fool?"

"Cee aspires to nothing more than an endless parade of party skanks."

"Has he ever shown any interest in Kinitra?"

Rondell shook his head. "She's not his type. Besides, if he goes anywhere near her, Jamella will tell Tyrone to send him packing."

"You say that Tyrone thinks you're a fool for feeling like you do about Kinitra. But he's a married man himself now, soon to become a father. Doesn't he feel that way about Jamella?"

"Love her, you mean? No, that's not actually possible. Tyrone doesn't know how to place someone else's happiness ahead of his own. He's not made that way. Jamella is what you'd call a career move. His future in the NFL depends upon him proving to the commissioner that he has matured. And nothing says maturity like a wife and a child."

"You make it sound awfully calculated."

"Only because it is. I'm not being critical. I love my brother. But he is who he is. And I-I . . ." Rondell choked back a sob. "I don't know *anything*." He hiccoughed, his eyes twirling around in their sockets. "Mitch, I don't feel so good. . . ."

A swarm of media people surrounded Stewart Plotka and Andrea Halperin as they stood outside the Grantham estate, holding their press conference. Andrea was waving an article of clothing for all of the cameras to see. It was red. A shirt or blouse.

Mitch had to honk at a dozen cameramen to move so he could pull into the driveway. Trooper Olsen was on duty there at the gate.

"What's the earth-shattering news, Oly?"

"Plotka claims he has Katie O'Brien's blouse with Grantham's semen all over it. The lawyer's demanding Grantham give up a DNA sample." Trooper Olsen shook his head in disgust. "That Plotka comes off like a no-good shakedown artist."

"Only because he is one."

"But the insane thing is he could be telling the truth. Given Da Beast's history with the ladies."

"Yes, he could. I'm afraid there are no clear-cut heroes in this movie."

Trooper Olsen peered across Mitch at his unconscious passenger. "Did Rondell get trashed or something?"

"Just had a bit of a shock. I didn't think he should drive."

The trooper opened the gate. Mitch drove on in and parked by the front door behind a black Escalade. He got out and rang the doorbell. No one answered it. He rang it again. Finally, he heard footsteps and the door was opened by the immensely fat Chantal Grantham. She had a Swiffer Duster in her right hand, a bucket of soapy water in her left hand and an intensely hostile expression on her face. A vacuum cleaner was running loudly in a nearby room.

"What do *you* want?" Chantal demanded. Before Mitch could respond, she turned around and hollered, "Don't forget *under* the sofa cushions, too, Monique!" Then she turned back to him, eyeing him suspiciously. "Well? . . ."

"I've driven Rondell home, Mrs. Grantham."

"Why you want to do that for? His Porsche break down?"

"His Porsche is fine, but he wasn't in any shape to drive it."

"He sick or something?"

"He's passed out drunk."

Chantal shook her head. "That can't be. Rondell doesn't care for alcohol. Never touches it."

"Well, he touched it today."

She glared at Mitch accusingly. "You got him drunk, didn't you? I knew I didn't like the look of you. Sneaking around in the woods like you was."

"Mrs. Grantham, he was already drunk when he showed up at my place. He's very upset about Kinitra."

"Oh, I get you . . ." Chantal's gaze softened a bit. "He's so young. All of those college degrees of his yet he's still a little boy when it comes to women." She hesitated, her brow furrowing. She seemed to be making up her mind about something. "You be seeing that girlfriend of yours today?"

"Yes. We're having dinner later."

"Tell her from me that today was laundry day, okay?"

Mitch stared at her. "Laundry day?"

"Laundry day."

"And she'll know what that means?"

"Just shut up and tell her, will you?" Then she turned around and yelled, "Cee, get your bony ass out here right goddamned now!"

Clarence came running, looking freakishly tall and wiry in his tank top and gym shorts. He was drenched with sweat, his muscles popping. "Yo, whassup?"

"Rondell's passed out drunk in this here gentleman's pickup. Put him to bed, will you? And don't say nothing to Tyrone."

"Awright." Clarence went out to Mitch's truck, opened the passenger door and threw his little cousin over one shoulder with ease. "You were at my party last night with the trooper, weren't you?" he asked Mitch.

"That's right."

"And you found Kinitra on the beach this morning."

"Right again."

"Hang out a sec. Want to talk to you."

Clarence carried Rondell inside. Chantal followed him. Mitch waited there by his truck until Clarence returned, pulling the front door shut behind him.

"Tyrone and myself been doing some reps in the weight room," he explained, mopping his sweaty brow with a gym towel. "Lifting settles him down some. Helps him deal with the monster inside. And the monster is definitely loose. I hear he almost tore up that whole clinic when he found out Kinitra's pregnant." Clarence glanced down the driveway toward the front gate. "We were watching ESPN in the gym just now. Saw that clown Plotka claiming he's got Tyrone's spooge all over some blouse. Big man was ready to sprint down the driveway and strangle the little bastard on live television. I told him, yo, that's what he *wants* you to do. He's *trying* to rile you." Clarence wadded up the towel and tossed it at the front porch. "He freaks me out when he gets this way. He needs Jamella to calm him down. But she has to be at the hospital with Kinitra." He eyed Mitch up and down curiously. "So what happened to little man?"

"He wanted to see where I found her. Showed up at my place drunk as a skunk."

"Where's his ride?"

"Parked at the foot of the causeway. It'll be fine there until someone has a chance to fetch it."

"I'll go get it right now. I can use a run. It's just under two miles from here if you cut through those woods at the end of Sour Cherry Lane."

Mitch looked at him in surprise. "I thought only the old-timers knew about that footpath."

"You thought wrong. I always familiarize myself with the surrounding terrain. Tyrone likes to take nature runs. Six, eight miles at a clip."

"I can give you a lift if you'd rather. I'm heading right back there."

Clarence's face relaxed into an easy grin. "You talked me into it. Let me just get his keys."

Mitch got in behind the wheel and waited for Clarence to join him, car keys in hand. The Studey's cab wasn't exactly spacious. Clarence had to fold his long self in carefully, limb by limb.

"You have enough legroom there?"

"Yeah, man. I'm good."

"Think I need a new truck?"

"Why would I think that?"

"Just asking."

Outside the front gate, Stewart Plotka and Andrea Halperin were still holding the media throng transfixed. No one paid any attention as Mitch rolled on out of there, working the Studey through its three-speed overdrive transmission.

Clarence said, "I wanted to thank you for that heads-up you gave the trooper about the hole in our fence. The fencing company's going to put in a whole new section tomorrow morning."

"What about until then?"

"I drilled some holes in a sheet of plywood and wired it into place over the hole. Should do the trick unless someone really wants in. And if they do, there's no stopping them, am I right?"

"I'm afraid you are."

"Chantal and myself paid a social call on the Joshua sisters and Mr. Lash. Brought them a mess of food."

"That was nice of you."

"Wasn't my idea. Let me tell you, those are some strange old ladies."

"Pretty standard for Dorset."

"And that house of theirs with all of those antique clocks tick-tocking away." Clarence shook his head in amazement. "I felt like

I was walking right into that Tennessee Williams play. The one with the little glass figurines."

Mitch turned onto Old Shore Road and started his way home. "You mean *The Glass Menagerie?*"

"That's the one. And kindly take the surprise out of your eyes. It so happens I majored in Performing Arts at Clemson—until they threw my ass out. That's a fine old house those ladies have. Real shame it's gotten so run down. I was able to fix a few things for them. The neighborhood where I grew up? You either do your own repairs or they don't get done."

"Did you get rid of that smell in their kitchen?"

"What smell?"

"Nothing. Never mind."

"I had no cause to hit Mr. Lash last night. It was a dumb move on my part. Guess I've just been living with too much drama for too long. That's life when you're in Tyrone Grantham's world. Drama twenty-four/seven. But I got to tell you—I've never known Rondell to take a drink. I doubt he even knows how to hold it."

"He doesn't, trust me."

"Poor little man's like a sad-eyed puppy around that girl. And she don't even know he's alive. I keep telling him to forget about her and have himself some F-U-N. Like last night. There was dozens of tasty young sisters in itty-bitty thongs out there by the pool. None of them Wharton graduates, I'll grant you. But who cares once you're between the sheets, know what I'm saying? I begged him to come on out and grab himself some. He wouldn't. Just sat there in his office working on his computer and pining away over that teenager playing her piano across the hall. Totally pathetic if you ask me. She's just a kid. I mean, yeah, she has ridiculous musical talent. But she's just a sheltered little schoolgirl. Jamella makes sure of that. Won't let no man near her."

"Kinitra didn't have a boyfriend this summer in Glen Cove?"

"Boyfriend?" Clarence gaped at Mitch incredulously. "What boyfriend?"

"A college football player from Georgia named Lonnie Berryman."

"Who, Raymond's friend? Yeah, I remember Lonnie. Stayed at Raymond's house for a few days. Nice enough dude. *Really* likes him to party."

"Did he party with Kinitra?"

"Why, is she saying he's the baby's father?"

"She's saying they had something going on."

"That's news to me. I never even saw the two of them talking to each other. Jamella don't allow it, like I said."

"Is it possible Jamella didn't know?"

"Anything's possible, but Jamella's *very* protective. Hell, if you'd asked me yesterday, I'd have sworn to you up, down and sideways that Kinitra was still a solid gold virgin." Clarence's face dropped. "But she's been with *somebody*, that's for sure."

"Who else could it have been? If it wasn't Lonnie, I mean."

"Don't be looking at me, man. I've made some mistakes in my life but I ain't that kind of dumb."

Mitch took the fork that led into the Nature Preserve, slowing as he left the smooth pavement for the narrow, bumpy dirt road. "How much did Tyrone tell you about Kinitra's condition?"

"She's pregnant is all I know."

"The trooper tells me certain things in confidence. . . ."

Clarence studied him curiously. "What things?"

"Kinitra's claiming that she's been in a consensual relationship," Mitch said. "But she's all scarred up down there. The sex has been very, very rough. She says she likes it that way. Do you buy that?"

"No way. She's strictly the dreamy romantic type. Love songs.

Nothing but love songs." Clarence fell into thoughtful silence for a moment before he said it again. "No way."

Mitch approached the bluffs now and pulled up at the barricade next to Rondell's Porsche.

Clarence didn't budge. Just sat there looking across the water at Big Sister Island. "She picked herself a nice spot to wash up."

"She was very lucky. Next time she might not be."

"Next time?"

"People who want to kill themselves usually keep trying."

"You think that little girl tried to kill herself?"

"I don't have a doubt in my mind."

Clarence ran a hand over his face. "Man, that is so wrong. She's truly gifted. If she ended her own life, it would be a horrible crime."

"You can do something about it, you know."

"Me? What can I do?"

"Tell me who's been raping her."

"I think we're all done here." Clarence abruptly opened his door and climbed out, slamming it shut. But then he lingered there by the open window, jangling Rondell's car keys in his hand. "What was Rondell drinking?"

"Grey Goose. A whole bottle of it."

"I've never seen him down more than a half a beer. Poor little man's totally blown away, I guess. He's so loyal to his brother. Tyrone is *everything* to him. That's why he can't deal with the plain truth of it."

Mitch leaned across the seat toward him. "Which is? . . ."

Clarence gazed out at the water for a long time before he turned back to Mitch and said, "The big dog takes what the big dog wants. Law of the jungle, man. Always has been. Always will be."

CHAPTER 11

THERE WAS A WHITE Escalade parked in her driveway when Des got home. When she went inside the house she heard voices out on the back deck. Found the Deacon seated out there at the umbrella table having lemonade with Jamella and her father, Calvin. The Deacon had already gotten dressed for dinner with the Bergers in his customary charcoal flannel suit, crisp white dress shirt and muted tie. It was the first time Des had seen him wearing normal clothes since his surgery and it thrilled her beyond belief. Calvin had on a No. 54 Tyrone Grantham football jersey and a showy oyster gray cowboy hat with a feather stuck in its band. Kid Rock sat in his lap padding at his big belly. Jamella was dressed in the same yellow shift that she'd been wearing all day long. She looked wilted, bleary eyed and distraught. Her lower lip was fastened so firmly between her teeth that it was a wonder she didn't draw blood.

"Ah, here she is," the Deacon said brightly as Des joined them. "I told you she'd be right on time. If there's one thing I taught Desiree it was punctuality." He not only looked like his old self, he seemed much more animated and engaged.

A few kayakers were out on Uncas Lake enjoying the late day warmth. Thin gray clouds were moving in, dimming the hazy sunlight a bit.

Des sat down at the table and said, "How may I help you folks?"

"Not so much me, miss," Calvin responded politely. "It's my oldest girl Jamella here. She wanted to speak with you on your home turf. Got herself a bit emotional after what's happened to our little girl Kinitra." He paused so that Jamella could take it from there. She just sat there in guarded silence, so he kept on going. "I felt she was too upset to drive over here by herself, especially being seven months along. So I offered to drive her." He sipped his lemonade, his face creasing with concern. "It turns out I'm an even worse father to my girls than I thought. Little Kinitra's got herself pregnant, too. And here I've been under the same roof this whole time and didn't even know anything was going on."

"Nobody did," Jamella said in a muted voice. "Don't blame yourself, Popsy."

"I wanted to visit her up at that hospital," Calvin added. "But Jamella said Kinitra don't want to see nobody or talk to nobody. You think she'll be coming home soon, miss?"

Des nodded. "Assuming she doesn't develop a lung infection."

"I imagine she needs a little time alone to sort this whole business out, too." Calvin let out a huge sigh. "I sure wish her mama was still around. She made sure both of my girls were quality young ladies. And they never gave her no cause to worry. Got good grades. Came right home when she told them to. My girls knew better than to hang around on street corners with trash. *I'm* the one was always in trouble," he confessed. "But those days are behind me now."

"That's right, Popsy," Jamella said reassuringly.

Des glanced over at the Deacon. His face revealed nothing. Never did. "So what did you want to talk to me about, Jamella?"

"I just thought that, I mean, I wanted to . . ." She broke off with a ragged sob. "God, this was a terrible idea. We should just go, Popsy. Stop bothering these people."

"You're not bothering us. What's this about?"

Jamella reached for her lemonade and took a small sip, the glass shaking in her hand.

"She's gotten herself all worked up," Calvin explained. "Wondering if it could be her Tyrone who fathered Kinitra's baby."

"Why would you think that?"

"I don't," Jamella insisted. "I'm just *wondering*—which I know is so unbelievably terrible. Not to trust the man who I love. But knowing what I know about his life before we met. All of those other women having his babies and . . ." She bit down hard on her lower lip again, her eyes puddling with tears.

"She did speak to Tyrone about it," Calvin said. "The man swore to her he's never touched Kinitra. But I could still see the doubt in her eyes. So I said, let's go talk to the resident trooper about it. She's investigating the case. She knows *facts*, not fears."

"Speaking of *facts* . . ." The Deacon gazed at Des with chilly disapproval. "I understand from Jamella that Lieutenant Yolanda Snipes and Sergeant Toni Tedone of the Major Crime Squad have launched a criminal investigation."

"That's correct," Des said, meeting his stern gaze before she turned back to Jamella. "Do you honestly believe Tyrone is capable of doing something like this?"

Jamella shook her head. "I don't know. I-I just don't . . ."

Calvin put his hand over hers. "Now don't get all upset again. Just ask the lady what you came here to ask her."

Jamella took another sip of her lemonade, her hand a bit steadier now. "I was wondering if Tyrone is a target of your investigation."

"Technically? No. Because, technically, no crime has been committed."

"How can you say that?" Calvin demanded. "Kinitra was raped."

"She insists she wasn't."

"But you *know* she was!" Now Calvin was the one getting worked up. "Jamella said the doctors found awful scars and suchlike."

"Kinitra's still your little girl," the Deacon put in, his voice calm and gentle. "But as far as the law is concerned, she's a grown woman. If she says no crime took place then no crime took place. We see this all too often with domestic abuse cases. A neighbor will call us up and tell us that the man in the apartment next door is beating the heck out of his wife. We get there and the wife's bleeding from the mouth and nose, her eye swollen half shut. She assures us she's perfectly fine. Just fell down in the park while she was walking her dog. And there's not a thing we can do."

"That's c-crazy!" Calvin sputtered in disbelief.

"That's the law," Des said. "But I promise you we're trying to find out what happened."

Calvin studied her from across the table. "You're going the extra mile for my girl, aren't you? You've got them investigating this thing even though she don't want you to. How come, miss?"

"Because she's afraid."

"You mean afraid of Tyrone?"

"I don't have anything concrete to implicate Tyrone at this point," she replied. Meanwhile thinking that Calvin wasn't exactly steering her away from Tyrone. Possibly the man knew something more. Something he wasn't willing to spill in front of Jamella. "Where *is* Tyrone?"

"He was lifting with Clarence when we left," Jamella said. "That's what he does when he's upset."

"Does he know that you've come here?"

She shook her head. "I told him we were going out for ice cream."

"And what about Rondell?"

"Working in his office, I imagine. I never know where he is. Rondell's got to be the quietest man I've ever met. Tyrone says he's been that way since they were boys and Chantal was into the drugs and all. Tyrone coped with it by getting so strong nobody could hurt him. Rondell shrank into the corner and got quieter."

She hesitated before she added, "He has a crush on Kinitra. I mean, it's pretty obvious. But he'd never get rough with her. He has no meanness in him."

"Yes, he does," the Deacon countered. "We all do—if we're riled a certain way."

"True enough," Calvin concurred, drinking down the last of his lemonade. "And you never know what'll set somebody off. I've seen men get shanked in the yard over a danged candy bar."

"What about Clarence?" Des asked Jamella. "Is he someone who we should be looking at?"

"Clarence has a big mouth. But he's a decent person deep down. Besides, he's got hot skanks coming and going. What does he need my baby sister for?"

"Maybe he's in love with her."

"Not so I've noticed. Have you, Popsy?"

"No, can't say as I've ever gotten that particular vibe off of cousin Clarence. He does spend a lot of hours with Kinitra in the recording studio. I hear them lipping away at each other all of the time. But he's strictly, you know, playful with her. Like she's his own kid sister."

Des found her thoughts straying to someone else who might know something—Chantal. She figured nothing went on there that Chantal didn't know about. But she also felt certain that Chantal would never say one bad word about either of her sons. "I just realized I'm being a terrible hostess. I haven't offered you folks more lemonade. I could go for a glass myself. Jamella, would you mind giving me a hand?"

"You sit, girl," Calvin said. "I'll help her out."

"That's okay, Popsy. If I don't keep moving around I feel like a beached whale." Jamella got herself up and followed Des inside with their empty glasses, leaving the two men out on the deck.

"Girl, this is a real nice place you've got here. You must feel so proud owning your own home."

"Yes, I do." Des pulled the pitcher of lemonade from the refrigerator and refilled their glasses. Found a glass for herself and filled that, too. She took a sip, lingering there in the kitchen with Tyrone Grantham's pregnant wife. "Excuse me for asking but has Tyrone ever gotten rough with you?"

"You mean like slapped me around? No, never. I'd never let any man put his hands on me that way. I've got too much respect for myself."

Des took another sip of her lemonade. Out on the deck, the Deacon and Calvin were talking softly. "Why are you really here, Jamella? What's bothering you? You can trust me. I won't tell a soul."

Jamella gazed at Des imploringly. "Word?"

"Word."

"I'm here . . ." She hesitated, swallowing. "Because I love Tyrone to death except I don't know if I trust him. And that's *so* messed up. I mean, how can you love a man and yet not be sure about him?"

"Easiest thing in the world. I did exactly that for three years with my ex-husband," Des told her, having learned one simple truth long ago: When it comes to confiding, you need to give some to get some. "I even took him back again a few months ago—even though the bastard had cheated on me the whole time we were married and lied to my face about it. Didn't matter. When it comes to men the heart wants what it wants and the head gets a great big dose of stupid. Hell, I actually convinced myself it would all be different this time."

Jamella's eyes searched hers. "And it wasn't?"

"Not a chance."

"How about Mitch?" she asked. "Do you trust him?"

"Yes, I do. I feel safe with him. How do *you* feel with Tyrone?"

"I don't *know* what I feel," Jamella answered wearily. "He's never been anything but a perfect gentleman the whole time we've been together. But these stories about other women keep dogging him. Like this whole Stewart Plotka mess. Tyrone keeps telling me, 'Baby, I don't even know who Katie O'Brien is.' And I've been believing him. But that man showed up outside our house today with a blouse of hers he says has Tyrone's stuff on it. And now my own baby sister is pregnant. And, suddenly, I don't know who to believe anymore. I feel like such a horrible person. But I want to know—really *know*—that it wasn't him who went after Kinitra. Can you understand that?"

"I totally can. And I don't think you're a horrible person. You're just watching out for yourself. I respect that. Now I need for you to respect me. Give us some time to do what we do. We'll find out what really happened, okay?"

Jamella thought this over for a moment before she nodded and said, "Okay."

Then they returned back outside to the deck.

"What you two ladies been jawing about in there?" Calvin asked them.

"I was just assuring Jamella that we'll figure out who the man is," Des answered. "And deal with him."

"It's *me* who he's got to deal with," Calvin said in a low, menacing voice. "Kinitra's my little angel. No thug's going to treat her like trash and get away with it. He'll pay, all right, but not your kind of justice. *My* kind."

"Don't go making threats in front of us," the Deacon said to him. "Your girls need you to be around for them. Not back in lockup."

"You're right about that, sir," Calvin allowed. "But I just get so crazy when I think about it."

"Why don't you two go get that ice cream?" Des suggested. "And then head on home and relax. There's an officer at your front gate twenty-four hours a day. And I'm five minutes away." She handed Jamella her business card. "My cell's right there at the bottom. Call me day or night."

"Thank you," Jamella said quietly. "And thank you, too, Mr. Mitry. Sorry to intrude on you like we did."

"You didn't intrude," the Deacon said. "The door's always open."

Des showed Jamella and Calvin out. The Deacon was still seated there on the deck when she returned. "Thanks for playing host, Daddy. Just let me get out of this gunnysack and I'll be ready to go."

"Not so fast, young lady," he growled. "Get back out here and sit yourself down *now*!"

She sat herself down, blinking at him in surprise.

"What in the *hell* did you think you were doing calling in the Major Crime Squad in the absence of a complainant?"

"I have a bad feeling about this one. Something very nasty has been going on in that house. Kinitra's afraid to speak up. She needs me to look out for her. That's what a resident trooper does."

"I do *not* need a lecture from you on the job specifications of a resident trooper. It so happens I'm the man who has administered the entire program for the past eleven years. You have involved Major Crime Squad investigators despite the clear and obvious absence of a crime. You have squandered precious investigative man hours—"

"*Woman* hours."

"To follow up on nothing more than a—a cowboy hunch."

"Cow*girl* hunch."

"Desiree, you're lucky I don't pick up the phone this very minute and have a talk with Yolanda's captain. I can guarantee you he knows nothing about this little adventure and he will *not* be pleased to find out she . . . why in the hell are you grinning at me like that?"

"Because this is the first time you've acted like *you* in I don't know how long. I've tried everything. Honestly, Daddy, I was at my wit's end. And the answer's been staring me in the face all along— I just had to go rogue."

"This is not funny, Desiree. There are rules. And those rules—"

"Exist for a very good reason, I know."

"I cannot believe you roped in Yolanda."

"She was free to say no. She's her own woman."

"Nonsense. She looks up to you. And who in the hell is *Toni* Tedone?"

"Their first *she* on Major Crimes. They call her Toni the Tiger. You'll like her a lot."

"That'll be the day." The Deacon despised the Tedones with every fiber of his being. It was Captain Richie Tedone of IA who'd tried to squeeze him out when he went in for his heart surgery. The asshole would have succeeded, too, if Des hadn't squeezed back. "I *should* apprise their captain of what you have them doing. You're just lucky that, technically speaking, I'm still on medical leave."

"You could still pick up the phone. Why don't you?"

He looked out at the lake. "Because I happen to agree with you. This one smells nasty."

"Jamella has genuine doubts about Tyrone."

"With good reason."

"He says he's cleaning up his act."

"Not a chance. Men don't change. They are who they are. He's been *Da Beast* for his entire adult life. He's made millions of dollars being *Da Beast*. He relishes it. This suspension by the NFL is nothing more than a minor bump in the road for him."

"You haven't met him, Daddy."

"Don't have to. I've known his kind since I was a boy in the schoolyard."

"He's complicated."

"He's a bully. There's nothing complicated about it."

"What did you and Calvin talk about while we were inside?"

"Calvin's failure to assume responsibility for his own life. He's filled with regret. And he knows more about this matter than he was willing to let on."

"What makes you say that?"

"Calvin has spent a big chunk of his life in the yard. A man like that always holds on to a choice morsel or two of information. Information is power." The Deacon thumbed his chin thoughtfully. "He's also frightened."

"Of? . . ."

"A few months ago the man was scuffing around the streets of Houston. Now he's living in a waterfront mansion. If Jamella leaves Tyrone over this mess, he'll be back out on the street again. He's feeling vulnerable. And a little bit ashamed. It's no fun for a middle-aged man to be dependent on his daughter."

"Are we still talking about Calvin?"

The Deacon fell silent. He'd always been emotionally walled off. It had driven Des's mother so nuts that she'd finally left him after twenty-five years of marriage.

"Daddy, you can go home tomorrow. And back to work whenever you're ready. The doctor has cleared you. The only thing holding you back is your own uncertainty. Which I totally get. But you've still got game."

"I couldn't even hold off that piece of dirt Richie Tedone. You had to step in and save me."

"Which I was glad to do."

"There was a time when I would have eaten Richie Tedone for breakfast."

"You were sick. You're not sick anymore. You're fine."

"Sure, I'm fine," he said in a hollow voice.

"Just let me change my clothes lickety-split, okay? You ready to go?"

"I don't feel like company this evening, Desiree. Think I'll just stay here and watch some TV."

"But you're all dressed."

"So I'll get all *un*dressed."

"Please don't do this to me, Daddy. The Bergers have flown all the way up here from Florida to meet you. They're nice people. And you like Mitch. *Please* come to dinner with me."

He looked down at his big hands. "Sure, okay. . . ."

Des darted into her bedroom with her stomach in knots. Changed from her uni into a white silk blouse and tan linen slacks. She was trying to decide whether or not to dab on lipstick when her cell rang. It was Yolie.

"What's up, Miss Thing?"

"Just had a surprise visit from Jamella and her father," Des informed her. "She's afraid that Tyrone's the father of Kinitra's baby."

"Well, that's fairly damning."

"Yeah, we thought so, too."

"By 'we' you mean? . . ."

"My father and me."

Yolie let out a gasp. "The Deacon know I'm working this with you?"

"I'm afraid so. But he's cool. Well, not cool but he won't say anything to your captain. What've you picked up?"

"Toni tracked down Lonnie Berryman through the University of Georgia Athletic Department. I just spoke to him on the phone.

He told me Kinitra has been leaving him like twelve, fifteen text messages every day. Keeps telling him how much she loves him and wants to be with him again like when they were together in Glen Cove. Except, hear this, Lonnie swore to me they never *were* together. He told me he spoke to her for a little while at a pool party. She played him some of her music. And that was that. He never went near her. Just thought she was a cute kid. And now she's practically stalking him. I asked him if he'd submit to a DNA test should it become necessary. He said he'd be happy to comply. Has no reason not to. The man *sounded* credible—unless he's a lying dog."

"Which is always a distinct possibility. What else?"

"We just caught up with Stewart Plotka and Andrea Halperin having themselves a drink by the pool at the Saybrook Point Inn. She jumped *all* over me when I asked Plotka where he was last night. Demanded to know why the Major Crime Squad was interested in his whereabouts *and* whether there was a criminal investigation underway *and* if so, what kind. I told her it was an unofficial inquiry. She told me I could unofficially go to hell. After some more warm, fuzzy sparring she decided to cooperate. Realized it was the only way she might learn something. Plus Plotka has nothing to hide. Or so she's been led to believe. The two of them had dinner together last night right there at the inn. She went up to her room after dinner and worked until bedtime. Plotka hung out at the bar by himself and tried to hook a hottie. The waitress there, a good-looking blonde, told me Plotka kept bragging to her that he'd be coming into a lot of money soon. She was incredibly not interested. Thought Plotka was total scum."

"This is a girl with keen instincts."

"Plotka left the bar at about eleven. He told me he went straight to bed. But he has his own car parked out there in the lot. A Toyota

Camry. The guests can access their rooms directly from the parking lot. Don't have to go in and out by way of the front desk. Meaning he could have slipped out and driven to the Grantham place. Burrowed through that hole in the fence, gone after Kinitra and then returned to his room undetected. Toni's at the New Haven newsroom of Channel Eight right now running their footage of the party for license plates. Maybe she'll turn up Plotka's Camry. She tried to get a guest list out of cousin Clarence but he wasn't very helpful."

"I smelled reefer smoke when I got there. He's probably afraid that this could lead to a drug bust—which is the last thing in the world Tyrone needs right now." Des dug a pair of sandals out of her closet and stepped into them. "Plotka's media savvy. I don't believe he'd park his car in full view of the news cameras. He's not that dumb."

"He's that *something*."

"Are you liking him for it?"

"Let's just say I object to him using up our planet's air, water and non-renewable fossil fuels."

"But other than that, you're a fan."

Yolie let out a laugh. "Oh, yeah. Other than that, I am crushing on him huge."

She drove her cruiser, the Deacon riding shotgun. He sat there straight and solemn in his gray flannel suit, big hands flat on his thighs, gaze fixed straight ahead. Didn't say one word until she turned off Old Shore Road onto Turkey Neck.

"Since when is this the way to Big Sister Island?"

"I just have to make a quick stop, Daddy. It won't take long."

The usual mob of news crews, paparazzi and gawkers were

clustered outside the Tyrone Grantham estate. The through-traffic was at a standstill despite the presence of the trooper who was trying to move drivers along.

The Deacon watched him with keen-eyed disapproval. "Does that trooper actually believe he's helping matters by standing in the *middle* of the road?"

"I don't know, Daddy. Would you like to ask him?"

"No," he said stiffly. "Just drive on *if* you can. Paying a call on Mr. Grantham?"

"His next door neighbor." Des inched her way past the Grantham place and pulled into the driveway of Justy Bond's waterfront home. Two cars were parked out front. She parked alongside them and shut off her engine. "Couple of questions I need to ask, okay?"

"Whatever you need to do, Desiree. I'll wait right here."

"You will not. You're coming with me. You were a big help just now with Calvin."

"Don't patronize me, young lady."

"I'm not. I would never do that. But you don't seem to realize how much *gravitas* you bring to the table. Please join me, will you?"

He climbed out of the car, glowering at her. "*Now* what are you grinning about?"

"This is epic, Daddy. I dreamt about this moment when I was a little girl but I never actually thought it would happen."

"*What* would?"

"You and me—we're actually working a case together."

"We're not 'working a case.' You're playing a hunch *and* making a supremely clumsy effort to pump up my ego. You're not fooling me, you know."

"Daddy, I have no idea what you're talking about."

"I swear, sometimes you're just like your mother."

"Um, okay, is that good thing?"

Bonita was swimming laps in the pool, her stroke steady and strong, the water gleaming on her tanned flesh. A shirtless, broad-shouldered June was down on the dock buttoning up the *Calliope* for the rainstorm that was forecast for later that evening. The sky was definitely turning grayer.

When Bonita noticed them there, she swam to the shallow end and got out, looking trim, toned and fabulous in her white bikini. "How nice to see you again, Trooper Des," she said with a complete absence of warmth.

"Bonita, this is my father, Deputy Superintendent Mitry."

She raised a speculative eyebrow at him. "Pleased to meet you."

He studied her curiously. "Don't I know you from those commercials? You used to be the Bond Girl."

Bonita let out a throaty laugh. "You have a good memory. It's been a while since I retired. These days I'm what's known in polite Dorset society as a trophy bimbo." She fetched a beach towel and dabbed herself dry. "Justy's not here, I'm afraid. He's got a regional dealership pow-wow up in Hartford. Probably won't come rolling home until after eleven."

"Actually, we're here to speak to June."

"In that case you're in luck." Bonita glanced down toward the dock at him. "He's like a mother hen with that boat of his, I swear."

Des and the Deacon started their way across the lawn toward him. No more than a hundred feet separated the *Calliope* from the dock where *Da Beast* was moored, looking long, low and positively obscene in the water. Tyrone Grantham's little strip of private beach was plainly visible from there, too. The very beach from where Kinitra had taken her near fatal swim late last night.

"Hey, Des," June said brightly as he scampered fore and aft, securing the *Calliope*'s lines.

"June, this is Deputy Superintendent Mitry. Also known as my father."

"Glad to know you, sir. What can I do for you?"

"I understand you've been sleeping out here on the *Calliope* lately," she said.

June's eyes flicked across the lawn toward Bonita, who was now stretched out in a lounge chair. The Deacon followed his gaze, his own eyes narrowing fractionally. "Well, yeah," June acknowledged. "Mitch . . . told you about that?"

"He told me you were prepping for an epic sea voyage. Wanted to get used to sleeping aboard."

"Yeah, that's right. I'm sailing her down to the Florida Keys."

"June, there was an incident next door late last night. I wondered if you might have heard something."

"I heard their party, if that's what you mean. It sounded outrageous. Tons of people, great music. Did my dad call you and complain? Because they quieted down real fast at around eleven o'clock. I'm guessing that's when you showed up."

"You're guessing right."

"He was out of line, Des. The party wasn't that loud. Besides, people have a right to enjoy themselves, don't they?"

"I was interested in something that happened later on."

June lowered his eyes, swallowing uncomfortably. "Later on?"

"Maybe two, three o'clock in the morning. It was a warm night. I'm guessing you had your hatch open. Wondered if you might have overheard an altercation between a man and a woman on the beach over there. *Did* you have the hatch open?"

"Yeah, I did," he murmured.

"Were you on board alone?"

"Callie didn't stay over. She was pulling an all-nighter at the studio."

"You didn't answer the question, son," the Deacon pointed out. "She asked if you were alone."

June reddened. "Yeah, I was alone."

No wonder June was no good at selling cars. He was one sucky liar.

"And I think I did hear something going on over there—now that you mention it. A couple woke me up some time in the middle of the night. I don't know when. But it didn't sound like any altercation. More like they, you know, snuck away after the party and were getting busy on the beach."

"Did you hear anything besides them getting busy?"

June frowned. "Yeah, I heard someone spashing around in the water. I think it was her. Yeah, it was definitely her. Because the guy called out to her."

"How did he sound? Was he angry?"

"No, more like he was afraid she'd drown or something." June's eyes widened. "Did somebody drown?"

"Nobody drowned. Did you get a look at either of them?"

"No, I was below deck. Just woke up for a second and then went right back to sleep. I'd completely forgotten about it until you mentioned it."

"June, do you remember if he called her by her name? Or used a term of endearment of any kind?"

June pondered this for a moment. "He called her 'girl.'"

"Can you tell me anything about his voice?"

"Not really. Just that he sounded . . . black. Not that I'm trying to racially profile him or anything. It was just the impression I got."

"Understood. Did you get any kind of impression in regards to his age? Was he young? Educated? Not so educated?"

"I really didn't get any kind of read on that. Sorry."

"That's okay. You've been a huge help, June. Thanks."

"No problem. And, hey, please thank Mitch, will you?"

"For? . . ."

"Callie's been conflicted about some things. She told me he's been helping her sort them out."

"That's my man."

Des and the Deacon started back across the lawn now toward the patio, where Bonita lay stretched languorously in that lounge chair, her long, lovely legs crossed at the ankles.

"June's not in some kind of trouble, is he?" she asked them.

"Not at all," Des assured her. "I was just asking him if he heard a disturbance down on your neighbor's beach late last night— perhaps two or three o'clock. Were you up that late by any chance?"

"Why, no. That party of theirs was so out of control that I took an Ambien. As soon as you quieted them down, I went to sleep and stayed asleep."

"And how about your husband?"

"He drank an entire bottle of Scotch and conked out, too."

"How do you know that?" the Deacon asked her.

Bonita batted her baby blues at him. "How do I know what?"

"That he drank an entire bottle of Scotch and conked out. You just said that you were asleep."

"Well, I don't *know* it. But that's what he does every single night of the year. Why would last night be any different?"

"No reason at all," he said to her politely. "Lovely home you have here."

"Why, thank you, Deputy Superintendent Mitry."

They took the bluestone path back toward her cruiser.

The Deacon was a very patient man. He waited until he got back in the car, closed his door and fastened his seat belt before he turned to Des and said, "How long has that boy been sleeping with his stepmother?"

"You don't miss a thing, do you?"

"I'd hardly classify that lady as subtle."

"I'd hardly classify that lady as a lady. Think she took that Ambien?"

"Not a chance," the Deacon replied. "I don't think she slept in her own bed either."

"June told Mitch that it was she who initiated things—for whatever that's worth. He's sailing out of here before she gets her nasty on and tells his dad."

"And this girlfriend, Callie, of his? How much does she know?"

"Poor girl hasn't got a clue. June wants her to drop out of school and come with him. Mitch is trying to talk her into finishing out the semester first."

He gazed through the windshield at the Bonds' picture-postcard home with its multimillion-dollar view of the Sound. "These people make me sick."

"Welcome to Dorset, Popsy."

"Get us the hell out of here, Desiree. And don't you *ever* call me 'Popsy' again."

CHAPTER 12

"So, Buck, what do you think about these two crazy kids of ours?"

The icebreaker play. Unreal. His father was actually going for the old icebreaker play. Hell, he'd probably been rehearsing that lame line all day.

"I think," the Deacon replied slowly, "that we all deserve a chance to be happy in this life. And no one should judge what does or doesn't make someone else happy."

"Amen to that, Buck."

Damned if it didn't work, too. The two fathers actually clinked glasses over the picnic table and took sips of their Sancerre.

Seventeen minutes. Mitch began to breathe in and out normally for the first time since Des and her steely, six-feet-four-inch ramrod of a father showed up seventeen minutes ago. Seventeen whole minutes of forced small talk, awkward silences and even more awkward silences. There wasn't a natural ease between the Deacon and Mitch's incredible shrinking father. The Deacon wasn't a relaxed or easy man. He'd shown up for dinner wearing a gray flannel suit. Chet had on a madras shirt and a pair of mango-colored Florida slacks snugged up to his sternum. Mitch really wanted to floor it to the Frederick House and nuke his father's entire wrinkle-free wardrobe. Instead he got busy lighting the grill. Des was inside the house with Ruth fetching some nibblies.

"Sa-weet spot Mitch has here, isn't it?" Chet said as the two fathers gazed out at the Sound.

"Beautiful sunset tonight, too," the Deacon observed.

Beautiful and rare. It was a blood red sunset. The western sky was pure crimson and the water had a rosy glow unlike anything Mitch had ever seen before. Meanwhile, from the south, ominous gray storm clouds were rolling in.

Des and Ruth came out of the house now, Ruth carrying a bowl of those healthful unsalted soy nuts that taste remarkably like packing material.

"This sure beats the early bird special at our coffee shop, doesn't it, Ruthie?" Chet called out to her.

"Yes, it does."

"I hope I can get our dinner cooked before it starts to rain," Mitch said, studying the dark clouds.

"It's not going to rain," Chet said with total certainty. "It can't."

"Why do you say that, Pop?"

"Because the sky's all red. 'Red sky at night, sailor's delight.' Everyone knows that."

"The Weather Channel's ace storm tracker, Jim Cantore, predicted rain."

"Then the Weather Channel's ace storm tracker, Jim Cantore, is wrong."

"Not possible. Jim Cantore's never wrong."

"Don't get between Mitch and Jim Cantore," Des advised Chet. "He has a huge man crush on him."

"I do not. I just happen to think he's the greatest weatherman ever."

Which led to yet another awkward silence. The four of them sat together at the picnic table, Mitch glancing over at Des. She had a slightly panicked expression on her face. And he swore he could hear her stomach churning in the evening quiet.

Happily, the Deacon dove in with an uber-lame icebreaker of his own: "Do you folks enjoy being retired down there in Vero Beach?"

"No, we do not," Chet replied. "That's why we're moving back to New York."

Mitch stared at him in shock. "I'm sorry, what did you just say?"

Chet beamed at him. "We're coming back. We've been saving the big news for tonight, what with this being a special occasion with special friends. We miss the city. We miss being alive. You know what Vero is? An outpost for a bunch of self-satisfied *schnorrers* who never did a goddamned thing for anybody else their whole lives. And all they do now is *kvetch* about their bunions and their lazy, ungrateful kids. We thought we'd be happy down there. We thought it was time to collect our pensions and take it easy. We were wrong. This whole retirement thing is a crock. If you're not *doing* something then you're not alive. Am I right, Ruthie?"

"Absolutely right," she agreed.

"So *that's* what these 'appointments' have been about?"

Chet nodded. "We've been apartment hunting. I don't think we can swing Manhattan anymore. You've got to be some kind of hot-shot film critic to do that. But we found a very nice two-bedroom in Jackson Heights yesterday."

"I have a better idea," Mitch said. "Why don't you just stay in my place?"

"Nah. We don't want to cramp your style."

"But I'm out here most of the time. Besides, I don't have any style."

"We've also been talking to people," Chet went on. "An old pal of mine who's got pull in the superintendent's office, the folks at the

Teacher's Union. We're still sorting out our options. It's no secret that the city's hurting for money. But they still need substitutes. And they always need volunteers. If just one kid at Boys and Girls High wants to sit down after school with a math tutor then I'm going to be there for that kid. I don't care whether they pay me or not. Same goes for Ruthie." He smiled at her. "Buck, this little lady was school librarian at a middle school in Washington Heights. Latino kids, mostly. English was a second language for a lot of them. She didn't just check books in and out. She taught hundreds of them how to read those books. Their teachers didn't have time. Their parents didn't know how. Ruthie stayed after school with them in that library for hours. Then she'd walk the girls home through the lousiest neighborhoods you ever saw. But no one ever messed with Mrs. Berger. They didn't dare. There are hard-working people out there, true American success stories, who never would have made it if Ruthie hadn't been there. And nothing has changed. Those kids still need us. Especially the boys. But I don't have to tell you that, do I?"

"No, you don't," the Deacon said solemnly. "Too many of them are growing up in the street. No family structure or sense of belonging. So they end up in a gang and then we lose them."

Mitch raised his wine glass to his folks. "Well, I think this is great."

"Do you really?" Ruth asked, her eyes shining at him.

"Really. It'll be great to have you back."

Chet said, "Thanks. And if you feel like baking in the sun with a bunch of boring old people, the condo in Vero Beach is all yours. You, too, Buck. If you and a lady friend are ever looking to get away for a few days."

The Deacon said nothing to that.

Chet didn't leave it there. He couldn't. He was obsessively nosy. Always had been. "Mind if I ask what happened between you and Desiree's mother?"

"Dad, maybe he doesn't want to talk about it," Mitch cautioned over the sound of Des's churning stomach.

"It's okay, I don't mind," the Deacon said quietly. "She felt she wanted something else. *Someone* else."

"And how long ago was this?"

"Three years ago."

"Have you been dating?"

"Not really."

"It was a yes or no question, Buck."

"Then the answer is no."

"You ought to. We're not meant to be alone. I know a terrific guidance counselor at Boys and Girls High. Marcia's a widow of color in her early fifties. Good-looking woman. I talked to her yesterday on the phone."

"He's had a crush on her for years," Ruth said tartly.

"Does Sharon Gless know about this?" Mitch asked.

"Buck, you're coming into the city and the four of us are having dinner, okay?"

"I'm still recuperating from my bypass surgery," the Deacon said.

"I know, but you *will* recuperate. And you *will* come to dinner."

"Go for it, Daddy," Des said encouragingly.

The Deacon hesitated. "It's nice of you to offer. I'm just not sure when that will be."

"Sure, sure. I understand. But I also know this—before long you'll be back on the job kicking *tuchos* and feeling like a rooster again. Trust me."

Des stared across the table at Chet with a startled expression on her face. "I just realized something awesome. . . ."

"Which is what?" Mitch asked her.

"How *you* became *you*."

Chet let out a laugh. "Who, this freak? We're nothing alike. All Mitch ever did was watch old movies on TV. He was a walking encyclopedia of film credits by the time he was twelve. Why, I'll bet he can still tell you . . . okay, who was the set decorator on *Casablanca*?"

"George James Hopkins," Mitch answered.

"And the assistant director of . . . *The Glass Bottom Boat*?"

"Al Jennings. You're lobbing me nothing but softballs, Pop." Mitch munched on a handful of flavor-free soy nuts as the blood red sky turned to purple. Dusk was coming fast. "We're losing our daylight. Would you care to move inside?"

"Maybe we'd better," Des said. "Sorry it took us so long to get here. We had to make a stop at Justy Bond's house."

"Was this about that poor girl who we found?" Ruth asked her.

"Yes, it was."

Inside the house, Mitch got busy turning on lamps while the others headed for the love seat and overstuffed chairs.

"Mitch told us that she's pregnant," Ruth said.

Des nodded. "Someone's been sexually assaulting her—not that she'll admit it."

"They never do. They're too afraid. Believe me, I had more than my share of them. Nice, studious little thirteen-year-olds with baby bumps out to here. It broke my heart."

They settled around Mitch's coffee table. Mitch filled everyone's glasses. Clemmie checked out the Deacon's lap and found it very accommodating. He stroked her gently.

"Why were you at Justy Bond's place?" Mitch asked Des.

"Wanted to find out if June heard anything last night. The *Calliope*'s well within earshot of Tyrone Grantham's beach."

Mitch grinned at the Deacon. "So you two are working this case together?"

"There *is* no case," the Deacon responded, stone-faced.

"June heard a struggle at two, maybe three a.m.," Des reported. "Someone, presumably Kinitra, splashing around in the water. And a man calling to her. He called her 'girl.' June thought he sounded black."

"Do you have a suspect in mind?" Chet asked her.

Des glanced uncertainly over at Ruth. "Are you sure this is what you want to be talking about?"

"Absolutely. I want to know who did that to her."

Des took a small sip of her wine. "Tyrone's wife, Jamella, is pretty much convinced that it was Tyrone."

"Clarence is right there with her," Mitch said. "And you can put Rondell on the list, too. He showed up here this afternoon blind drunk. I had to drive him home. Which reminds me—I have a message for you from Chantal. She said to tell you that today was laundry day."

Des frowned at him. "Laundry day?"

"Laundry day."

"And I'm supposed to know what that means?"

"She wanted me to tell you. She was real intent about it."

Des glanced over at her father. "Maybe she found the rest of Kinitra's clothing."

"Will that help you build your case?" Mitch asked.

"There *is* no case," he stated once again.

A brisk wind picked up and began to blow through the cottage. Off in the distance, Mitch could hear a rumble of thunder.

Chet eyed Des shrewdly across the coffee table. "You've got your eye on somebody other than Tyrone Grantham. Boo-Boo's told us how razor sharp your mind is."

"Boo-Boo has a habit of exaggerating."

Mitch sighed. "Is there *any* chance I can get you to never call me that?"

She looked at him through her eyelashes and said, "None."

"So who do you like?" Chet pressed her.

"Stewart Plotka has a major grudge against Tyrone. He was in and around the Glen Cove vicinity eight weeks ago, and he and his lawyer are presently staying at the Saybrook Point Inn. The lawyer went to her room after dinner last night. He stayed at the bar until eleven. Maybe he slipped out after that and drove to Turkey Neck. Maybe he's the one who made that hole in Tyrone's fence. Maybe he burrowed through that hole and—"

"And *what?*" Mitch interjected. "Waited around on the patio until Kinitra just happened to slip out in the middle of the night for a swim?"

"Maybe they had a prior arrangement to meet."

"If that creep raped her, why on earth would she agree to meet with him?"

"Because he told her he had some important information about Tyrone."

"Or possibly her sister," the Deacon put in.

"That's good, Daddy. That totally works. The man's shameless. And I wouldn't call Kinitra overly bright."

Mitch nodded his head slowly. "Okay, but how did he set up the meeting?"

"Easy. He bumped into her at the store some time in the past couple of days. Passed her a note. I'm not saying that's what happened. I'm just saying it's possible."

"Who else?" Chet asked. "Who else could have bumped into her and arranged this clandestine meeting?"

"Des never uses the word 'clandestine,' Pop."

"She doesn't? I thought all the pros used it."

"Maybe they do, but she doesn't."

"How about hush-hush? Does she say hush-hush?"

"No, I don't think I've ever heard her—"

"Boys, *please!*" Ruth scolded them.

"There's the neighbor, Justy Bond," Des continued. "He's clashed with Tyrone from Day One. His auto empire is collapsing. He drinks. The man's your classic all-American mess. His wife, Bonita, claims he drank himself to sleep last night same as always. Except Bonita wasn't in bed with him and therefore can't be sure he didn't go next door and attack Kinitra."

"Wait one second," Mitch said sharply. "Where was Bonita?"

"On board the *Calliope* with June. Not that either of them will admit it."

"But you can bank on it," the Deacon said.

Mitch reached for another handful of soy nuts. "So it's like that?"

Des nodded. "It's like that."

Ruth said, "Desiree, is this Justy Bond devious enough to trick the girl into a late night meeting with him?"

"He's a car salesman. Need I say more?"

"And what about his son, June? Is he a suspect, too?"

"In theory? Yes. But I seriously doubt June is involved. He already has enough going on." Des gazed down into her wine glass. "We also have to consider Tyrone's other neighbor, Winston Lash. The old man knew about the hole in the fence. And he did bite that girl on the butt at Clarence's party."

Chet's eyes widened, "He *what?*"

"Winston's a dementia patient, Pop. He's lost his sexual inhibitions, but he's basically harmless. Hell, half the time the old fellow doesn't even make any . . ." Mitch trailed off, scratching his head.

Des narrowed her gaze at him. "Make any what?"

"Never mind. I just thought of something I forgot."

"Are you going to share it with the rest of the class?" Chet asked.

"It's nothing. My point is he's no rapist."

Chet said, "The girl consented to a rape examination at the clinic this morning. Clearly, she wants your help. So why won't she accept that help and tell you the truth? Who is she so afraid of?"

"Her big sister," the Deacon answered quietly. "This is just us folks talking. But my own view is that Kinitra swam away like she did because of Jamella. Jamella has made a home for her, cared for her, supported her musical ambitions. Kinitra owes her a lot. And it's eating her up inside."

"What is, Buck?" Ruth asked.

"That she 'let' her sister's husband have his way with her. Not that she could have stopped a two-hundred-forty-pound bully like Tyrone Grantham. If he was intent on having his way, there wasn't a thing that girl could do."

"So *you* think Tyrone Grantham is your man," Chet said.

"There's very little doubt in my mind that Tyrone Grantham is the father of that girl's baby," the Deacon said. "He wanted her. He took her. He's been a taker all of his life. The league's given him an official spanking. And he's been mouthing all of the right words about changing his ways. But men like that don't ever change."

Des stiffened, staring at the Deacon with a startled expression on her face.

"What is it?" Mitch asked her.

"Nothing. I just thought of something that I forgot."

"Yeah, there's a lot of that going around." Mitch heard another rumble of thunder. This one a bit closer. "The coals should be ready by now. I'd better put our fish on before the rain gets here."

Des's cell phone rang. She glanced at the screen and took the call. "Hey, Yolie . . . No, no, it's okay. What's? . . ." Her face dropped as she listened to what Yolie Snipes had to say. "Okay, I'll be there in five." She rang off, jumped to her feet and darted toward Mitch's wardrobe cupboard, where she always kept a spare uniform. "Daddy, we officially have ourselves a case now."

The Deacon peered at her. "What case is that?"

"Somebody just shot Stewart Plotka in the parking lot of White Sand Beach. He and his lawyer Andrea Halperin. They're both dead."

Chapter 13

White Sand Beach, which was the only stretch of precious sand anywhere in town that was open to all Dorseteers, was a dinky little public beach by most people's standards. Two hundred yards wide at most, with parking for no more than a few dozen cars. There was a covered picnic area with a couple of picnic tables. And, during the peak summer months, there was a lifeguard on duty watching over a roped-off swimming area. After Labor Day, there was nothing. Just sand.

A pair of troopers from the Troop F barracks had secured the perimeter a half-mile back where Old Shore Road intersected Brighton and Seaside, the two roads that led down to the beach. News vans and satellite trucks were already crowded there. TV reporters were busy doing their stand-ups for the cameras. It sure hadn't taken them long. They were the same mob who'd been camped out on Turkey Neck in front of the Grantham place. And nothing, but nothing, jump-starts news crews like a 911 call about a multiple homicide. They love blood. Anything with blood.

The trooper who'd sealed off Brighton Road let Des in, and she eased her cruiser through the two-block-long colony of summer cottages, slowing for the speed bumps that had been installed years ago for the safety of the children who lived there. They were small, squat cottages that were nestled close together. Almost all had been in the same working-class New Britain and Hartford-area families for generations. Almost none were winterized. Since the calendar said it was nearly November, most of the cottages were already shuttered for the season. Only a few lights were on here and there.

As she inched along between the speed bumps, Des saw a flash of lightning in the southern sky over Long Island. The storm was moving in fast. Soon, Mitch would be taking the salmon off the grill and the Bergers would be sitting down to eat. Des had insisted they go ahead without her. Ruth hadn't cared for that idea. She wanted to wait for Des to return.

"That's very sweet of you," Des said to her. "But I'm liable to be gone for hours and hours. Please enjoy your evening, okay?"

The Deacon had come along for the ride. Sat right there beside her in the cruiser, big hands resting on his thighs, face impassive. The grown-up inside of Des was thrilled that he wanted to be at a crime scene again, be involved. This was a good sign. But her inner child definitely felt funny about him breathing down her neck while she was on the job. Not funny ha-ha. Funny freaked.

A trooper was stationed at the entrance to White Sand Beach's dimly lit parking lot. Another was posted over at the lot's exit on Seaside. Traffic in and out of the lot was routed that way so the streets absorbed the beach flow evenly. When Des pulled into the lot, she encountered a hive of activity. The crime scene techies were there with their blue and white cube vans. So was the death investigator. Everyone was crowded around Andrea Halperin's black Mercedes sedan. Bright camera flashes kept going off as they photographed the bodies, the car, the pavement surrounding the car, it all.

"Your instincts were good," the Deacon said as she pulled up and parked. "You thought something nasty might go down. You had it right."

"Daddy, that's not giving me a whole lot of comfort right now."

"Wouldn't expect it to. Sometimes, being smart can be a real curse."

"Now you tell me." Des climbed out, giving her big hat a tug against the wind that gusted off the water. A few raindrops were starting to spatter.

Yolie spotted her and came right over, shaking her head in amazement. "Damn, girl, I *forgot* how whack this town of yours is. It's so peaceful here that you'd swear everyone's on Prozac. Except every time I turn around somebody's getting shot or poisoned or bashed over the head with a-a-a . . ." She broke off with a sputter, her eyes growing round as she realized who'd just climbed out of the passenger door of Des's cruiser. "Deputy Superintendent Mitry, it's great to see you up and around again, sir. How are you feeling?"

"Hungry, Lieutenant. I was just sitting down to dinner when you called."

"I'm so sorry to break into your evening."

"You didn't. Your shooter did. Besides, I'm not on active duty. Merely observing."

Toni scurried over to them now like an anxious little spaniel. "Good evening, Deputy Superintendent Mitry," she exclaimed with a big smile. "So pleased to meet you, sir. I'm Sergeant Toni Tedone."

"Of course you are," he said to her dismissively.

Toni stood there with her mouth open. No sound came out.

"Would you like me to run it for you, sir?" Yolie asked him.

"Well, I *didn't* come down here to inhale the sea air, Lieutenant," he barked in response.

This was the Deacon who Des knew. The Deacon whose intimidating presence could make even a hardened twenty-year veteran lose his lunch. She hadn't seen this Deacon in a long while. It made her smile inside, she had to admit.

"Sir, we have two victims in the front seat of the vehicle," Yolie reported. "The passenger's Stewart Plotka. The driver's Andrea

Halperin, his attorney. If you'll come with me . . ." She started toward the Benz, Des and the Deacon following her. "Guys, could you step back for just one moment, please?" she asked the techies. "Thank you. . . . Her window was rolled down, sir. His wasn't, as you can see by the shattered glass. The engine was running when we got here, and the air conditioning was on. It would appear that they were idling in comfort while they waited."

The Deacon stared at her. "Waited for? . . ."

"I'm surmising that they had a prearranged meeting here with someone."

"You're surmising this based upon what, Lieutenant?"

"I'll get to that in a moment, if you don't mind. Miss Halperin probably rolled her window down when the shooter arrived. She took two in the forehead from point-blank range, here and here . . ." Yolie pointed to the wounds with a Bic pen. Andrea's eyes were open wide. She had a totally shocked expression on her dead face. An expression that Des doubted she'd ever had in life. "Mr. Plotka took two to the left side of the head, as you can see. He was also shot once through his left hand and twice more in the chest. We make seven shots fired altogether. We just dug a nine-mil slug out of the armrest on Mr. Plotka's side. It's likely to be the shot that went through his hand."

"Did you find the weapon?" Des asked, head spinning and spinning.

"No weapon."

A powerful gust of wind buffeted them. It was a chill wind. The air suddenly felt ten degrees colder. Lightning crackled in the sky over the Sound, followed one, two, three, four seconds later by a clap of thunder.

"We'd better let these people get their work done before the rain comes," the Deacon said, stepping under the overhang of the covered picnic area. Des, Yolie and Toni joined him there. "When did it go down, Lieutenant?"

"A neighbor one house up on Brighton Road heard shots fired at two minutes past seven and phoned it in. And a young couple out walking on the beach phoned it in three minutes after that when they came upon the scene. The shooter was long gone by then. We took their statements and sent them on their way. The girl was pretty upset. We can reinterview them tomorrow."

"Did this neighbor hear the shooter drive away?"

"No, sir. But if he exited the lot over there on Seaside, then our Brighton Road caller wouldn't necessarily have heard him. I have men canvassing the neighbors on Seaside now."

"How about prior to the shooting? Did your Brighton Road caller observe either car entering the lot?"

Yolie nodded. "The Benz. Not a second vehicle."

"And what does that tell you?"

"The shooter could have come and gone on foot," Des suggested. "Parked his car up by Old Shore Road. Approached the Benz nice and quiet in the darkness, let them have it, then hightailed it back to his car."

Yolie nodded. "I'm with you. We're asking the neighbors if they saw anybody out walking or running." She glanced uneasily at the Deacon. "Sir, we sealed off the perimeter ASAP but a couple of tabloid photographers slipped through and ID'ed the victims before we could chase them off. So I'm afraid we've got ourselves a real circus."

"That can't be helped. Just do your job and accept the fact that they're doing theirs."

"Yes, sir."

There was another crackle of lightning followed almost instantly by a deafening clap of thunder. Rain began to hammer down on the roof over their heads.

"Before I jump to an obvious conclusion I always pause to consider the less obvious," the Deacon said, thumbing his jaw thoughtfully.

Yolie frowned at him. "As in? . . ."

"Is there any chance that your victims had become romantically involved? That they were down here admiring the sunset together and were attacked by a jealous lover?"

"Stewart Plotka's lady friend, Katie O'Brien, presently lives and works down in Boca Raton," Des said. "I'm not up on Andrea Halperin's love life but I doubt she'd go there. She was way out of Plotka's league."

"There's no telling who a woman will fall for," he countered.

"True enough," Des allowed, wondering if she'd imagined that extra little edge she'd heard in his voice.

"Lieutenant, you were surmising that your victims arrived here for a prearranged meeting with someone. Possibly a seven o'clock meeting given the time of the shooting. Who would that someone be?"

"Well, *that's* pretty clear," Toni the Tiger spoke up. "I mean, isn't it?"

He turned his frosty gaze on her. "I've only been on this job for thirty-two years. Absolutely nothing is clear to me."

"If you ask me what *I* think, it reads Tyrone Grantham all the way," she went on. "Da Beast made up his mind that Plotka raped Kinitra Jameson and decided to make him pay. The lawyer's merely collateral damage."

The Deacon nodded his head slowly. "Fair enough, Sergeant. Except you neglected one critical detail."

"Which is what, sir?"

"I didn't ask you what you think."

"Yes, sir." Toni gulped, her big-haired head beginning to swivel spasmodically atop her neck. "I mean, no, sir."

He turned back to Yolie now. "You had something more to tell me."

"Yes, I was just coming to that, sir." Yolie held up a plastic evidence bag that had a cell phone inside. "It's Andrea Halperin's. Her most recent incoming call, at 6:33 p.m., came from the landline inside the Grantham home."

"Therefore, you're surmising that someone in the Grantham home called her and arranged the meet. Does the time frame work?"

"The victims were staying at the Saybrook Point Inn," Des said. "That's a fifteen-minute drive from here. Twenty if there's traffic. It works."

The Deacon considered this for a moment. "What sort of a call would prompt the victims to jump in her car and drive down here at the drop of a hat?"

"A settlement offer," Des answered, shoving her heavy horn-rimmed glasses up her nose. "A nice, quiet settlement offer in a nice, quiet place. The victims stood outside Tyrone Grantham's house this afternoon waving a red blouse for the cameras and challenging him to take a DNA test. It was not a good day for Team Grantham. Maybe Tyrone decided he was ready to shove some cash at them so they'd go away."

"Who's authorized to negotiate such a settlement? Is Grantham's attorney currently in Dorset?"

"He wasn't as of a few hours ago," Des replied. "Although it's certainly possible that he came out from New York late this afternoon."

"That's not an acceptable answer," he growled at her.

"I'll find out," Des said quickly.

"Much better." The Deacon never showed her any favoritism—especially in front of others. "If his lawyer *isn't* present then who would be authorized to negotiate a settlement?"

"His brother, Rondell, handles all of his business affairs," Yolie said. "Rondell also happens to be madly in love with Kinitra. I have a trooper posted outside her hospital room in case someone decides to pay her a visit. No one has, according to hospital security, but there's no telling what we're into now."

"It appears as if you've done a pretty fair job so far, Lieutenant," the Deacon said. "Although your shooter did serve it up awful nice and easy by leaving Miss Halperin's cell phone behind that way. You wouldn't figure someone who's smart enough to lure her down here would be dumb enough to leave such incriminating physical evidence behind. In fact, if I were you, I'd be wondering if someone's playing with my head."

"I *am* wondering that, sir."

"What's your next move?"

"Paying a call on Tyrone Grantham."

"Mind if we tag along?"

"Not at all," Yolie responded, raising her chin at him. "As long as you remember one thing. . . ."

The Deacon looked at her, stone-faced. "And what's that?"

"It's *my* case."

"Good answer, Lieutenant."

By the time they got to Turkey Neck the rain was coming down in blinding sheets. Des could barely make out Yolie's taillights ahead of her as they sloshed around the bend to the Grantham place. And it was drumming so hard on the roof of the cruiser that she practically had to shout when she asked the Deacon if he wanted to borrow her hooded rain slicker. He didn't. Of course he didn't.

When they reached Tyrone's driveway, Yolie pulled in and lowered her window to talk to Oly, who'd taken cover inside his cruiser next to the gate. Most of the media throng had relocated to the double-homicide scene. The few who'd stayed put had sought refuge inside their own rides. But at the sight of two cruisers pulling into the driveway they jumped out and came splashing toward them, hollering and screaming for an update, a quote, something, anything. Des had nothing to say and refused to roll down her window. Just waited for Oly to open the gate so she could follow Yolie inside, the gate closing behind them.

Yolie came to a stop almost immediately and got out.

Des rolled down her window, feeling the hard, chilly rain on her face. "What's up?"

"Tyrone's not home," she reported, huddled inside her hooded rain jacket. "Oly said he drove off in his Escalade at about six-thirty and hasn't come back."

"Was he alone?"

"He was alone. Told Oly he was going to get some ice cream for Jamella."

"Ice cream," the Deacon repeated, staring straight ahead.

She dashed back to her car and jumped in and they followed her to the front entrance to the house.

Clarence answered the door, looking wide-eyed and tense. He was also not his usual yappy self. Led them in silence into the vast, high-ceilinged living room where those six sharks swam restlessly, endlessly, inside their giant aquarium. Rondell, Jamella and Chantal were seated on the white leather sofas grimly watching CNN's live news coverage of the White Sand Beach murders on the flat-screen TV. The rain-soaked correspondent, who stood under an umbrella at the Brighton Road perimeter, was reporting that Stewart Plotka and his attorney, Andrea Halperin, had been gunned down "gangland style" in the front seat of her late-model Mercedes at approximately 7:00 P.M. The correspondent also pointed out that Tyrone Grantham had left his luxurious waterfront estate on nearby Turkey Neck Road at approximately 6:30 P.M. in a black Cadillac Escalade and had not yet returned home. Thereby leaving viewers to connect the dots for themselves. It wasn't exactly hard.

When Rondell noticed them standing there with Clarence, he muted the sound on the TV. It fell silent in the room—except for the wind-driven rain that was pelting against the glass walls.

Rondell and Chantal hadn't met the Deacon yet. Des made the introductions. They were so distraught they barely seemed to hear her.

"He just went out to get me some ice cream," Jamella protested, plopped there forlornly on the sofa, her hands folded across her big belly. "That's all he did."

"That's right, hon," Chantal said to her comfortingly. "Ain't no law against that. Is there, Trooper Mitry?"

Des mustered a faint smile. "No law at all."

Rondell could not stop fidgeting or clearing his throat. He was dressed way sportier than usual. Instead of a sober, neatly tucked oxford button-down, he wore a loose-fitting electric blue Hawaiian shirt emblazoned with a white palm tree. "I—I've tried him numerous times on his cell," he stammered nervously.

Yolie narrowed her eyes at him. "And? . . ."

"He's not picking up. Here, I'll try again. . . ." Rondell hit speed dial and listened, shaking his head when the call went to voice mail. "It's *me*, big man," he said into the phone. "*Please* call me, will you?"

He rang off, aware of Des's eyes on him. "This shirt's not me at all, is it?" he acknowledged self-consciously. "Tyrone bought it for me in Honolulu. It's a genuine Tori Richard, whatever that means. Silly thing's made of silk."

"It's not silly at all," Toni spoke up. "I think it's beautiful."

Rondell looked at her in surprise. "Really?"

"Where's Calvin?" Yolie asked, glancing around.

"In the pool house, last time I looked," Chantal responded with a discernible chill in her voice.

Yolie nodded to Toni. She immediately went marching off to fetch him.

"And how about Monique?" Des asked Chantal.

"She's up in her room watching the TV."

"Ask her to join us, please."

"The girl's simple. She don't know nothing."

"Please ask her anyway."

Chantal craned her head around and yelled, "*Monique? . . .*"

"*What? . . .*" Monique hollered back.

"*Get your ass in here, girl!*"

It took her a while but Monique came scuffing in. At the sight of all of them there, her dull-eyed gaze went down to the floor. "I do something wrong, Chantal?" she asked, standing there knock-kneed in her T-shirt and cutoffs.

"You got nothing to worry about. Just sit right here next to me. These folks want to talk to us, that's all."

Toni returned now with Calvin, who was clutching a fresh can of Bud.

He popped it open and took a thirsty gulp. "What's all of this fuss?"

"Have you been watching the news?" Yolie asked him.

"Naw, I was playing around on my laptop."

"Watching that filthy online porn of yours again," Chantal said reproachfully. "It's *sick*, you ask me."

"Who's asking you?" he shot back, bristling. "You're just jealous because there ain't no man alive wants to look at you that way no more."

"Please shut up," Jamella begged them wearily. "Both of you."

"Don't tell me to shut up in my own son's home," Chantal huffed. "Tell *him* to shut up—insulting me to my face that way."

Lightning flashed outside the glass walls, followed by a tremendous clap of thunder. The household lights flickered but stayed on.

Toni said, "He *was* watching online porn, Loo. I could see it on his screen through the window."

Calvin shrugged his shoulders. "So what? That's no crime, is it?"

"No, it is not," Yolie said to him. "But murder is."

His eyes widened. "Who's talking about *murder?*"

"Stewart Plotka and Andrea Halperin are dead, Mr. Jameson," the Deacon informed him. "Someone just shot them in the parking lot of White Sand Beach."

"Dang . . ." Calvin exhaled slowly, glancing over at Rondell and Clarence. They sat there in tense silence, staring down at their hands. "Hey, where's Tyrone at?"

"He's out getting me some ice cream," Jamella answered in a small voice. "He's been gone for over an hour."

"Don't take but five minutes to get to that ice cream parlor you like."

"I know that, Popsy."

Calvin frowned. "I'm not liking the sound of this at all. . . ."

"Don't you be thinking what you're thinking," Chantal said to him. "My boy wouldn't kill *nobody*."

Des's cell phone rang on her belt. She answered it and listened to the voice on the other end, then rang off and said, "That was Oly. Tyrone's home. He just passed through the gate."

"Well, praise the Lord for that," Chantal said.

Des heard the slam of a car door outside, then the front door to the house open and close.

"I'm back, girl!" Tyrone called out from the entry hall. "Got your pistachio for you! Yo, what's up with those police cars parked out in our? . . ." He trailed off as he arrived in the living room and saw all of them. Stood frozen there in a tank top and spandex shorts, his giant tattooed muscles bulging, rain drops glistening on his shaved head. In one hand he held a bag from Clancy Muldoon's ice cream parlor, in the other his car keys.

"Good evening, Tyrone," Des said to him quietly.

"Evening, Trooper Mitry," he responded guardedly. "Who's the suit?"

"The suit happens to be my father, Deputy Superintendent Mitry. He and I were having dinner together when I got the call."

"What call? You got some news for us about Kinitra?"

"They're not here about Kinitra," Rondell informed his brother somberly.

"Well, then what's going on? Somebody tell me, will you?"

Jamella swallowed, her eyes puddling with tears. "Baby, where have you *been* all of this time?"

"I told y'all I'd be gone for a while. Was starting to feel like a caged tiger. Needed to take a drive and clear my head. You heard me say so. You and Cee both. Right, Cee?"

"True that," Clarence acknowledged. "I heard you."

"Where did you drive to, Tyrone?" Des asked.

"What difference does that make?"

"Please answer the question," Yolie said to him.

"Up into the hills by that Devil's Hopyard waterfall. Man, it is peaceful up there. I could listen to that waterfall all night long."

"Did anyone see you there?" Yolie asked.

"*See* me? How would I know? I was just kicking it. Minding my own business—until it started to pour down rain. So I came back to town, got my girl's pistachio and here I am."

"I called you a million times on your cell," Rondell said. "Why didn't you pick up?"

"Didn't feel like it." Tyrone's voice had a definite edge now. "And I'm all done answering questions. Somebody tell me what's going on right this goddamned minute."

"Stewart Plotka and his lawyer got themselves shot in the parking lot of White Sand Beach while you were out," Yolie informed him.

Tyrone seemed genuinely shocked. He breathed in and out for a long moment before he said, "Are they . . . *dead*?"

Yolie nodded her head.

"Wait, wait . . ." Tyrone looked around at everyone. "Y'all think *I* shot them?"

"Did you?" Yolie asked him.

"No, ma'am. Wasn't me. You got to believe me."

"I don't *got* to do anything—except get to the truth. Tell me, do you own a handgun?"

He looked at Des and said, "You know I do. I told you I keep a Glock 19 for our protection."

"Where do you keep it?" Yolie asked him.

"In our bedroom. It's in my nightstand."

"Let's go get it, okay?"

"Not a problem."

"Hold on a second," Rondell cautioned him. "Perhaps we had ought to contact your lawyer before we proceed any further."

"I don't need no lawyer, little man. I didn't *do* anything."

Yolie went with Tyrone to fetch his gun. Not one word was said while they were out of the room. Everyone just waited in taut silence as the rain whipped against the glass walls.

When they returned Yolie was empty-handed.

And Tyrone had a stricken expression on his face. "My Glock's *gone*."

"When did you last see it?" Des asked him.

"This morning, I guess. When I was fetching my shades out of the drawer."

"Do you generally keep the weapon loaded?"

"Hell, yeah. Don't do you no good if it's empty."

"Did you have any visitors today?" Toni asked him.

He shook his shaved head at her. "Just y'all."

"So whoever lifted it, assuming someone *did* lift it . . ."

"You calling me a liar?"

"Either lives here or snuck onto the premises," Toni concluded.

"I fixed that hole in our fence," Clarence spoke up defensively. "Wired a board over it."

Des mulled this over, her mind working it, working it. "Are there any other guns in the house?" she asked, her gaze boring in on Clarence.

"What are you looking at *me* for?" he demanded.

"This is a homicide investigation, son," the Deacon said in a calm, measured voice. "Best get it all out now."

"Okay, yeah, I've got a Glock of my own," Clarence admitted grudgingly. "Only, it's not exactly registered or what have you."

"Where did you get it?" Yolie asked him.

"A friend loaned it to me."

Toni let out a snort. "A *friend?*"

"Go and get it, Clarence." Yolie nodded at Toni to tag along as he went loping out of the room.

When they returned Toni was wearing a pair of white latex evidence gloves and holding a Glock 19 with a pencil she'd poked into its barrel.

"Has it been fired recently?" Yolie asked her.

Toni shook her head. "Smells fresh as a daisy, Loo. And the clip's full." She yanked an evidence bag from the pocket of her rain slicker, tucked the Glock carefully inside and then stuffed it back in her pocket.

Slowly, each and everyone's eyes returned to Tyrone Grantham.

"I'm telling you, I'm totally innocent," he insisted angrily. "I didn't shoot nobody. I didn't rape nobody. I didn't do nothing. Go on, tell 'em, baby. *You* believe me, don't you?"

Jamella sat there in silence, tears spilling from her eyes.

Tyrone let out a gasp. "My God, you *don't* believe me. . . ."

"I believe you, big man," Rondell spoke up.

Tyrone shook his head at him. "No, you don't. I can see it in your eyes, little brother. In *all* of your eyes. You *all* think I been forcing myself on that sweet little girl. And that I took my gun and capped those two people. You actually think I'd do those things."

"What I think," Yolie said, "is that we need to continue this conversation in official surroundings."

"What, you're *charging* me?" he demanded.

"No, but you are a person of interest and we need to have a talk. You have the right to have your attorney present."

"He's in New York."

"I'll call him right now," Rondell said hurriedly. "He'll have

Yale's best criminal defense attorney here from New Haven in thirty minutes."

"Tell him the attorney will find us at the Troop F barracks in Westbrook," Yolie informed Rondell.

"I'll do that. Thank you."

There was a loud tapping now on the French doors over next to the fireplace. Des turned and spotted Mitch standing out there on the halogen-lit patio in the pouring rain. He was not alone. Winston Lash was with him.

She went to the door and let them in. Both men wore hooded rain jackets but their legs were soaking wet. "Mitch, what are you doing here?"

"We thought we'd get in out of the rain," he replied, grinning at her in that boyish, maddening way of his. "Hey, we're not interrupting anything, are we?"

CHAPTER 14

"DOES THIS SORT OF thing happen often?" Chet asked as Mitch came sprinting back inside with their rain-drenched, semi-raw slab o' salmon.

Five more minutes. Just five more minutes on the grill and it would have been toothsome and smoky good. But, no, the torrents of rain had outraced him. *This* was what he got for his loyalty. *This* was how Jim Cantore repaid him.

Mitch peeled off his rain slicker as a bolt of lightning crackled overhead, followed by a booming clap of thunder. His lights flickered. Uh-oh . . . "Yeah, we get these storms all the time, Pop. The bad news is that out here on the island we almost always—"

"No, I meant Desiree dashing off at a moment's notice."

"Afraid so. That's what happens when the love of your life is sworn personnel. Any minute the phone may ring and out the door she goes." Mitch set the platter of cold, wet fish down on the kitchen counter and returned to the living room, where his folks were huddled on the love seat with Clemmie and Quirt, all four of them looking a teensy bit spooked. It was a violent storm. The wind was howling. The surf was crashing against the rocks. His valiant little cottage was shuddering. "Listen, I hate to say this but I have to take off, too."

"Take off for where?" Chet demanded.

"I have to go see a friend."

"Right now?"

"I'm afraid so, Pop."

"But what about dinner?"

"We can eat when I get back. I won't be gone long."

Outside, there was another snap, crackle, pop of lightning—followed by a deafening cannonade of thunder. And this time the power went out, plunging the house into total darkness.

"I'm afraid this happens all the time, too." Mitch fetched the kitchen matches from over by the fireplace and started lighting his oil lamps. "We almost always lose power out here when we have a thunderstorm. It's nothing to be concerned about. You just won't be able to use the water, as in flush the toilet. My well pump runs on electricity. So does the oven, for that matter." Mitch paused, furrowing his brow. "I guess this dinner party has to rate as an epic disaster."

"Nonsense, we're having a terrific time, sweetheart," Ruth said bravely. "This is fun. It's like camping out."

"You're a good sport, Mom."

"She's always been a good sport," Chet said. "That's why I've kept her around. That, and she has one sa-weet *tuchos*."

"Chester, behave yourself!"

"Like I said, I won't be gone long. Mom, if the power comes back on you can finish the salmon in the oven. I would set the temperature at around—"

"Sweetheart, I've been baking salmon since the 1970s."

"Right, right. I forgot who I was talking to. If you guys get cold you can build a fire in the fireplace. There's plenty of seasoned wood. Kindling's over in that crate. Flue's open. You know how to build a fire, don't you, Pop?"

"Of course I do. I was a Boy Scout. Remember when I was in the Scouts, Ruthie?"

"I hadn't met you yet, dear."

"Sure, you had."

"No, I hadn't."

"But we went to the Jamboree together."

"Chester, that wasn't me."

"Well, then who was it?"

"How would I know?"

"And help yourselves to more wine," Mitch said, topping off their glasses.

"Thanks, I believe I will." Chet took a sip. "Maybe I'll get shnockered and make a pass at your old lady."

"Chester! . . ."

"Hey, what happens on Big Sister stays on Big Sister," Mitch said as he got back into his slicker. Then he dashed out into the pouring rain to his truck.

A crackle of lightning lit up the night sky as he piloted the Studey slowly across the rickety causeway. The angry surf was foaming up and over the wooden planking. Twice since he'd moved out to Big Sister whole sections of the causeway had been washed away by violent storms, stranding Mitch and the other residents out there for days. But he'd seen no reason to bother his parents with that worrisome little detail.

His windshield wipers could barely keep up with the rain as he slogged his way through the Nature Preserve. When he made it to Old Shore Road he was happy to see plenty of lights on. The mainland still had electricity. He headed straight for Turkey Neck, where the news crews and gawkers had all but vanished from the Grantham place. The storm had sent them running for cover. The storm and the small matter of that double homicide over on White Sand Beach.

He found Winston Lash and the Joshua girls seated at their kitchen table dining on fried chicken and potato salad. The kitchen windows were closed against the windblown rain, which was really too bad. That horrid smell still hadn't gone away.

"Pull up a chair, Brubaker!" Winston called out cheerily as Mitch stood there dripping on their floor. "Chantal from next door brought us a ton of grub. Now *there* is a handful of woman. *Two* handfuls."

"I'm good, thanks. I have dinner waiting for me at home."

"What brings you out in such awful weather, Mitch?" Luanne asked, nibbling daintily on a chicken wing. "Did poor Callie phone you?"

"Why, what's wrong with Callie?"

"She's up in her room weeping," Lila answered breathlessly. "Mr. June Bond has informed her that he'll be sailing with the tide tomorrow and never coming back."

"Just between us, she's better off without him," Mitch confided.

Luanne shot a knowing look at him. "It's Bonita, of course. It was only a matter of time before that steamy little tramp set her sights on him."

"Are you sure you won't join us, Mitch?" Lila asked.

"Positive. I just wanted to ask Winston a quick question."

"Why sure, Brubaker. Fire away."

"Have you seen your buddy lately?"

The old fellow looked at Mitch blankly. "My buddy?"

"Last night, when we were burrowing through that hole in the fence, you told me you had a buddy who shares your appreciation for tender young flesh." Mitch glanced over at the sisters. "Please pardon my earthiness."

"Think nothing of it, Mitch. We've heard it all," Lila said, reaching for a drumstick. "That black woman sure can make fried chicken, can't she, dear?"

"She sure can," Luanne agreed. "They're very clever with their hands, you know. And such a musical people."

"Winston, you told me your buddy understands you."

The old man toyed with his handlebar moustache, grinning at Mitch devilishly. "You bet. My buddy and I understand each other."

Luanne looked at him pityingly. "Which 'buddy' would this be, Winnie?"

"He may very well be talking about an imaginary friend," Lila whispered to Mitch.

"That's exactly what I thought last night. But then I got to thinking about it some more and . . . Winston, have you seen him this evening?"

"Sure thing, Brubaker."

"When was this?"

"Just before it started to rain."

"Where?"

"Out in our backyard."

Luanne peered at him suspiciously. "What were you doing in our yard?"

"Attending to some personal business."

"Winnie, were you peeing on those trees again?"

"What if I was?" he replied defiantly. "A man *needs* to mark his territory. It's an animal instinct. Tell her, Brubaker. You know what I'm talking about."

"Winston, what was your friend doing?" Mitch asked him.

"Passing through."

"Is that what he usually does? Pass through?"

"Sometimes he stops by late at night to watch Callie fling paint on the sun porch in her birthday suit. He told me he can see her plain as day from out there."

"But tonight you say he was passing through."

"That's right."

"Where was he heading?"

Winston shrugged. "Search me."

"Well, where does he usually come from?"

"That-a-way." Winston waved in the direction of the Grantham estate.

"Do you mean the house right next door or Justy Bond's place?"

"That-a-way," the old man repeated with maddening vagueness.

"Would you mind showing me?"

"Be happy to, Brubaker. Any time."

"How about right now?"

"Why, Mitch, we're in the middle of dinner," Luanne said.

"*And* it's teeming bricks out there," Lila added.

"I'm sorry, ladies, but this is really important."

"Very well. But wait a second . . ." Luanne grabbed her napkin, leaned over and wiped the fried chicken grease from Winston's moustache and mouth.

Winston beamed at her. "When you bend over that way I can almost see your boobies."

"You're as bad as a schoolboy, you old fool."

Winston got up out of his chair and drew himself up to his full height, his shoulders thrown back. "Shall I lead on, Brubaker?"

"Please do."

Lila fetched the old fellow's yellow rain slicker from the mudroom and helped him on with it, zipping it up to his throat.

"I'll be back soon, girls," he announced in a booming voice. Then he went charging out the kitchen door into the pouring rain, striding gallantly across the soggy lawn toward the trees where the fence stood.

Mitch had to run to catch up with him.

CHAPTER 15

"GOOD TO SEE YOU again, Yolie," Mitch exclaimed as he and Winston Lash stood there dripping all over Tyrone's polished hardwood floor.

"Back at you, Mitch," Yolie responded grimly.

Toni the Tiger marched right up to him and said, "I've heard a lot about you, Mr. Berger. I'm Toni Tedone."

Mitch smiled and said, "Of course you are."

"Why does *everyone* keep saying that to me?"

"My, you certainly have a pair of big ones," Winston observed, his eyes zeroing right on her ta-tas.

"*What* did you just—?"

"Don't mind Winston," Mitch said as Des studied him, wondering what in the hell he and the old man were doing here. He glanced around at the very tense group of people who were gathered there, his gaze settling on little Rondell. "Hey, man, how are you feeling?"

"Better, thank you," Rondell answered quietly.

"I love that shirt you have on."

Rondell looked down at his Hawaiian shirt doubtfully. "Do you really mean that?"

"I do. It's totally you."

"Good evening, Chantal," Winston said. "The girls and I were just enjoying some of your delicious fried chicken."

"Glad you liked it," Chantal murmured, seated there next to Monique.

Des said, "We're, um, into something kind of heavy right now, Mitch. What's up?"

"Maybe something, maybe nothing. And if it's nothing I apologize in advance for barging in like this. You know how I hate to interrupt an official inquiry."

Yolie nodded her head. "Oh, I do. You've only done it, what, six times?"

"Actually, I think this might make eight," Des said.

"Say what you came to say," the Deacon interjected with quiet authority.

"Thanks, I will," Mitch said, scratching his curly head of hair furiously. It was a thing he did sometimes when he was trying to collect his thoughts. Reminded Des of an inquisitive organ grinder's monkey. "Last night, when I was leading Winston home through the woods after that unfortunate incident at the party—"

"I'm all done apologizing for that," Clarence blustered at him.

Mitch held up his hands as a gesture of surrender. "We're good. This isn't about that. As we approached the hole in the fence Winston started telling me about a buddy of his who happens to share his predilection for lovely young ladies. At the time, I thought Winston was talking about, well, an imaginary friend. Given what we know about his current state of mind." Mitch glanced over at him. "No offense, Winston."

"None taken, Brubaker," Winston assured him.

Clarence frowned. "Brubaker? I thought his name was Berger."

"Shut up, Cee," Tyrone growled.

"But here's the thing," Mitch continued. "Winston just informed me that he ran into his buddy this very evening—shortly before it started to rain."

Des narrowed her eyes at Mitch. "Where was this?"

"In his backyard. His buddy was cutting through the Joshua property."

"From where?"

"That's exactly what I wondered. Winston said he didn't know. But when I asked him where his buddy lives, he led me right to this place." Mitch paused, scratching his head again. "I could be way off base here but Winston does like to wander in the night and he did know about that hole in the fence. So here's what I'm thinking: What if his buddy *isn't* imaginary? What if Winston has actually seen the man who made the hole? That would mean he may be able to identify Kinitra's attacker. Possibly even your White Sand Beach killer. The shooting did take place just before the rain started, correct?"

Yolie nodded. "Correct."

"Did any witnesses see the shooter drive away?"

"No, they did not," she answered.

"Possibly because he was on foot," Mitch suggested. "It's just a quick scoot from White Sand Beach into the Nature Preserve. And two miles from there to here if you take the footpath at the end of Sour Cherry Lane. Even less than that if you cut through the Joshua sisters' property and go through that hole in the fence. I'll bet you could make it in fifteen minutes if you had to."

"This is all very interesting, Mitch," Des said tactfully. "But Mr. Lash doesn't exactly qualify as a credible witness."

"Still, it's worth finding out if he can identify someone here, isn't it?"

Clarence let out a guffaw. "Show that old man a picture of Mr. Barack Obama and he'll tell you *he's* his buddy. Besides, I fixed that hole."

"Are you talking about that sheet of plywood you wired in place?" Mitch asked him. "Because it took me less than ten seconds to undo the wire with my fingers in the pouring rain. It hardly even slowed us down, did it, Winston?"

Winston didn't answer him. He was too busy staring across the living room at someone. "Why, *there* he is!" he exclaimed, his eyes fixed on one man and one man only. "*There's* my buddy!"

He was gazing at Calvin Jameson.

"Don't be looking at me," Calvin grumbled at him. "Only time I ever seen you was last night when you *bit* a young lady."

"You don't remember me?" Winston seemed hurt by Calvin's chilly rebuff. "We've talked in my yard many times about the blessed beauty of tender young fruit. I like to think we understand each other."

"Popsy, what is he talking about?" Jamella asked Calvin.

"Don't ask me. Old man's sick in the head."

"Did you happen to go out for a while this evening, Calvin?" Mitch inquired. "Possibly slip through that hole in the fence so Trooper Olsen wouldn't see you leave by the front gate?"

"I don't know what you're talking about," Calvin responded gruffly. "And you're not the law. I don't have to answer none of your questions."

"That's very true, Mr. Jameson," Yolie acknowledged. "But you do have to answer mine."

Calvin looked at her in disbelief. "That old man has Alzheimer's."

"Frontotemporal dementia, actually," Mitch said.

"Are you taking his word over mine?" Calvin demanded.

"I can't speak for the others," Mitch said. "But I'm going with the old guy with dementia."

"You shut up!" Calvin blustered at him. "Who are you to come in here making all of these wild accusations?"

"He's with me," Des said. "And I'd advise you to answer his question."

"*Which* question?"

"Did you go out earlier this evening?"

Calvin took a long, slow drink from his can of Bud. "The answer is no. I've been entertaining myself in the pool house all evening. Downloaded a movie onto my laptop from one of them amateur sites. Bunch of college girls at a frat party having themselves a wild time. Run a check on my computer if you don't believe me. I've been logged on all evening."

Yolie shook her head at him. "You'll have to bring something better than that, Mr. Jameson."

"What's *that* supposed to mean?"

"It means that you could have downloaded a ninety-minute movie and left it playing on your computer while you took off and came back."

"Ask the trooper at the gate," Calvin said easily. "I never left the property. He'll tell you."

"See above," Mitch said. "Re: Hole in the fence."

"I never left through any hole in any fence," Calvin insisted. "That's bull."

Yolie puffed out her cheeks. "Okay, let's back this up. Before you walked in that door, Mitch, we were discussing that Mr. Tyrone Grantham had no one to account for his whereabouts at the time of the White Sand Beach shootings. His Glock nine-mil is missing from his nightstand—or so he's alleging—and the murder weapon happens to be a nine-mil. One of the victims, Stewart Plotka, had a physical altercation with Mr. Grantham that led to Mr. Grantham's suspension from the NFL. The other victim, Andrea Halperin, who was Mr. Plotka's lawyer, was on TV this very afternoon demanding a DNA sample from Mr. Grantham as part of the civil case they were pursuing against him. The victims claimed that Mr. Grantham raped Mr. Plotka's fiancée, Katie O'Brien, three years ago. Meanwhile, Mr. Grantham's sister-in-law, Kinitra Jameson, is at Middlesex Hospital after her near-fatal drowning early this morning. She is eight weeks pregnant and a physical examination revealed extensive scarring from repeated, forcible sexual contact." Yolie raised her chin at Mitch. "Real world? Mr. Tyrone Grantham appears to be our chief person of interest. So if you're offering an alternative scenario I sure would like to hear what it is."

"I'd like to ask Chantal a question first, if you don't mind," Des said, looking over at her. "Are you just going to let them take your son away in handcuffs or are you going to speak up?"

"Speak up?" Chantal blinked at Des in alarm. "Speak up about what?"

"What's she talking about, Moms?" Tyrone demanded.

Chantal lowered her eyes. "I don't know. . . ."

"Yes, you do," Des said to her sharply. "You asked Mitch to let me know that today was laundry day. What were you trying to tell me?"

Chantal took a deep breath and let it out, her mountainous chest rising and falling. She glanced over at Monique next to her on the sofa, then at Tyrone and Rondell. Then she lowered her eyes again. "I didn't mean nothing."

"It sure sounded like something to me," Mitch said.

"You was mistaken. Wasn't nothing."

"Yeah, it was, Chantal." Monique tugged at the woman's sleeve. "They talking about them clothes I found in the hamper this morning, remember?"

"Hush, girl."

"Don't you remember them clothes, Chantal?"

"Girl, this is serious business. You hush, hear?"

"Whose clothes did you find, Monique?" Des asked gently. "Were they Kinitra's clothes?"

Chantal's eyes widened. "Keep your mouth shut, Monique!"

"Let her speak, Mrs. Grantham," Yolie said. "Or we'll *all* be taking a ride to the barracks."

"Were they Kinitra's clothes?" Des asked Monique once again.

"N-No, ma'am." Monique's voice was trembling. "They was a-a man's clothes. They was all damp. And there was grass stains all over the knees a-and looked like blood on the shirt."

"Moms, what is this?" Tyrone demanded to know.

"I still got 'em in the laundry room," Monique added, trying to be helpful.

"Go with her," Yolie told Toni.

Toni escorted Monique off to the laundry room. Chantal bowed her head and closed her eyes. Her lips were moving—in silent prayer.

Outside, the hard, windblown rain continued to whip against the glass walls.

Winston moved over toward the huge aquarium, transfixed by Tyrone's sharks. "Amazing," he said in childlike awe. "What kind are they?"

Tyrone shot an angry, distracted look at him. "What'd you say?"

"What kind of sharks are they?"

"Black tip reef sharks."

"They're positively hypnotic. I must get some of my own."

"Yeah, you do that, old-timer."

Toni and Monique returned now, Toni clutching a plastic trash bag in one latex-gloved hand. She set it down on the coffee table.

"Let's have a look, Sergeant," Yolie said.

Toni reached into the bag and carefully removed a lime green polo shirt that was speckled with dried blood, then a pair of tan slacks covered with grass stains and more dried blood.

"Are these the items of clothing you brought to Chantal?" Yolie asked Monique.

"Yes, ma'am."

"And why did you do that?"

Monique frowned at her, puzzled. "Sorry? . . ."

"Because that's what I taught her to do," Chantal explained. "Any time she finds something out of the ordinary she brings it to me. She's fine with the regular wash but with something like grass stains she don't know whether to pretreat or soak 'em or whatever. Right, hon?"

Monique nodded eagerly. "That's right, Chantal."

"Whose clothes are these, Monique?" Des asked.

"I found them in Mr. Calvin's laundry hamper," she replied.

Every set of eyes in the room swiveled toward Calvin. In Tyrone's eyes Des saw pure animal fury. In Rondell's acute pain.

Jamella gaped at her father in shock. "Popsy, what's she talking about?"

Outwardly, Calvin couldn't have been calmer. He took another drink of his beer and set the can down on the coffee table, his hand steady as a rock. "That girl's simple in the head. All mixed up. Those clothes aren't mine."

"A simple DNA test can determine that easily enough," Yolie said. "It was a warm night. That shirt's bound to have perspiration on it. Refresh my memory, Sergeant Tedone. Kinitra scraped up her knees pretty good, didn't she?"

"She sure did, Loo."

"Mr. Jameson, if that's her blood on your shirt and pants then you'll have some explaining to do."

Calvin sat up a bit straighter, his jaw muscles clenching. "I don't have to explain a thing. I been in trouble with you people my whole life. You're always blaming me for every little thing. Never giving me a chance."

"I'm giving you a chance," Yolie responded evenly. "Are these your clothes or aren't they?"

"So what if they are?" he demanded. "And so what if they're dirty? That's why I put 'em in the danged hamper."

"How did those grass and bloodstains get on them?"

Calvin stared at Yolie coldly. "You want to know how they got there?"

"What I'm asking."

"We had us a party here last night. I had me some fun out on the lawn with a certain young lady, okay?"

"A certain young lady named? . . ."

"We didn't exchange no business cards. Her and me got to talking by the pool. Hit it off real fine. The wine was flowing. And one thing led to another, okay?" He tugged at his ear thoughtfully. "Shaniqua, maybe. I do believe her name was Shaniqua. She was a pretty young thing. Blond streaks in her hair."

Chantal curled her lip at him. "What would a pretty young thing be doing with old trash like you?"

"Having herself a fine time. We made sweet love out on the lawn under the stars. That's how those grass stains come to be there."

"And the blood?" Yolie asked him.

"Couldn't say, miss. I was surprised to see it there myself when I got undressed. She must have scraped her elbows or knees on something. We got going pretty wild there."

"You are a no good lying punk," Chantal said in a voice that had turned ice cold. "You are lying right now just like you been lying all along."

Calvin stared at her long and hard. "You shut your mouth, woman."

"I *won't* shut my mouth! I've been keeping quiet for too long. I'm all done keeping quiet. You are *evil*, Calvin Jameson. You have been raping that sweet young daughter of yours for months under my son's roof and you belong *in eternal hell!*"

Jamella gasped. "Popsy, what is she? ..."

"Don't pay her no mind," Calvin said dismissively. "The woman's an old crack whore. You going to listen to her or to me?"

"I can't speak for the others," Mitch said. "But I'm going with the crack whore."

"She's crazy," Calvin insisted. "If you believe her, you're just as crazy as she is."

"Look me in the eye," Jamella said to him pleadingly, her eyes huge and shiny. "Look me in the eye and say it isn't so."

Calvin looked his older daughter right in the eye and said, "It isn't so, girl, I swear. Chantal's just trying to get rid of me. She's never liked me being around here with y'all. You know that."

"Don't listen to him," Chantal begged Jamella. "He's lying to you. I'm the one speaking the truth. I saw what I saw."

"What did you see, Mrs. Grantham?" Yolie asked.

"The two of them together in Glen Cove—maybe five, six weeks ago. Everyone else had gone out on *Da Beast* for the afternoon. Me, I don't like that boat. Get seasick soon as I'm out on the water. So I didn't go. And Kinitra stayed behind to work on her music. So did Calvin, who said he wanted to take himself a nap. I-I was walking down the hallway, minding my own business, when I heard a little cry coming from the den. Looked in and he had her cornered in there. His pants was down around his ankles and h-he was making her *do* him from down on her knees. I let out a scream. Poor Kinitra went running to her room, crying her eyes out. And this thug zipped up his pants, yanked a huge knife from his back pocket and held it right to my throat. He said he'd *kill* me if I ever breathed one word about it to you, Jamella. Sneak into my room while I slept and slit my throat ear to ear. I-I didn't doubt for one second he'd do it either. That man is pure thug. I know he's your daddy and you love him, but he would have *killed* me. So I-I couldn't tell you."

"Moms, why didn't you tell *me?*" Tyrone demanded to know.

Chantal heaved her chest. "I was afraid for you. You already got so much trouble in your life. You don't need no more. I was doing what I should have done for you when you were young—except I was too messed up back then. I was protecting you, understand? Your little brother, too."

Rondell peered at her, mystified. "How were you protecting *me?*"

"I know how you feel about that girl. I-I didn't want you finding out such a horrible thing about her. Maybe I was wrong to keep quiet. Maybe I should have let Calvin slit my throat in the night. Maybe that was the Lord's plan for me and I was just too blind to see. I've prayed on it long and hard, night after night. You can't imagine how hard I've prayed. But I still don't know the answer. I don't. I-I just . . ." She broke down and sobbed.

"It's okay, Moms." Tyrone said down beside her and hugged her gently. "Hey, it's okay."

Little Rondell was so upset he couldn't sit still. Jumped to his feet and paced his way around the entire room, shaking his head, before he returned to the seating area and came to a halt in front of Calvin. "*You* got her pregnant," he said hoarsely. "You forced yourself on your own daughter."

Calvin crossed his arms in front of his chest defiantly. "Your mama's lying to you, boy. Wasn't me."

"It *was* him, little man," Chantal cried. "I swear it. And I'm so sorry I didn't speak up, Jamella."

"And yet you gave Mitch that message for me today," Des pointed out. "Why, Chantal?"

"Because that poor girl tried to take her own life, that's why. Hers and her baby's. There is no greater sin than that."

Tears were spilling out of Jamella's eyes and streaming down her chiseled cheekbones. "If what you say is true . . ."

"Oh, it's true," Chantal swore.

"Why didn't she come to *me*? I'm her big sister. I'd do anything for her. I-I don't understand."

"I think I do," said Des, who'd seen this sort of thing happen before. Too damned many times. "She didn't come to you because she's been blaming herself for what's been going on. Plus she's humiliated, ashamed and really, really frightened." Des looked over at Calvin. "But not nearly as frightened as you. You panicked when Kinitra was admitted to the hospital, didn't you? Especially after you found out she didn't want you to visit her."

Calvin reached for his beer can and took a swig. "I don't know what you're talking about," he said, sounding a bit less sure of himself now.

"Sure you do, Calvin," Des went on. "You had to know that the doctors would discover she was pregnant. You also had to know that once she was tucked away safe and snug, talking to the law about her situation, she'd eventually summon up enough courage to bring the hammer down on you. So when Tyrone went out for that ice cream, you cooked up a scheme on the fly. He said he'd be gone for a while, felt like clearing his head. The timing couldn't have been more ideal. The second he walked out the door you called Andrea Halperin on her cell and told her to meet you at White Sand Beach. Then you snatched Tyrone's Glock from his nightstand, hightailed it there on foot and shot her and Stewart Plotka, figuring if you framed Tyrone for their murders that Kinitra's rape would land on him, too."

"That makes perfect sense, Master Sergeant," Mitch said slowly. "Except I have a mighty huge icebox question for you."

"What's an icebox question, Loo?" Toni asked.

"It's some weird Hitchcock old movie thing," Yolie replied. "Trust me, don't go there."

Des stared at him. When Mitch had an icebox question, he was not kidding around. "Okay, lay it on me. . . ."

"How did Calvin know Andrea Halperin's cell number?"

"I ain't saying nothing," Calvin grumbled in response.

"Yes, you are," said Rondell, who in the blink of an eye no longer stood facing Calvin. He stood behind him holding a Glock 19 to Calvin's head—a Glock 19 that he'd whipped out of the rear waistband of his slacks. He'd had it hidden under that damned Hawaiian shirt. And made his play so fast that not one of them had a chance to react. Not Des. Not Yolie. Not the Deacon. Not Toni.

And for damned sure not Calvin, who sat there frozen and wide-eyed.

"Don't anybody move!" Rondell warned them. "Keep your weapons holstered or I swear I will blow his brains all over this beautiful white sofa!"

"Whatever you say, Rondell." Yolie's voice was calm and quiet. "Just take it easy."

"I'm *taking* it easy!"

"Then why don't you put that gun down?" Des suggested. "Let's not make this situation any worse."

"She's right, little brother," Tyrone said. "Put that thing away. This ain't your style."

"My *style*?" Rondell shoved the Glock's nose harder against Calvin's head, the gun trembling in his hand. "My *style* is to treat a fine young lady like Miss Kinitra Jameson with *respect*. And just look where that got me, will you?"

"Is that your brother's Glock?" Des asked him. She wanted to keep him talking. Maybe cool his jets a little.

"No, it's *my* Glock," he answered angrily. "I keep it in my desk at all times in case some nut like Stewart Plotka tries to go after him. You people made sure you asked Clarence if *he* kept a weapon in the house. But not one of you thought to ask *me*—because you think I'm a-a helpless little wonk. A weakling. You *all* think that."

"That's not true," Jamella said, as he continued to hold that Glock to her father's head. "I think you've got a whole lot to offer. You're smart. You're compassionate. I've always said that."

Tyrone nodded his head. "That's right, she has. Let the police handle this, little brother. Stop and think, will you? What in the hell are you doing?"

"I'm taking care of myself." Beads of sweat had formed on Rondell's forehead. He was so overheated his glasses were practically fogging up. "That's what you always told me a man does, right? Well, I've got some news for you. All of you. I'm a man. And I can take care of myself just fine."

"Sure you can, son," the Deacon said. "No one in this room doubts that for one second. But what's important right now is for you to put that gun down and let the law take over."

Rondell shook his head. "No, sir. I'm sorry, but this is a family matter. And *I'm* in charge now. So y-you answer the question, Calvin. Answer it right goddamned now."

Calvin gulped. "*Which* question?"

"Mitch's ice chest question."

"Actually, it's an ice*box* question. The term dates back to when folks still owned . . ." Mitch broke off when he noticed Des's warning glare. "But you can say it either way."

"How did you get Andrea Halperin's cell number?" she asked Calvin.

"She . . . gave me her business card at the store." Calvin's eyes shifted uneasily as Rondell pressed the Glock to his head. "In case I ever wanted to sell her some inside info to help her case."

"And did you?"

"Naw, never."

"Keep talking," Rondell commanded him.

"About *what*?"

"What you did tonight, you sick bastard!"

"Okay, okay. I phoned that Miss Halperin, like the trooper said. Told her I might have some news to sell her. We agreed to meet in that parking lot at seven. I-I took Tyrone's gun from his nightstand and hoofed it there, like the fellow said. Took that shortcut through the woods at the end of Sour Cherry."

"How did you know about that path?" Mitch asked him.

"Cee mentioned it to me."

"It's true, I did," Clarence said.

Rondell jabbed the Glock at him even harder. "Who made that hole in our fence?"

"It was me," Calvin admitted. "I can appreciate Tyrone wanting his privacy and all. But I lived inside the wire for too many years. Don't like to be fenced in. I need to roam—without some state trooper at the front gate knowing my business. So I took some wire cutters to the thing first night they put it in. Moseyed around the neighborhood and found me this fine white girl next door who likes to paint buck naked on the sun porch after dark."

"Her name is Callie. Have you ever laid a hand on her?" Mitch demanded.

"No, sir. I looked, that's all."

"You met them at the White Sand Beach parking lot," Yolie said. "Then what happened?"

Calvin let out a sigh. "I-I capped them, okay? Then I came straight home."

"Where's the weapon?" Yolie asked.

"Tossed it in the woods."

"With your prints on it?"

"Naw, I wiped it clean. How stupid do you think I am?"

"Don't know yet," she replied. "Still getting there."

Rondell took a ragged breath, the Glock shaking in his hand. "Was Trooper Mitry right? Did you kill those people to make it look like Tyrone was a cold-blooded murderer? A-And everyone would figure *he* raped Kinitra?"

"It worked, didn't it?" Calvin retorted. "Not a one of you believed him just now when he swore he was innocent. Not you, Jamella. Not you, Rondell. You *all* thought he did it. Hell, these police people were ready to take him away in cuffs until that crazy old man showed up with his mouthy friend."

"He's not crazy," Mitch said indignantly. "And I'm not mouthy. I choose my words very carefully. Force of habit. The first magazine I ever worked for only gave me fifty words to dissect an entire movie. Why, I could barely even—"

Des said, "Mitch . . ."

He moved it along. "I simply like to get to the bottom of things. Like, for instance, how long have you been raping your own daughter, Calvin?"

"I never touched a hair on my beautiful Kinitra's head."

"Try again," Mitch urged him. "And I'd be a bit more careful about how you answer. Rondell's hand is getting kind of twitchy. Rondell, we're making excellent progress here. Sure you don't want to put that thing down and have a seat?"

"Positive," he replied between gritted teeth.

Jamella's shiny eyes searched her father's face. "Is it true, Popsy? Did you . . . do those things to her?"

"Naw, girl," Calvin said reassuringly. "You know me."

She flared at him suddenly. "Yeah, I *know* you. I *know* that after I got to be twelve years old you started looking at me up, down and sideways, licking your chops. That's why Mama threw you out, wasn't it? Because *she* knew you."

Tyrone began breathing in and out very hard. And that vein was throbbing in his forehead now. "Did he *ever* come near you?"

"No, never," she replied. "Mama made sure he never got the chance. He was out of our lives for years. And he's been nothing but decent since you invited him to move in with us. Sure, I've seen him flirting with the pretty young girls by the pool. But he never got out of line. He was strictly being playful. Chantal gets upset about him watching his porn. But there isn't a man in America who doesn't watch porn. He's been a good father to Kinitra and me since he moved in. Or so I thought." She glared at Calvin. "I should have known the real deal."

"Which is *what?*" Rondell demanded, blinking at her.

"That I'm not Daddy's little girl anymore," Jamella said bitterly. "I'm Tyrone's. Huge with his child. But Kinitra's still young and sweet and innocent. So he went after *her.*" She glowered at her father accusingly. "You forced yourself on my baby sister. You've been forcing yourself on her ever since Tyrone was kind enough to give you a nice home with us. And *this* is how you repay him—by trying to make him out to be a murderer a-and rapist. I'm the fool here. I kept telling myself you'd turned over a new leaf. That you weren't the same awful scum Mama said you were. I should have known better."

"I should have known better, too," Des said, glancing over at the

Deacon. "You said something to me earlier today that should have set off alarm bells in my head. Only it didn't—not until we were sitting down to dinner."

The Deacon frowned at her. "What did I say?"

"That men don't change. That they are who they are." She looked back at Calvin. "You are a low-life street hustler who only looks out for himself—even when you're living large in a waterfront mansion. You have no moral code and zero conscience. You helped yourself to your own daughter because you felt like it. And when things started to go south, you tried to push the blame off on the son-in-law who took you in. You're sly and you're devious, Calvin. But you're not smart. The state can't bring Tyrone to trial on the rape charge unless Kinitra swears out a criminal complaint against him. And she'd be compelled to give up a sample of her baby's DNA—which would prove that *you* are the father, not Tyrone. There was no way in hell you were ever going to get away with this. Don't you see?"

"Wasn't thinking that far into the future," Calvin grumbled. "I was strictly thinking survival. Get the other cat before he gets you. I've spent half my life in a cage. I live by the code that I learned there, thanks to y'all. You're the ones put me in there. You made me the man I am today."

"So these murders are *our* fault," the Deacon said to him.

"Absolutely."

Rondell's finger tightened on the trigger. "And what about Kinitra?" he cried out, trembling with rage. "Whose fault is that?"

"I got me a likeness for the young girls. I ain't proud about it. But it is what it is. And I take what I want. That's what a man does. He don't ask for permission. He takes."

"She's your own daughter, you filthy bastard!"

"Kinitra is one fine-looking young girl. And once my blood gets to boiling, there ain't much I can do to stop myself. The good Lord knows that. He's always testing me. Sometimes I fail."

"You will *die* for this!" Rondell snarled.

"We all die," Calvin said with a shrug.

"And we all know the truth now," Des said. "You've forced it out of him, Rondell. Good job. Why don't you let us take it from here? Just put that gun down. It's over now."

"It's *not* over," Rondell said with chilling certainty.

"You folks don't have to worry yourselves none," Calvin said, sneering at Rondell. "He don't have the balls to pull that trigger. I can tell from a man's eyes if he's got 'em. This one's just a little bitch."

"You shut up!" Rondell screamed at him.

"Don't do it, little brother," Tyrone said pleadingly. "You'll mess up your whole life."

"I-I *have* no life," Rondell sputtered at him. "Don't you get it? I loved her. And he destroyed her. She's *gone!*"

"She's not gone, Rondell," Jamella spoke up. "She'll be home from the hospital tomorrow. And she'll need you now more than ever."

"Son, I want you to listen to me," the Deacon said. "I've been around a lot longer than you and I know a few things. I know that right now you can't see how you will ever deal with your pain. But you will deal with it, I promise you—provided that you act like the responsible man you are and put down your gun. You did what needed doing just now for the girl who you love. Now let us prosecute Calvin through the proper channels. Believe me, he will pay."

Rondell kept the Glock pressed to Calvin's head. "Yes, he will. He will pay right now. On your feet, Calvin."

Calvin's eyes widened. "Why, what are you—?"

"On your feet!" Rondell ordered him.

Calvin got slowly to his feet. Rondell used the Glock to prod him over to the edge of the sofa so that he could get right behind him, his left forearm wrapped around Calvin's throat. He was using the bigger man as a shield.

"He will pay right now," Rondell repeated, backing the two of them toward the rain-spattered French doors that Mitch and Winston had come through. "He will pay." When they reached the doors, Rondell groped around with his left hand for the wall switch, flicking off the outdoor floodlights. He and Calvin were no longer backlit. There was only darkness behind them. "He will pay."

Rondell paused there for a brief moment now with his Glock against Calvin's head, the two men lit from above by the beams of the ceiling track lights. There was an incredible intensity to that light. An incredible intensity to that moment. Neither man moved. Not one person in the whole room moved. Time seemed to stop. Everyone was frozen there in place, their eyes gleaming, faces drawn tight, bodies poised for action. For an eerie instant, Des felt as if they were all living inside "The Night Watch" by Rembrandt.

But this was no painting.

And Rondell's finger on the Glock's trigger began to move now. Not at normal speed. In slow motion. It all seemed to go down in slow motion. . . . The shift in Calvin's posture as he waited for the fatal shot, expecting it, resigned to it. His eyes closing one last time as Rondell fired off the round that blew away the side of Calvin's head. Calvin sagging to the gleaming hardwood floor, a lifeless sack of meat and bone . . . Until suddenly everything returned to normal speed and Rondell was dropping the gun and running out of the French doors and into the pouring rain, Monique shrieking in horror from the sofa.

Toni was the first one out the door after him, flicking on the floodlights as she ran by, her SIG drawn. Rondell was splashing his way across the lawn down toward the beach.

"No, don't hurt him!" Tyrone barked as he went sprinting right past Toni, leaving her far behind. Tyrone Grantham possessed extraordinary speed for his size.

Clarence, the former Clemson small forward, raced right past her, too. Toni dropped to one knee on the wet grass, aiming to take Rondell down with a leg shot. But she had no shot. Not with those two very large men between her and Rondell.

"Come back, little man!" Tyrone hollered after him. "Come baaaack!"

Jamella stood in the doorway weeping over the body of her father as he bled out onto the floor. Chantal led Monique out of the room, her hand over the traumatized girl's eyes so she wouldn't look at him anymore.

The rest of them hurried across the lawn in the chilly, wind-driven rain—Yolie and Des in the lead, Mitch, the Deacon and Winston bringing up the rear.

Rondell had made it down to the dock. He cast off the lines and jumped aboard *Da Beast,* which no one had bothered to cover against the rain. But Rondell didn't care if its seats were wet. And with a *varrroooooom* he had its mammoth 1200-horsepower Cobra supercharged engines roaring. He was just starting to pull away when Tyrone came hurtling down the dock toward him. Tyrone didn't stop running. He dove right off the end of the dock—only he was a fraction of a second too late. Instead of touching down aboard *Da Beast* with his fleeing brother, he ended up in the river with a tremendous splash.

"Help me, Cee!" he cried out frantically. "Help me!"

"Man can't swim!" Clarence roared as he dove in after him

with all of his clothes on. "Here, cuz, I got ya! Don't flail your big arms—you'll drown us both! Relax, I got ya. You're okay."

He swam them away from the dredged dock area to shallower water where they could stand, water streaming from their clothes as they watched Rondell speed out into the middle of the choppy, mile-wide Connecticut River, the cigarette boat's xenon running lights swiveling left-right, left-right as he steered frantically down-river toward Long Island Sound. There were no other boats out. Not in a storm like this.

"Call the Coast Guard," Yolie ordered Toni. "We'll need launches out in the Sound. And chopper support if they can fly in this. He can outrun whatever they've got but he can't go forever." To Tyrone she called out, "How much fuel have you got in that thing?"

"Maybe a quarter of a tank," he called back, his eyes never leaving those swiveling lights. "Needed filling next time we took her out. He won't get far."

"He won't get far is right," Clarence said. "I swear, he's going to flip that damned thing. Don't know how to leave the wheel alone."

Jamella joined them out there now. She wore some of her fa-ther's blood on her yellow shift. And a strangely impassive expres-sion on her face.

"You okay?" Des asked her, concerned that she might be in shock.

"I'm fine," she answered quietly, shivering from the cold rain.

Des took off her hooded rain jacket and put it around her.

Tyrone rushed out of the water to her. "Girl, you got to go back inside in the house."

"I don't want to go inside," she said in that same quiet voice. "I don't want to be there with him."

"But you'll catch cold out here. That's no good for you or the baby. Go back inside, okay? We're okay."

"We're *not* okay. I'm so sorry, Tyrone."

"What for? You got nothing to be sorry about." He kissed her softly on the mouth, caressing her smooth cheek with the back of his battle-scarred hand. "We'll get through this, I promise you. We just got to get that freaked-out little man back on dry land. He'll be all right. He's a respectable individual with a spotless record. Can plead temporary insanity or something. People will understand."

"Where in the hell is that little dude going?" Clarence cried out.

Where indeed. Because Rondell was no longer streaking downriver toward the open water of the Sound. Instead, he was coming around in a wide arc that was sending him *up* the windswept river in the direction of the old stone railroad bridge and, beyond it, East Haddam and Hartford.

Toni, who'd just put out her distress call to the Coast Guard, said, "I'll call them back and tell them him he's changed course. And notify our own marine responders up the line. But I don't get it, Loo. What's he doing? Now he *can't* get away."

"Makes no sense," Yolie agreed, watching him in bewilderment.

"Sure it does," Mitch said. "Because he's not trying to get away."

The Deacon glanced sharply at Mitch before he turned to Yolie and said, "I agree. You can call off the pursuit, Lieutenant Snipes."

"Call it off?" Tyrone protested angrily. "Why?"

"Because he's not trying to get away," Mitch said again.

"Man, what in the hell are you? . . ." Tyrone's eyes widened. "Oh, Lord." He no longer had to ask Mitch what he meant. It was obvious to him.

Obvious to all of them now that Rondell was headed straight upriver, letting *Da Beast* loose with a tremendous roar. The supercharged cigarette boat had to be going at least seventy-five miles per hour as he closed in on the railroad bridge, its running lights casting bright beams on the granite pilings that had been stoutly supporting the old bridge for more than a hundred years. The pilings were spaced wide enough apart to allow dredging barges and other big ships to pass on through. Each of the supports was marked with bright red warning lights that could be seen from miles away. There was no mistaking where the pilings were. Consequently, hardly anyone ever rammed a boat into one of them.

Not unless they really wanted to.

Rondell drove *Da Beast* directly into one of the bridge's centermost granite support pilings. The boat exploded on impact. Its quarter-tank of fuel was plenty enough to set off a ball of fire that shot at least 500 feet into the rainy air. Witnesses later reported seeing it from as far as ten miles upriver. The explosion was felt by residents twice that far away.

"Call Amtrak," Yolie ordered Toni. "Alert them that their bridge just took a major hit. They'll have to shut down all of their trains between New York and Boston. I'll call Homeland Security. They'll probably be getting a hundred calls in the next sixty seconds from neighbors who think we just got attacked by Al Qaeda. Des, could you? . . ."

"On it." Des got busy contacting the emergency marine responders who'd close off the river and deal with the burning wreckage.

The Deacon stood by quietly and observed. He did not interfere.

Tyrone, Jamella and Clarence could only huddle there together, hugging each other and sobbing.

"I'll see you a little later," Mitch said to Des somberly when she'd finished making her calls. He was profoundly shaken by what had happened. "I'm going to walk Winston home. The girls will be worried about him. And I want to check on my parents. The power was out when I left. I want to make sure they're okay."

"Tell them I'm sorry about dinner. We'll try dinner some other night, okay?"

"Sure, I'll tell them," he said, his gaze fastened on the dock at their feet.

"You did good tonight."

He looked up at her, his eyes searching hers. "Did I?"

"Hell, yes. You cracked the Plotka-Halperin killings wide open."

"Des, I didn't crack anything open. And now two more people are dead."

"Calvin got what he deserved."

"But Rondell didn't. He was a nice guy. He didn't deserve this."

Des looked out at the flaming pieces of wreckage that were strewn across the oil-slicked water. Then she took his hand and squeezed it. "You're absolutely right, he didn't. Neither did Kinitra. Now you know why I sit up all night drawing portraits of victims until my fingers bleed."

"No offense, but I wish I didn't know these things."

"So do I, boyfriend. Believe me, so do I."

Epilogue

THE FOUR VIOLENT DEATHS that occurred that stormy evening went 24/7 on the cable TV news channels, sports channels and Internet gossip sites. The public just couldn't seem to get enough of the story. Not that the public actually knew the real story. Only the people who were actually there in Tyrone Grantham's living room knew the real reason why Rondell shot Calvin. But they weren't talking. And Kinitra certainly wasn't. In fact, the name Kinitra Jameson was never so much as mentioned. The public only knew the version of the events that was fed to the media by Yolie—which was that Calvin had confessed to several Connecticut State Police officers, as well as members of his own family, that it was he who had murdered Stewart Plotka and Andrea Halperin. An enraged Rondell had shot Calvin and then taken his own life despite everyone's best efforts to stop him.

The public wasn't totally satisfied with this version. They wanted more. And got more. One authoritative cable TV talking head after another held forth in sonorous tones about what *really* happened. That Tyrone had *really* sent Calvin to White Sand Beach to scare Plotka and Halperin off and things got out of hand. Or that Calvin, who had a long criminal record, had *really* been taking money under the table from Andrea Halperin to feed her dirt on Tyrone and got found out. Or that straight-arrow Rondell, who *really* had a serious drug problem, had *really* brokered a settlement with Plotka without telling Tyrone. There was a ton of speculation, most of it outright fiction. Usually, the talking heads cited "friends close to the family," which Des had learned from Mitch was reporter-speak for *"I'm totally making this shit up."* She already knew from her own personal experience that any time there was a violent family dispute involving black people, the media automatically assumed that drugs were involved.

No one had the real story. And that was as it should be, as far as Des was concerned. No one outside of the family needed to know that Kinitra's own father had raped her and gotten her pregnant. It was no one else's damned business. Kinitra's privacy was being zealously protected by the family. And Yolie had made it very plain to anyone who'd come in contact with Kinitra at Middlesex Hospital or Shoreline Clinic that she'd land on them super-hard if they ever breathed a word about her. The Jewett sisters didn't have to be told. They always kept their mouths shut.

The murder-suicide rampage was one more giant blot on Tyrone Grantham's troubled reputation. Even though Tyrone wasn't personally responsible, the NFL commissioner wasn't happy. The events of that night brought just the sort of "unsavory" attention to the league that he'd warned Tyrone about when he suspended him. Consequently, it was no longer a sure thing that Da Beast would be back on the field next season. A lifetime ban from the league was a distinct possibility.

Not that Tyrone was thinking about his career just now. He'd returned to his hometown of Los Angeles to lay Rondell to rest in the cemetery where their grandparents were buried. Lay his soul to rest, that is. There were no earthly remains—Rondell's casket was empty. But Tyrone wanted to give him a proper burial. Chantal and Clarence went out there with him, as did Monique. And more than a dozen of Tyrone's teammates flew to L.A. for the funeral, which Des thought was very nice of them.

Jamella, who was entering her thirty-fourth week of pregnancy, stayed behind. Her blood pressure had gotten a bit high and her doctor didn't want her to fly. Plus, she had Kinitra to take care of. And, after the Medical Examiner released the body, she had to arrange to have Calvin cremated. There was no funeral service. She and Kinitra simply stood together at the end of Tyrone's dock and scattered their father's ashes into the Connecticut River.

Jamella told Des this when Des dropped by the estate on Turkey Neck at her request. Actually, Kinitra's request. "My sister has something to say to you," was how Jamella put it to her on the phone.

It was a blustery, slate gray day, the temperature in the upper forties. Indian Summer was now officially over. And Des now had on her normal cold weather wool uniform and a Gore-Tex jacket. A skeleton crew of tabloid TV cameramen and paparazzi remained camped outside the estate.

It was moving day. Giant vans lined the long driveway. Justy Bond had won out. He was getting his precious neighborhood back, although the proud owner of Connecticut's highest volume G.M. dealership could hardly be called a happy fellow. June had sailed off for the Florida Keys on the *Calliope* just as he'd promised he would—and taken Bonita with him, much to the giddy delight of the village gossip hens. Justy was devastated. He also needed to find himself a new Bond Girl. Callie Kreutzer had informed him that she did not intend to utter the words "Just Ask Justy" aloud on TV, or anywhere else, ever again for as long as she lived.

A dozen or more movers were busy loading the vans with furniture and boxes. The front door to the house was braced open. Des found Jamella standing in the living room gloomily watching a crew from the aquarium company perform the delicate task of transferring Tyrone's precious sharks to temporary holding tanks and disassembling the giant tank, coral reefs and all.

"Taking them with you?"

"Moving them next door," she answered softly. "Tyrone wants Mr. Lash to have them. A bunch of electricians are over there right now rewiring the whole downstairs. Tyrone told them to just put it on his tab."

"That was nice of him."

There were dark circles under Jamella's eyes, which had a haunted look in them. "Things got so crazy that night that I forgot to thank you."

"For what?"

"Trying to help my sister."

"I was just doing my job."

"And *I* wasn't. I was supposed to be looking out for her. I let her down. Popsy was doing those horrible things to her all that time and I didn't know. I should have known." She looked at Des accusingly. "Did *you* know?"

"No, I didn't."

"Is that for real?"

"I wouldn't lie to you, Jamella. That's not how I roll. How are you feeling?"

"I don't *feel* anything. I'm just about keeping busy. Tyrone's lawyer rented us a big apartment near Lincoln Center. We're going to try the City for a while. I want to hook Kinitra up with Julliard. If not enrolled there, then at least taking private piano lessons from somebody who's on the faculty. She has to get back into her music. And she has an appointment tomorrow morning with a therapist who has an office on Central Park West. I'm meeting with my new obstetrician tomorrow, too. I'll be having my baby in the City."

"Is Kinitra planning to have her baby?"

"We'll talk about her options when she's ready to have the conversation. She . . . isn't ready yet. She's just so filled with guilt.

Blames herself for every single thing that happened." Jamella glanced at Des hesitantly. "I'm kind of beating myself up, too."

"Why's that?"

"Tyrone swore to me that night—swore to all of us—that he didn't do it. I-I didn't believe him. And he knows that. He saw it in my eyes. I don't know if we'll survive this. I can't hardly blame him if he doesn't want me anymore. I don't deserve his love. And I sure don't like myself very much right now."

"I'm not real proud of myself either. I was standing right there when Rondell drew his Glock on your father and I didn't react in time to stop him. None of us did. We're all pretty down on ourselves."

Especially Yolie. It was her case. And the Internal Affairs fallout for Calvin's murder, if there was to be any, would land on her. But the sad truth was that not one of them, not even the Deacon himself, had considered the possibility that little Rondell might be armed and dangerous. Yolie had attempted to determine if there were any weapons in the home. Clarence had coughed one up. True, she hadn't asked Rondell if he owned one. But if she had, he would have lied and said no. True, in an ideal, perfect world, he should have been patted down. But it wasn't an ideal, perfect world. Real world? Not one law enforcement person in the entire state would have patted Rondell down for a weapon that night. You could replay it a million times and it would always turn out the same way.

It shouldn't have happened, but it did.

Des had been drawing like crazy ever since it happened, working off of the grisly crime scene photos. Stewart Plotka and Andrea Halperin dead in the front seat of her Mercedes. Calvin Jameson lying on Tyrone's living room floor with his head blown open. If there'd been any photographic evidence of Rondell's remains, she'd have been all over that, too. It was the only way she knew how to cope with her overwhelming sense of powerlessness with a chain of events that had outpaced her ability to grasp them and act upon them. In that ideal, perfect world, Rondell wouldn't be in smithereens at the bottom of the Connecticut River right now. He'd be holding Kinitra's hand and telling her in a soft, reassuring voice what a terrific person she was. Instead, he was gone.

It shouldn't have happened, but it did.

And so Des drew, deconstructing the horror one stroke at a time, knowing that this one would stay inside of her for keeps.

"My sister's anxious to talk to you," Jamella said. "Are you ready?"

"I'm ready."

Kinitra was stretched out in a lounge chair on the patio by the pool. She wore a chunky wool turtleneck, fleece pants and UGG boots. She was staring out at the river. Upriver, actually, at the blackened but structurally sound railroad bridge. Amtrak service between New York and Boston had been restored that morning.

Des showed her a smile and said, "Hey."

Kinitra turned and looked at her, but her mind was somewhere else. A place far away. She seemed to have aged five years in the past seventy-two hours. She'd lost that doe-eyed, childlike quality of hers. She was a young woman now. "Thanks for coming, Trooper Des." Her voice wasn't sing-songy anymore either. It sounded flat and tired. "I wanted to apologize for lying to you and being such a total brat."

"Not a problem. I understand where you were coming from."

"I also wanted to thank Mitch and his parents for saving my life. I don't think I ever did."

"I'll be sure to pass that along. And, for what it's worth, I've got my dress all picked out."

Kinitra frowned at her. "What dress?"

"The one I'm going to wear when you play Carnegie Hall. I'll be there."

"I'll write you a song. Would a love song be okay?"

"A love song would do just fine."

She smiled at Des faintly, then gazed back at the railway bridge and was someplace else again. Someplace where no one should ever, ever have to go.

They tried doing brunch this time. Scrambled eggs, bacon and biscuits for those who could eat such things. Irish oatmeal for those who couldn't. There was fresh-squeezed orange juice. There was piping hot coffee. It was a brisk, beautiful autumn morning. Mitch had a big fire going in his fireplace.

"I've got some news to impart," the Deacon announced between spoonfuls of oatmeal. "I'm returning to work next week on a part-time basis. And I'm moving back into my own place. Giving my girl her life back. I've imposed on her long enough. I've got you to thank for this, Chet. You inspired me."

Mitch's dad looked at him surprise. "I did?"

"You did. You made me realize that I'm not ready to be put out to pasture yet. I'm just like you—if I'm not helping someone, or at least trying, then they may as well dig a hole and cover me over."

"Here's to you, Buck," Chet said, raising his coffee cup to him.

"I'm going to miss you, Daddy," Des confessed.

"No, you're not."

"Yes, I am. I've gotten used to you prowling around the house in the middle of the night."

"I could move in with you for a while if you'd like," Mitch offered. "I'm a consummate night prowler. Mind you, that's not all I know how to do in the dark."

"Behave, Boo-Boo," she chided him.

"Des, I'm still not totally comfortable with you—"

"Tough," she said, feeling Ruth Berger's eyes on her. The little lady had been staring at her all through the meal.

After they finished eating, Ruth insisted on helping her clear the table, her jaw clenched with determination. *The Talk*. Des had been waiting for this. Dreading it. Because there was no avoiding the reality of their situation. Mitch was a Jewish widower. Des was a divorced woman of color. She wasn't sure exactly how Ruth's words would go. But she was fairly certain what her message would be:

You've had your fun—now stay away from my son.

Des piled their plates in the sink, steeling herself as Ruth set the serving bowls down on the kitchen counter.

When the words came they weren't what Des was expecting at all.

Ruth Berger said, "Thank you, Desiree."

"For what, Ruth?"

"Saving my boy. We thought we were going to lose him after Maisie died. He didn't smile for two whole years. Now he can't stop smiling. He loves life again. And it's all because of you."

"You're giving me too much credit."

"Nonsense. You've made him whole again."

Des heard hearty male laughter from the other room. The men enjoying each other's company.

Ruth glanced at the doorway, lowering her voice. "After Maisie's funeral, he just sat in their apartment for months watching old movies and stuffing his face. When we tried to visit him he wouldn't let us in. He wouldn't even speak to us on the phone. His editor, Lacy, was planning to put him on medical leave. She phoned me, you know."

"No, I didn't."

"Neither does Mitch. Please don't tell him."

"I won't."

"The lady absolutely could not figure out what to do about him. I told her that when he was a little boy all he ever wanted to do was sit in the apartment watching old movies on TV. Sometimes I had to turn off the set and shove him out into the sunshine to play with the other boys. So Lacy did. She sent him here to Dorset to write a weekend getaway piece. She didn't think he'd agree to go, but I assured her he would. He's always been very conscientious."

"So Mitch coming here was *your* idea?"

"I suppose it was."

"Ruth, if it hadn't been for you we would never have met."

Ruth looked at Des curiously. "His life is so much better now. Is yours?"

"Yes, it is. That's not to say that everything's been perfect. We've had our ups and downs."

"Oh, hell, all couples do. I left Chester for three months. Moved in with my girlfriend Lenore on West 78th Street. This was before Mitch was born. He doesn't know. Don't ever tell him."

"I won't. Why did you? . . ."

"Because I wasn't in charge of my own life anymore. Chester was. He could be very bossy when he was younger. I persuaded him to accept me as his equal and stop telling me what to do. We worked things out. We just had to grow up a little. By 'we' I mean Chester. My point is, we were totally right for each other. Same as you and Mitch are totally right for each other. And if you ever decide you want to make me a grandmother, I wouldn't say no." Ruth hesitated before she added, "Mitch was all wrong, you see."

"All wrong about what?"

"He thought Maisie was his soul mate for life. She wasn't. *You* are."

Damn.

Des bit down hard on her lower lip, her eyes misting over.

"Oh, dear, now I've upset you. I'm sorry."

"No, no. You didn't upset me. You made me feel good all over."

Ruth smiled at Des and said, "I'm glad. That makes us even." She glanced around at the cluttered counter. "Are we done here?"

Des said, "We're done." Then she took Mitch's mother by the arm and led her back into the living room to join the three good men in their lives.